The
Spirituality of Music

THE SPIRITUALITY OF MUSIC

by Selina Thielemann

A.P.H. PUBLISHING CORPORATION
5, ANSARI ROAD, DARYA GANJ 2001
NEW DELHI-110 002

Published by
S. B. Nangia
A.P.H. Publishing Corporation
5, Ansari Road, Darya Ganj
New Delhi-110002
☎ 3274050
Email : aph@mantraonline.com
Website : aphbooksindia.com

ISBN 81-7648-249-8

2001

Typesetting at
NEW APCON
25/2, Panchsheel Shopping Centre
New Delhi - 110 017
☎ 6490802
6494336

Printed in India at
Efficient Offset Printers
New Delhi-110 035

Preface

Writing a scholarly book about music is like drawing a picture of a flower: the resulting account offers an accurate and elaborate description of the depicted reality, in which each and every detail is subjected to painstaking analysis, and if the investigation is masterfully done, it finally comes forth with a perfect imitation of the material phenomenon sublimated to an extent that the layman will not tell the copy from the original. Just as the painting portrays the flower in full resplendency of colors with all its petals and tender leaves, the musicological essay captures every single rhythmic-melodic turn of the musical construction, assesses one by one the words of the song and the notes of the instrumental play and interprets their intrinsic meaning and signification. But can the painted canvas convey the essence of the flower - its fragrance, its sweetness of nectar? No, it can not, because the subtle vibrations of joy, of which this spiritual substance is made, cannot be translated into material metaphors. And that is why any written account of music, however thorough and earnest in its intents, misses out on the vital essence of music which is joy, which is bliss, which is sweetness.

Consequentially, the idea of writing about the spiritual essence of music was born out of a spontaneous strain of responsiveness rather than from preplanning considerations. In the concrete, I felt inspired by reactions received from the audience in one of my recent lectures in which, stimulated by the presence of many excellent musicians, I had decided to deviate from a carefully prepared academic script on musical structuralities only to plunge into a lively discourse of music in its philosophical dimension. The inspirative spark came as a natural effect in the company of the musicians: like all scientists, the musicologist wants facts, but the music-maker, the artist is intuitively concerned more with the subtle emotional workings behind those facts rather than with the factual reality itself. Thus, while the musicologist runs after music in its material presence, directing his full endeavor at capturing the sounding reality and imprisoning it in his tape recorder, the musician keeps himself smilingly apart: he knows that all the eager scholar can obtain is the outer body, the physical phenomenon, while the soul of the music remains uncapturable, recorded in his - the musician's - heart.

What is more, the musicologist's way is constantly constrained by uncertainties, and material obstacles mount up to obstruct his progress in any conceivable manner: authorities refuse permission to record, locations become inaccessible because of riots or floods, equipment breaks down, tapes run out - but the Eternal Truth needs no technical accessories to be recorded, and its realization requires no prior sanction. And once that truth has been realized, once music reveals itself to man in its full cosmic sweetness, the emerging presence outshines in its blissful radiance all rational explanations and descriptive accounts, and the personality of the song ultimately excels all structural skeletons the academic has ever pressed in notations drawn on music-paper.

Responding to requests from readers and audience-members of my lectures, I have therefore decided to focus in the essays presented on these pages on music as the spiritual energy, as the cosmic personality whose essence of sweetness indwells the sounding phenomenon of music as its vital soul. It needs to be emphasized that the result cannot be more than a modest attempt at pointing into the direction of the universal flow of music, for the musical reality as such, the river in its transcendental essence cannot be made visible through the medium of language. And this is why I have abstained from too much quoting theoretical texts and philosophical scriptures while instead illustrating the theoretical tenets with quotes from poetry: because the poet is the artist, and from his heart speaks the music-maker who inspirits the philosophical facts with the melodiousness of the tune.

So though I have incorporated theoretical aspects, with natural emphasis on ideas emerging from Vedāntic philosophy which I have inherited through my own family's generation-old scholarly tradition, rather than fatiguing the reader with Upaniṣadic and Purāṇic quotes I have decided to bring over the living spirit of these texts through the charming expressiveness of Rabindranath Tagore's poems, and through the devotional depth of the songs of Bengal's Bāul mendicants. Why the Bāul singers? Because the Bāul's philosophy is his music; because the Bāul practices, or rather lives his religion through music. The *śāstra*, the didactic work provides the theoretical key to realization, yet this key is not sufficient to unlock the door that leads to the infinite. The Bāul, however, in his songs teaches his experience - he teaches *through* experience, and this teaching through music is the only didactic tool to emancipate not only the intellect, but the soul in its entirety.

A musical creation, like any creation in the cosmic play of becoming and being, cannot be brought forth by a single individual, but arises from the marriage of two creative forces. That is, one force who generates the imaginative spark, and one force who endows this germ of imaginativeness with concrete shape in the form of the creation. But once the creation has been completed into a perfect revelation of the imaginative energy, what is its primary intent? - surrender to the one from whom originates all inspiration, all imaginativeness, all creativity. Surrender to the one who comes forth through a multitude of finite manifestations, yet whose spiritual essence is the permanence of infinite oneness. And if ever I may have received any imaginative strain in my immodest attempt to capture the truth of music in words, then it is Him to whom is due all gratitude - to Him in His infinite essence, and to Him in His human manifestations.

SELINA THIELEMANN

Māgha kṛṣṇa ekādaśī
VS. 2057
20 January 2001

Life of my life, I shall ever try to keep my body pure, knowing that thy living touch is upon all my limbs.

I shall ever try to keep all untruths out from my thoughts, knowing that thou art that truth which has kindled the light of reason in my mind.

I shall ever try to drive all evils away from my heart and keep my love in flower, knowing that thou hast thy seat in the inmost shrine of my heart.

And it shall be my endeavour to reveal thee in my actions, knowing it is thy power gives me strength to act.

Rabindranath Tagore, *Gītāñjalī*, IV

Contents

Introduction: Music - the divine art   1

Spiritual and mundane qualities of music   10
Offering and blessing: the dialectics of music   29
The infinity of music   48

Music and devotion   65
Music and beauty   81
Music and harmony   97
Music and love   113
Music and creativity   133
Music and spiritual union   148

Communication through music   165
Service through music   179
Realization through music   200

Introduction

Music - the divine art

Even if you forbid,
Dear friend,
I am helpless.
My songs contain
My prayers.

Madan[1]

1

My songs contain my prayers, for my music is my worship of thee, my music is my service rendered unto thee - my music is the outcry of my heart, my all that I can offer to thee, because my music is the essence of my being. What is it like, this essence of essences, the quintessence of existence, the core substance of life?

It is obvious from our poet's proclamation that his music is more than merely a harmoniously structured arrangement of sounds. The earnestness of his appeal, the fervor with which he declares his full submission to the power of a tune makes us wonder as to the true nature of the sounding reality to which he refers. Is it actually music, the melodious presence evoked by the voice of a singer or through the play of a musical instrument, that the poet speaks about, or does he apply the musical metaphor to a larger concept of universal existence? Or could it be that perhaps the metaphor is no metaphor but reality? Could it be that music - known to us as a delightful, enjoyable amusement - is more than that which it appears to be? Could it be that deeper cosmic principles inhere in the sounding creations of music? Could it be...

No, not could be - it *is*. Music *is* more than bland entertainment. Music *does* reach beyond the limits of organized sound. Music *has* all the intrinsic qualities of a cosmic reality, and music *can* incite that which is never to be achieved by ordinary human faculties. But what is music?

Music is a cosmic energy. Music is an energy of bliss, of love, of joy - an energy sent out by the supreme transcendental reality from which emanates all being, all life, all existence. Who is this transcendental reality? He is the formless source of all form, the

---

[1] quoted in Deben Bhattacharya, *The mirror of the sky* (London: Allen & Unwin, 1969), p.93

nameless root of all names, the soundless essence of all music. He is the omnipresent force of motion, the all-pervading radiation of light, the inexhaustible flow of sweetness that fills the universe with bliss. He is the core inspirer of life on all planes of cosmic existence, who instigates and sustains the universal play of creation - the play in which the infinite and the finite, the formless and the form, the perennial and the fugitive continuously unite as playmates in the game of love. He is the one to whom our poet prays with his songs, the one whom the poet addresses as 'dear friend' - because He who is the lord of the universe is truly the most intimate friend of the human soul. It is Him who accompanies man throughout the unending cycles of coming and going, of being and becoming, of meeting and parting:

> With his morning songs he knocks at our door
>   bringing his greetings of sunrise.
> With him we take our cattle to the fields and play
>   our flute in the shade.
> We lose him to find him again and again in the
>   market crowd.
> In the busy hour of the day we come upon him
>   of a sudden, sitting on the wayside grass.
> We march when he beats his drum,
> We dance when he sings.
> We stake our joys and sorrows to play his game
>   to the end.
> He stands at the helm of our boat,
> With him we rock on the perilous waves.
> For him we light our lamp and wait when our
>   day is done.[2]

He is essence of all action, of all creativity - and the essence of all music. How does that supreme divinity reveal himself in music? The transcendental reality becomes manifest in multitudinous ways, and each manifestation, when translated into music, adds a different flavor to the sounding creation. The Supreme Being is by nature infinite, and so is music in its universal appeal. The Formless One delights in his own beauty of form, in his music which is the manifestation of beauty

---

[2] Rabindranath Tagore, *Crossing*, LX

beyond all forms. The Divine Lover dedicates himself to the human soul with unconditional affection, and music is the tuneful articulation of his devotion. The Infinite Reality incorporates the elemental principle of union between the contrary forces of existence, the principle of harmony which is established by the unifying potencies of music. The Supreme Divinity embodies the sweetest essence of love, and His call of love resounds in multicolored strains of musical cadences. The Creator's imaginative play finds its most sublime expression in the creativity of music. The Supreme Soul choses the human soul for his companion of eternity, and it is music that makes their marriage perfect. And through music, this marriage becomes consummate: through music the soul communicates her secrets to her lover, through music the soul renders her service to her master, through music this soul of man attains to her lord ever again in the unending play of love.

Music is not an abstract concept that exists outside the concrete reality of being, yet music is indwelled by the cosmic principles whose dynamics makes the universal mechanism function. Music is an energy, but at the same time it is the expression of that energy, the definite manifestation of an unmanifest force. Music penetrates the cosmos as an invisible, inaudible vibration of bliss, while music represents likewise the audible vocalization of that bliss. Therefore music comes forth as the immediate, sounding embodiment of the world in its infinity - of the world which is music, of the world of which the poet sings -

> Thou hast given me thy seat at thy window from
>   the early hour.
> I have spoken to thy silent servants of the road
>   running on thy errands, and have sung with
>   their choir of the sky.
> I have seen the sea in calm bearing its
>   immeasurable silence, and in storm
>   struggling to break open its own mystery of
>   depth.
> I have watched the earth in its prodigal feast of
>   youth, and in its slow hours of brooding
>   shadows.
> Those who went to sow seeds have heard my
>   greetings, and those who brought their

harvest home on their empty baskets have
passed by my songs.
Thus at last my day has ended and now in the
evening I sing my last song to say that I have
loved thy world.[3]

That "last song to say that I have loved thy world" is in reality the song
of eternity, the unending flow of music that ensures the unbroken
continuity of creativity, of creation.

How is the creative impetus of music invoked? What inborn
properties does music possess that qualify it as the core instigator of the
creative quest? The motivating strength of music lies in its inherent
ambivalence, in its capacity to embrace contrary forces and to unite them
in complete harmony: "In my room / live in total unity / the sage and the
thief, / the demon and the man - / poison and nectar..."[4]. In music come
to confluence all opposite currents to mingle into the great ocean of
harmoniousness, of sweetness, of bliss. In music, the infinite meets the
finite, the timeless meets the momentary, the divine meets the human.
Music melts dualities, music fuses the disconnected fragments of reality
in order to establish the eternal truth of unity. What is more, music fills
the separateness of dual entities with meaning, because it incites their
active interplay, because it inspirits the quest for union through
interaction. Interactive respondency, reciprocity is the primary quality of
music, which endows music with the ability to transcend its own limits
of phenomenality and to convert into the spiritual essence of its own
physical revelation.

The dual yet unifying nature of music becomes manifest in the
most elemental way in the very act of the musical performance. "Only
from a marriage of two forces does music arise in the world"[5] - music,
in order to be rendered, needs two: the music-maker and the listener, the
one who sings and the one who hears, the creator and the recipient. It
requires two, but these two must form a single entity; they must act, they
must react in unity, in harmony. That is to say, they must be mutually
respondent. It is for the sake of the listener that the music-maker unfolds

---

[3] Rabindranath Tagore, *Crossing*, LXXIII
[4] Ananta, quoted in Deben Bhattacharya, op.cit., p.53
[5] Rabindranath Tagore, *Broken Song*

his tune, and it is in response to the musician's melody that the listener partakes of the joy of music. More than that, the response from the listener inspires the musician ever anew to go on creating fresh cadences, and the continuity of the musical flow saturates the listener's heart with ever increasing delight. The music-maker not simply presents his sounding artefacts before the listener - he dedicates them to him, he renders them as offerings penetrated by a deep sense of love, of devotion, of commitment. It is this intrinsic spirit of surrender, the dedication that the music bears at its heart, rather than the aesthetic perfectness of the sounding reality which makes the listener truly blissful. But where then does music emanate from? Is music produced only and alone in the mind of the performing musician? No, it is not. The musician himself attains to his music by the grace of the Divine Music-maker. That means the musician who delights the Supreme Soul by dedicating the tune to Him partakes of the divine grace in the form of musical inspiration received as the highest blessing given out by the Eternal Musician.

Of what kind is this transcendental music, the imaginative spark that manifests itself through the sounding melody? The music of infinity carries at its core all the essential qualities of its infinite source. It is permanent in its substance but momentary in its appearance; it is formless in its essence but reveals itself in form; it is soundless from within but wells forth as never ending currents of melodious sound. Man conceives music as divine inspiration, but where rests the infinite reality from which all music is emitted? - in the heart of man. The illimitable reality indwells the human soul as the infinite within man, emerging from within the human heart in ever-changing expressions of man's creative action.

What is it that calls forth these continuous revelations of the divinity in the first place? And which power enables man to transcend his own finite existence by inviting the spirit of infinity to make the human heart his permanent abode? The secret of man's capacities is submission: *submission is the secret of knowledge*[6] - of knowledge which embraces knowing and feeling in one single act, of knowledge nourished by rationality and emotionality likewise, of knowledge

---

[6] Anon, quoted in Deben Bhattacharya, op.cit., p.41

sustained by devotion as its core essence. Devotion is the live-giving energy that emancipates the human soul from the bonds of finitude, because devotion motivates the vital flow of emotion that melts together the opposite forces of the universe and fuses them in an all-unifying instant of love. But which is the substance that forms the emotional fluid? It is music - it is music as the sounding manifestation of cosmic sweetness; it is music as the melodious revelation of universal love; it is music as the prime vocalization of the devotional quest.

The liquid at the core of the emotional current is music, yet music signifies but an embodiment of a higher aesthetic principle: of the principle of beauty. Music is joy, music is born of joy, music grows in joy, music is absorbed by joy, but how is joy itself expressed? - as beauty. The joy of the formless becomes manifest in the beauty of form, and the joy of the concrete finds its freedom in the beauty beyond all forms. Music is beauty in the most immediate sense of the word: music is formless joy abiding in the infinite essence of the musical idea, and music is the joy of form that comes forth through the definiteness of the musical creation. And more than that, music is the sounding articulation of that all-inspiring harmoniousness through which joy is established in the first place.

What is that to say? Joy arises from the harmony of contrary forces, and music is both the instigator and the expression of that harmony. Without joy, there can be no music in the world, but how could there be joy if the universe were not permeated by the all-pervading sweetness of music? Creation can only progress where there is a creative duality, yet the truth of being consists not in the duality as such, but in the constant longing of its two poles to merge into one. Music acts as the unifying agent that enforces their fusion, while at the same time music is in itself the quest for union. Music is the elemental manifestation of cosmic harmony, because music evokes harmoniousness - because music accomplishes the union of opposing entities and thereby fulfils the primal ambition of all beings: to become one with the supreme truth of existence.

How is this primeval intention raised at the heart of creation? How is it carried forward, how is it accomplished? Through the energies of love. Love is the universal breath of life whose inspiring touch sustains the world in its course. Love is the most sublime energy of transcendental sweetness, which assumes definite shape in the sweetness of music. Music therefore becomes the principal vehicle on the way towards love's fulfilment. In music, the call of love, the outcry of the lover's heart for union with the beloved, finds its most spontaneous and at the same time its most subtle articulation, because music possesses the capacity to express the unexpressible. Music is an emotional energy, music is an emotional tool, and the essence of music is emotion. The quest of love is an emotional quest, hence calls for an emotional agent to accomplish its fulfilment - and that agent is music.

In what way is the union of love established? Through play - through the cosmic play of love that takes its course in ever-varying streaks of creativity. In its essence, therefore, the creative quest expresses nothing but the perennial play of love on the level of universal existence. Creativity springs up from the imaginative play of contrary forces, from the play which is the play of love because its sole object is union, because its final goal is to transcend the existing duality through the joy of the play. It is this unending play of cosmic love from which music derives its creative energy. Yet it is music that inspires this very play because of its inherent motivating force. Music, in its full dialectic dynamism, functions as a continual process of being and becoming, of giving and receiving, of stimulating and being stimulated, hence music represents at once both the object and the cause of love's play.

When does the play of love become consummate? When does love reach its climax, when does music dissolve into silence, play still into bliss? The play of love culminates once the union of love has been accomplished, once the transcendental energies of bliss have been gathered into an immense cloud of joy pressing to be released. To be released in what? - in music. Union signifies silence: the moment of highest bliss is at the same time the moment of speechlessness, of overwhelming amazement; it is the moment of an overpowering sense of wonder. The state of union is the state of confluence, the instant when the current of love reaches the ocean of bliss, when the stream of music merges into the sea of silence. Music is the river, but music is also the boat that carries the searching soul along that river towards its ultimate destination - towards the meeting-place where the human soul and the Supreme Soul ever delight in their timeless dalliance.

But how could this union come true without the two lovers exchanging their secrets verbalized in the language of the heart? How could there be communion without communication? Yet how can such communication turn real if no language is competent to give voice to the soul's plea? It is true that words are improper tools to instigate the conversation of mutually committed hearts, but is there no substitute? Is there no medium of communication suitable to establish the contact of lovers? Yes, there is such a medium - it is music. Music appeals to the emotional faculties of man and is therefore able to articulate what words as the instruments of rationality could never express. Music, through its spiritual essence, ties the communicative bond, while at the same time music remains accessible for man on the phenomenal level through its very own phenomenality of sound.

And music instigates the highest form of communication, which is worship. Worship, dedicated service enlivened by the spirit of devotion is the primary way for the loving soul to communicate her emotional appeal to the beloved. Again among all forms of worship, music represents the mode *par excellence*, because music is nourished in its very substance by the spirit of devotion, and every act of music-making is essentially a statement of love, of dedication, of surrender to the soul to whom is offered all love, all worship, all music. Music is a statement of surrender; more than that, music is an act of surrender - of surrender which is the core tenet of the quest for realization, of the quest for attainment, of the quest for spiritual union. Because surrender is the essence of love, and love is the quintessence of joy - of joy which is the joy of music, of joy which is the life-breath of music, of joy which *is* music. Music embodies the highest ideal of perfection aspired by the spiritual quest, and therefore, it is through music that man realizes the infinite; it is through music that man attains to the infinite, and it is through music that the Infinite gives out his own blissful essence in the union of love.

So what is music, the cosmic energy, the transcendental fluid of bliss? As an aesthetic fact, music represents the innermost vein at the heart of art, the essential limb in the body of the artistic personality without which art would turn into a debilitated, lifeless cripple - just as would be a song without its melody: "the best part of a song is missed when the tune is absent; for thereby its movement and its colour are lost, and it becomes like a butterfly whose wings have been plucked"[7]. On the cosmic stage, music is the motivating energy that inspirits the personages in the great game of creation: "it is music that sets the personages on stage in motion, and that gives life to them as it is passed on to the spectator in the form of intense and profound experience"[8].

Music is experience, and music is bliss: the bliss of experience, the experience of bliss. Therefore it is music whose imaginative impetus stimulates creativity: "Bliss, received from the stage, becomes thus inspiration to act in the right spirit"[9]. Music is the vivifying emotional force that enlivens the rational facts on the universal drama-stage and adds the spiritual meaning to them: "When there is no visible scenic action, sound becomes even more important to vitalize the contents of the words"[10]. Music is accomplishment, and music comes true through accomplishment: the perfect tune possess the power of leading the soul to fulfilment of the aspired goal, hence "the correct intonation becomes the essential medium to convey the thoughts and to evoke the object of desire"[11]. But perfectness must be paired with beauty, with the concrete manifestation of love, in order to turn into bliss, in order to make the soul truly blissful: "If the tonal figures are moreover appealing, even beautiful, then the listeners become enjoyed, even excited"[12].

And that is the essence of essences. That is the quintessential meaning of music when we speak of it as a divine art - when we say that the divinity becomes revealed through the divine art: "This state of bliss is the ultimate quest of all beings, and whenever music is capable of evoking this state, in India, one speaks of a divine art"[13].

---

[7] Rabindranath Tagore, *Creative Unity* (New Delhi: Macmillan India Ltd., reprint 1995), p.78

[8] Josef Kuckertz, "What is Indian music" (English translation by Selina Thielemann), in Selina Thielemann (ed.), *Essays on Indian music by Professor Josef Kuckertz* (Bombay & Baroda: Indian Musicological Society, 1999), p.24

[9] ibid. (pp.24f.)

[10] ibid. (p.25)

[11] ibid.

[12] ibid.

[13] ibid.

Spiritual and mundane qualities of music

Music, the sounding manifestation of spiritual inspiration, has been surrounded by a flair of mystery ever since it entered the sphere of conscious human activity. Accepting its mystique, its hidden intrinsic qualities, man has made music his primary tool of emotional expression through which he communicates his own inner secrets to the outside world. But what is it that makes music eligible as a seemly cohabitor of human sensibilities? It is its mysteriousness - the mysteriousness of the musical sound that absorbs the mystery of the human soul and conveys it to the ear through the medium of sonic waves. Once the river of emotional moves merges into the ocean of sounding vibrations, their union becomes audible and the unspoken secret of the heart reveals itself in music. The sounding reality turns into a mirror of the soul that reflects the inexplicable emotional essence of human existence. Music, at its core, is a spiritual experience whose perceptibility remains out of the reach of most sense-organs: music is neither visible nor touchable, nor can it be tasted or smelt. Yet the phenomenon of music is not immaterial, and it can be perceived by the only sense which is alert at all times: music can be heard.

What happens when the human ear perceives the vibrations of the musical sound? Once a spark of spiritual inspiration converts into an audible musical reality, what reaction ensues from the mind of the recipient? Music, in the first place, prompts an emotional response in the heart of man, because its appeal is directed at the emotional sphere of human consciousness. The emotional response is intrinsically personal, even subjective, just as human nature itself is characterized by individuality and diversity. Music, therefore, is heard in different ways, perceived on individual grounds, and responded to according to the emotional potential of the listener. But, however broad the spectrum of reactions may be, the ensuent response will be in any case an emotional one. Why would it be emotional? What factors account for the emotional rather than rational appeal of music? What qualities, what energies does music inherit that make it grow beyond a merely physical phenomenon, beyond a mere accumulation of organized vibrations or sound waves? If we seek an answer, we need to cast off the limits of physical science and examine instead the fruits of age-old human experience - of experience which has settled in theories and scriptures, yet of experience which cannot be taught because it cannot be comprehended unless it has been tasted and lived through.

The *Oxford Wordfinder* defines music as 'the art of combining vocal or instrumental sounds (or both) to produce beauty of form, harmony, and expression of emotion'. This definition, however incomplete and unsatisfactory it may remain, indicates that music incorporates more than the mere phenomenon of sound. It speaks of art, of beauty, of harmony, and even more important, of emotion. But then, what is music? From where does music emerge, what is music born of? The physicist will readily offer his scientific explanation about regular and continuous vibrations of a surrounding medium causing a sensation in the ear, and he will point out how these vibrations are produced, maintained and stopped. Not so the poet, the one for whom music represents the essence of being, the basis of existence. He is not concerned with the physical origins of sound and its transformation into an organized entity called music. To him, music emanates from the heart - from the heart of man in response to the rays of all-pervading love sent out by that ultimate manifestation of sweetness that permeates the universe and keeps the cosmic cycle going. To the poet, music emanates from the heart and is also perceived by the heart: heard by the ears, the tune needs to descend into the depth of the heart in order to prompt an emotional response in the listener, because emotions are born from within rather than produced by the outward senses. That is to say the ear that perceives the sound of the music remains deaf to its beauty unless the sound enters the emotional sphere of man. The poet, therefore, addresses his heart whenever he speaks of his longing for spiritual perfection, and he knows that rational explanations can never adequately answer the question about the origins of music. And he transcends the physicist's scientific description when he says "He it is who puts his enchantment upon these eyes and joyfully plays on the chords of my heart in varied cadence of pleasure and pain"[1].

It is experience, intimate personal experience that makes the poet arrive at his conclusion. The one who has not himself experienced the thriving energy behind the mere physical phenomenon, who has not tasted the sweetness of the inexplicable, he will perceive the sound, but

---

[1] Rabindranath Tagore, *Gītāñjalī*, LXXII

not the music. Yet he will be affected by the emotional impact of the sounding reality, even if he is not aware of it. Music possesses the capacity to arouse sentiments of different kinds, depending upon its own inherent qualities and upon the emotional state of the listener. What is it that accounts for this capacity? What is the cause of the motivating power of music? Now it is the psychologist who comes with explications at hand, worked out in careful and thorough study and observation. The poet, however, tells of his experience: "He it is, the innermost one, who awakens my being with his deep hidden touches"[2]. The answer appears so strikingly simple that one wonders why generations of great thinkers invest so much energy and yet strive for it in vain. The way towards realization, however, is not that easy, because its ultimate destination can be reached only through living experience.

Experience of what? Experience of that Supreme Reality which cannot be described in words nor settled in mathematic formulae, which cannot be apprehended by science nor perceived by the sense-organs. Experience of that one about whom the materialist says in disbelief, 'show me that god of yours, let him appear in physical form so that I can see him, hear him, touch him, or else I will not accept his existence'. Yes, we may answer, the Supreme Being truly manifests himself in physical form, he is present everywhere in the material world and can be seen, heard, touched - but only once you have felt his spiritual touch, once you have seen him with your inner eye and listened to his music with the ear of your heart, then only you will be convinced of his physical existence. That experience, however, the emotional experience of the unexplainable, cannot be taught but requires the personal effort of the individual - as the English say 'you can take a horse to the water, but you cannot make him drink'. Once the emotional experience has been lived through, the senses too are activated to perceive the infinite reality in its finite forms. The sensual experience stimulates, but at the same time presupposes the emotional experience. That is to say, only once the Supreme Reality has been experienced emotionally, this experience can be enhanced through sensual involvement, but not otherwise.

Music, the prime instigator of emotional moves, is sensual and emotional experience both in one. Through its physical vibrations, music

---

[2] ibid.

exists as a material reality which is perceived by the senses but accessed and apprehended emotionally. Music thus becomes the object of the emotional experience, the material entity to be experienced. At the same time, however, music as a spiritual reality represents the very cause for that experience. How is this explained? Mere sound with its primarily physical appeal may or may not lead to an emotional reaction in man once it is perceived by the ear. Music, on the other hand, distinguishes itself from mere sound through its spiritual essence, the core substance of music which the *Oxford Wordfinder* attempts to describe as 'beauty of form', 'harmony' and 'emotion'. It is this spiritual essence that transcends the limits of physical form and accounts for the emotional appeal of music. Unlike mere sound, music prompts an emotional response in any case. Yet music, on the primary level, is perceived physically and thereby maintains its rational appeal. In this way music integrates both spiritual and material qualities, and as a result appears as both a transcendental and a rational entity.

What is the specific significance of this dual quality of music, its inherent spiritual and physical elements, in the context of human perception? Sound, as we have seen, is physically produced and also perceived, and the experience arising of sound is primarily sensual. Music, if we follow the definition of the *Oxford Wordfinder*, aims at a higher quality than bare sound by transforming it into a construction that generates 'beauty of form, harmony and emotional expression'. But what is it that calls for this higher quality? - the need to give voice to an emotional experience that cannot be described in rational terms. It is the desire to express one's feelings arising from the ultimate experience of the supreme transcendental reality that calls for a medium of spiritual substance, yet with a material basis. Why? Because man is linked to the material world through the medium of the human body, hence he tends to manifest his spiritual experience in physical terms. The tool of expression, the transformer that translates the spiritual input into a rational output, is the musical sound, equiped with a spiritual sensor and a physical emitter both activated by the current of emotion.

While music represents the primary medium to express the ultimate spiritual experience, it functions at the same time as the foremost mode to arouse that experience, and here again the interplay of rational and transcendental factors within the musical entity gains relevance. Music, on account of its motivating energy, advances to be the vehicle *par excellence* for man to reach the final destination of his spiritual voyage, to attain to his highest spiritual goal. What is this supreme object? It is the ultimate quest of mankind: to become one with the Supreme Being, to relish the essence of essences, the sweetness of sweetnesses - to experience the all-pervading energy of love, that ultimate transcendental reality whose beams of affection sustain the motion of the universe. The supreme transcendental reality is omnipresent in the nature, but it is not discernible by rational means because of its non-material essence. Man, however, is a rational animal who will apprehend only that which can be perceived by the senses as well. Therefore, in order to arrive at his spiritual aim, man requires a medium that can act as a link between his rational understanding and the transcendental reality. This connecting medium is music with its dual capacity to appeal to both the emotional and the rational spheres: spiritual in its essence, music manifests itself as a physical reality to be sensually perceived.

But does music - played, heard and perceived - always necessarily result in ultimate spiritual fulfilment? Is it always the utmost delight, is it always unbounded bliss that arises from the musical experience? No, it is not. Not always, not in any case, because music is more than an unqualified expression of sheer joy. Music gives voice to the ultimate transcendental experience, to the sentiments aroused through the touch of the infinite. But that experience, that aggregation of emotions, is it always pleasure? No. It can be pain, excessive pain: agony of separation springing to consciousness at the very moment of union. Why else would the poet say, the one who has lived through that experience, that "days come and ages pass, and it is ever he who moves my heart in many a name, in many a guise, *in many a rapture of joy and sorrow*"[3]? Why else would he admit that the Supreme Being "joyfully plays on the chords of my heart in varied cadence of pleasure and pain"? Yet at the time of fulfilment, even pain is perceived as pleasure because it originates from the very source of all delight, and our poet readily accepts the experience of pain without which no pleasure can be derived: "No, I will never shut the doors of my senses. The delights of sight and

---

[3] ibid.

hearing and touch will bear thy delight"[4] - for the Supreme Soul will delight even in separation, but not so the human soul who is in constant search to overcome this separation. Music as the primary tool of emotional respondency reflects the quest for union in all its shades and nuances on a continuous scale between agony and bliss.

The rôle of music, however, does not remain restricted to merely reflecting man's spiritual journey. Music turns at the same time into the principal motivator that stimulates the spiritual search and makes it meaningful. It is through music that man strives to attain to his highest goal, and it is through music that the unattainable reality becomes accessible. In which way? The ultimate reality becomes emotionally accessible once the musical sound prompts an emotional response in man, and thereby sensitizes the mind to the abstract vibrations of the universe. The emotional response accordingly reveals the innermost desires of the heart, and if these desires are directed towards the Supreme Being, the spiritual contact with the object of desire is instigated through the connecting flow of emotions set afloat by the music. Music thus activates the emotional sensor in man, resulting in both incitement and, once the emotional connection has been established, fulfilment of the spiritual search.

Music advances the search for spiritual accomplishment, but what is it that incites music in the first place? It is the imperfection within perfection, the impossibility of the absolute, the unattainableness of the eternal that nourishes the musical flow and ensures its uninterrupted continuity. What does this mean? Man may obtain the object of his search, but he is not competent to retain it. Why? Because attainment is temporary by nature; it can never be constant for the reason that constancy implies unchangingness, and the very state of unchangingness contradicts the vital principle of creation. That is to say union is always followed by separation, delight by disenchantment, fulfilment by distress - only to stimulate the search anew in order to achieve an even higher degree of perfection. Impermancence, therefore, is not primarily a defect but rather a cosmic law, the vital reproductive energy lest the universe dies in stagnation. It is on the grounds of this impermanence inherent in all things that man's quest for his highest

---

[4] Rabindranath Tagore, *Gītāñjalī*, LXXIII

spiritual goal is a permanent quest, that his search for ultimate attainment remains a continuous search, and that his music as the vehicle for this search sounds in an unbroken current of notes.

But what is it that motivates man ever again to continue his search? If the setback is predestinate, is it not foolish to keep running after something that cannot be obtained? Is it not better to accept the ultimateness of failure, the unreachableness of an irrational quest, the inadequacy of an unreasonable demand? Yes, the sceptic will say, it is nothing but an illusion, the vain chase for something which cannot be accomplished. The shaky seeker, who has never even once reached the aim of his journey and does not know the sweetness of the infinite - he may capitulate at these words of the disbeliever, but what happens to the one who has already experienced the Supreme Reality? The one who, after attaining supreme bliss, is now pained by the pangs of separation? Would he not sit down and say to himself, yes, you have had it and that is it - fulfilment is achieved but once and comes never again, so do not ungratefully cherish inordinate desires. But are his desires truly inordinate? The innermost yearning of the human soul, can it ever be inordinate? No. The longing of the human soul for union with the divine can never be inordinate, because it is the Supreme Soul himself who desires this union. The one who has ever experienced the bliss arising out of the touch of the infinite, who has ever even once obtained the vision of the undescribable, he will never get away from this ultimate reality and readily accepts to bear the agony of separation only to delight in union time and again in endless cycles of pleasure and pain.

It is the knowledge that the object of his spiritual search will be attained which stimulates man to continue on his chosen path and not to resign in disbelief. Where lies the source of that knowledge? It lies in the Supreme Soul's own yearning to meet the human soul - in the longing of the infinite to manifest itself in finite form, in the longing of the unbounded to find its freedom within bounds, in the longing of the perfect to unfold in the unfinished design of creation. It is the supreme manifestation of love thirsting to consummate itself in the love of the human being, the desire of the supreme divinity to give himself away to his human lover, that inspires man ever again to continue his spiritual search. It is the infinite reality with its continuous whispers of 'yes, I am coming, I will meet thee in this thy life and bless thee with the taste of infinite sweetnees' that implants in man the knowledge of ultimate fulfilment to come, and it is the confidence that his search will be fruitful at last which emboldens the poet to call out to his god: "If it is not my portion to meet thee in this my life then let me ever feel that I have missed thy sight - let me not forget for a moment, let me carry the pangs of this sorrow in my dreams and in my wakeful hours"[5]. No, it is not the pain of having lost his dearest treasure, the agony of staying apart from the object of his aspirations that our poet wishes to feel. The intent of his prayer is rather to end that very state of separation, to liberate himself from "the pangs of that sorrow" which accompanies his spiritual journey as long as its final goal remains unfulfilled. And yet, just as the songbird intones her melodies while it is still dark, knowing that daylight will eventually break through, our poet knows that sorrow cannot be the ultimate truth but is to make way to boundless joy.

While proceeding on his spiritual path, man resorts to music as a vehicle to take him ahead in order to reach his destination. Music qualifies as a suitable tool to attain to higher spiritual ends because of its capacity to intensify the emotional potential of man. A person, therefore, who noble-mindedly and with pure intentions strives for spiritual perfection will obtain the object of his search helped by the medium of music, because the emotional impact of the musical sound enhances his positive inclination and sensitizes him to the transcendental reality. But is the influence of music always beneficial? Does music actually purify a person, or does it only respond to the virtuous essence within the individual? And, if the latter were true, what happens when music is heard by an ill-natured person? Would such a person at all be able to perceive the music, and how would he perceive it? Yes, music can be perceived even by the evil-doer, because every individual capable of expressing himself emotionally is substantially fit for listening and responding to the musical construction. Music takes effect by instigating an emotional reaction in the listener, but the quality of this reaction depends on the emotional condition of the recipient.

If the ensuent influence of music is derived from the preliminary human potential, music naturally exposes both positive and negative effects. The positive or negative disposition is however not inherent in

---

[5] Rabindranath Tagore, *Gītāñjalī*, LXXIX

the music itself, but in the individual who perceives the music. That is to say if the listener is positively inclined, music will activate and enhance the positive vibrations within the person, but the same music may lead to negative reactions in a negatively inclined individual. In practice, though, the emotional reaction of man represents a complex psychological process composed of a multitude of subtle nuances of mental vibrations resulting in an either predominantly positive or predominantly negative response. This is explained by the relativity of human nature, by the fact that no person is inhabited by exclusively positive or exclusively negative qualities. The two poles of the dialectic construction, the positive and the negative elements, are inherent in every individual, and the predominance of the one can only suppress but not extinguish the other. This imperfection is immanent in the human character and is indeed the prime cause for all evolution in the human realm. In the context of musical perception, it is the complex mental disposition of man that forms the active factor of the perceptive process, while music with its inherent spiritual qualities remains the neutral agent.

If music as such is neutral in its qualities, then why is the effect of music generally described in terms of qualifying attributes? Why is it that one speaks of the bliss-giving or purifying effects of music, or, negatively, of its intoxicating or even poisoning influence? The reason is the capacity of music to prompt a qualified reaction while retaining its own essence as an attributeless, unqualified energy. In the same way as light-beams become visible only when they fall on a material object, music can unfold its inborn qualities only once it is absorbed by a qualified medium, and that medium is nothing else than the human soul, the emotional property of man. It is therefore true that the effect of music is beneficial and purifying, but it is so only if the listener possesses the necessary emotional potential to instigate the purifying effect. It is likewise true that the influence of music can be polluting, as it is the case with music heard by and prompting a response in a mentally polluted individual. Music is inherently neutral in its qualities, while positive and negative attributes arise out of the human potential and the resulting emotional reaction provoked by the music.

The inborn qualities of music are not only neutral, but also essentially spiritual in their character. Would it then be justified at all to speak of mundane qualities in the context of music? Unlike spiritual qualities, mundane aspects are not implicit in the musical reality as innate features, but occur as specific factors resulting from the context into which music is brought. Once music is perceived by the human being and causes an emotional response, the positive and negative effects, the spiritual and mundane substances of the music are set free through the ensuent reaction. The two-sidedness of the musical influence occurs as a logical result of the natural ambivalence inherent in all things, reflecting the constant struggle between the two currents within the human soul flowing into opposite directions. It is nothing but this fundamental dialectic principle, the inborn duality of creation, which the mendicant poet pronounces when he sings: "Poison and nectar / are mingled in one - / like music / played and heard / in one single act"[6]. The prior potential, positive and negative, is latently there in the musical reality, but it becomes manifest only once the musical vibrations penetrate the emotional consciousness of man. Therefore our poet continues: "The human heart / free from flaw, / forever enlightened, / sees good and evil / same time / same place"[7]. The human heart, the abode of qualified emotions, is the very place where the musical flow is distilled and its spiritual essence extracted. The liquid contains both positive and negative qualities, constructive and destructive potential, but it is the human being who, according to his mental disposition, extracts either good or bad, nectar or poison. Music is the nourishing substance for the craving heart, yet differently inclined individuals feed themselves on different emotional ingredients: "A child sucking his mother / draws milk, / a leech at the breasts of a woman / draws blood..."[8].

The musical fluid is indeed a multicolored mixture of emotional qualities whose effects are set free once the liquid is consumed. From where do the emotional qualities emerge? From the heart of man, where music arouses an emotional experience whose impact unchains the dormant emotional potential. Music, however, releases only those qualities from within the heart that are already there; it does not - and cannot - implant or induce other qualities, both positive and negative, which do not exist at the core of the individual. The neutral, spiritual qualities inherent in the musical reality, therefore, translate into both

---

[6] Lālan Bāul, quoted in Deben Bhattacharya, *The mirror of the sky* (London: Allen & Unwin, 1969), pp.86f.

[7] ibid.

[8] ibid.

spiritual and mundane reactions once the music is played, heard and perceived by the human being. Through this capacity to instigate a qualified and motive-oriented response, music becomes a suitable tool for man to attain to a particular spiritual or rational aim. A person striving for spiritual accomplishment thus utilizes the motivating power of music to enhance the intensity of his spiritual search. In that case, the indwelling spiritual qualities of music serve an entirely spiritual purpose and remain settled on the transcendental level. What happens, however, if the same qualities are lowered onto the plane of mundane existence?

The precondition for the transfer of the inborn qualities of music onto the mundane level is a prior intention within the individual which is not exclusively directed at the spritual realm; a mundane or even utterly materialistic intention related to the phenomenal world. Such an intention does not necessarily bear a negative implication, though negative influences are more likely to enter the emotional response than in a fully spiritualized perceptive process. If, however, the response to the musical sound appears negative in its character, this negativity is not primarily caused by the music itself, but arises out of a negative impetus implicit in the prior intention. Such qualitative impulsions are immanent in the emotional potential of man, and they are released to manifest themselves as positive and negative reactions once the musical reality enters the human heart and activates the emotional sensor. Music thus does not establish new qualities within the heart, it only extricates those qualities that are already dormant. Music, therefore, cannot purify an individual or refine his emotional qualities unless a certain purifying potential exists in the person, but *vice versa*, there is likewise no danger that the influence of music might pollute an otherwise pure human being - for the heart which is flawless and free from evil intentions does not possess the potential that enables unfavorable reactions. That is to say, to put it in the words of the 9th century Islamic mystic Abū Sulaimān al-Dārāni, "music and song will not arouse *those* things in the heart that are not contained in it". And therefore it is not the music to be banished in order to retain mental purity, but the contaminating influences within one's own heart.

Pureness of the mind is thus not attained through abstinence from music. To the contrary, by means of its positive powers, music will even help to arouse and maintain those motions within the heart that have purifying influence on the individual. How do these positive powers of music become effective? - through the capacity of music to enhance the positive substance in the heart of the listener. In the same way, however, music is also capable of amplifying the immanent negative vibrations, hence how does one protect oneself from these? Protection is achieved not by abstaining from music, but in the first place by spiritual discipline, that is by not indulging in negative intentions in order to prevent the contaminating emotional forces from taking possession of the mind and heart. Spiritual discipline is the necessary condition to develop and bring forth the positive potential of man, to extract the virtuous essence of the human soul and strengthen the pure substance of the human heart. Why is spiritual discipline indispensable? The reason is the inherent ambivalence of the human soul, the dialectics of positive and negative currents, purifying and polluting elements, good and evil, poison and nectar - the vital principle of opposing energetic forces which is immanent in the nature and which guarantees the organic flow of creation. Because of this inherent ambivalence, no human heart is entirely free from negativity, but it is through spiritual discipline that the individual can prevent the negative influences from being released and developing their destructive potential.

How is spiritual discipline exercised? At what point should evil effects be averted, and how? Should one ward off unfavorable conditions through avoidance or through defiance? But is it possible at all to completely avoid, to annihilate negativity? No, it is not, because the negative and positive aspects are vital to maintain the inherent polarity of the cosmos. Keeping a neutral balance by eliminating the negative elements means therefore to eradicate the positive powers as well. Avoidance of negative influences thus cannot be the key to spiritual freedom. Confession to the constructive energies immanent in all things signifies at the same time acceptance of the likewise indwelling destructive potential, and it is the spiritual challenge that every individual encounters on his journey towards perfection: to defy the destructive capacity of the adverse forces and to tranform their energetic potential into positive currents.

What consequences does the inborn duality of things bear for the practice of music? Music as the motivator of the emotional currents is endowed with positive and negative capacities, and acknowledgement of the one requires admission of the other. That is to say, in order to efficaciously employ the inherent spiritual qualities of music, one has to be aware of the implicit mundane effects of music and their latent negative potential. If, however, worldliness prompts negative responses, would it not be better to turn away from the world, to renounce all influences related to the phenomenal world and to entirely spiritualize one's intentions? No, complete retreat from the sphere of mundane existence is neither possible nor sensible. If mundane qualities arising out of the musical reality due to a worldly context lead to negative effects, it is not necessarily penance and abstinence from the world that induces positive reactions. If music is negatively associated with orgies, with overindulgence in food and drink, then one does not have to stop eating and drinking at all in order to experience music without evoking its negative powers. To the contrary, it is the one who knows to enjoy good food who will be able to delight in music, because it is him who maintains a healthy emotional potential - rather than the ascetic exercising penance beyond good and evil, beyond all emotional perception. The one who appreciates aesthetic beauty accepts the ugliness, for he is aware that without ugliness there is no beauty. The one who enjoys music and explores its beneficial effects is likewise aware that the influence of music can be malefic, but he accepts that danger because without it there can be no benefit. And he knows that the danger is not immanent in the music but in the human being - it is immanent in man who hold the decision in favor of virtuous or evil, nectar or poison in his own hands.

But what happens to the ascetic, to the one whose aim is to reach beyond the realm of good and bad, to the one who strives after an attributeless condition? Will he ever be able to see the beauty of things? Will he ever absorb the all-pervading energy of love sent out by the soul of the universe? No, he will not. He will never revel in that ultimate bliss arising from the experience of the infinite, he will never relish the delight of aesthetic beauty, because he is so much obsessed with eliminating the negative forces that he willingly throws those very energies that would take him to his desired goal - the positive streams flowing into the ocean of bliss where good and bad merge into one single current of love. The one who renounces the world renounces also the joy that emanates from the touch of the indescribable. The one who rejects the momentum of imperfection refuses also to see the unbroken perfection of creation.

Penance, therefore, can never be the way to spiritual fulfilment, because penance dries out the emotional flow, and once emotions are dead, the vital senses for the experience of the ultimate transcendental reality are gone. Why then renounce the world if He Himself delights in it? Why turn away from material existence if the creator himself takes pleasure in his material creations? There is truly no sense in mindless penance, in closing one's eyes before the fascinating beauty only to avoid seeing the ugliness of the vulgar. With mind directed at the Supreme Being, even material enjoyment will lead to spiritual perfection, and the one who becomes immersed in the musical flow while opening his heart to the infinite will certainly not yield to the latent maleficent effects of music.

How is music enjoyed without inviting unfavorable emotional influences? In which way does one open oneself to the positive powers of music while at the same time preventing the release of averse effects? The essential factor to control the emotional impact of music on the individual is the individual's own prior mental disposition. That is to say, a person who directs his mind entirely on his spiritual goal and eradicates mundane interests from the sphere of his inner intentions, if such a person plays or hears music, he will extract spiritual benefit from the sounding reality but remains unaffected by the negative implications that may bear effect on a person inclined towards worldly intents. Why? Because the one who, striving for spiritual ends, concentrates upon the object of his emotional search, perceives the music of the soul first before he hears the musical sound that enters through the ear. The one whose mind is twisted up in worldly entanglements, on the other hand, hears the musical sound but is unable to delve into the deeper spheres where music emerges as a meaningful reality. It is however those deeper regions of the ocean of music where the positive essences are hidden, while the negative potential accumulates on the surface. Therefore, if man fully opens his mind and heart to the Supreme Being, to the ultimate object of his spiritual quest, he will hear the music that emerges from the rays of eternity, and he knows that it is this infinite music omnipresent in the universe which manifests itself in the vibrations of sound and takes the finite shape of the musical construction.

Indeed music is but a sounding expression of the silent energies of the universe, a material manifestation of the beams of joy immanent in the waves of creation. Music is the source of unbounded bliss, yet if we listen to it, it is not always the feeling of perfect happiness that we derive from music even if our mind were completely immersed in the spiritual essence of the sound. Music makes us sad, it makes us angry or distressed, even disgusted. What is the reason for this varying spectrum of emotional reactions caused by music even in spite of a primarily positive inclination of the listener? The reason is founded in the emotional disposition, in the prior emotional state of man. A person who is positively inclined, is his inner disposition always necessarily positive as well? No, it is not, even though the individual himself may not be aware of his actual state of emotions. Thus, a person inclined towards happiness may be intensely sad within, though he perhaps denies the momentum of sadness even to himself. Music, however, possesses the emotive capacity to elicit the emotional essence of man - so what happens if an outwardly happy but inwardly suffering person listens to music? The entire amassment of suppressed sadness forces its way out of the human heart where it had been held captive, and merges into an uncontrolled current of tears that washes away the joyous façade of feigned happiness - only to bring about true happiness once the emotional cloudburst has cleansed the heart of even the slightest particle of sorrow.

On the one hand it is the prior emotional state, the - sometimes even unconscious - innate potential for sadness, aggression, indifference or similar emotional reactions, that determines the quality of the response to music independent of one's own conscious inclination and intentions. In certain cases, however, music evokes reactions in the listener that do not necessarily arise out of his own mental predisposition. Listening to music may awaken sentiments of sadness in a perfectly happy person; it may cause aversion or anger in a peacefully inclined individual, and, *vice versa*, music may console the grievous and calm down the infuriated. How is this explained? In the context of musical perception, a second factor becomes relevant besides the emotional state of the listener: the emotional potential immanent in both the musical construction and the musical performance.

The phenomenon of music always involves three categories of individuals: the composer who receives the inspiration out of which he creates his musical work, the music-maker who presents the sounding construction, and the listener who responds to it. These three categories can be united in one person who conceives, renders and hears his music at the same time. More frequently, however, the functions of the composer, performer and listener are distributed among three different individuals - with the only specification that the performer is always himself a listener, for music becomes audible as soon as it is intoned: "played and heard in one single act"[9]. Music addresses not only the listener, but the composer and the performer as well. The emotional input relevant in the process of musical perception, therefore, results from three sources: in the first place, music arises out of the emotional potential which the composer has woven into his musical work and which bears effect upon the performer who plays or sings the musical composition. The performer himself, at the time of the rendition, passes his own momentary sentiments on to the musical presentation. The accumulated potential of both the composer's and the performer's emotions is finally perceived by the listener, and it is this prior potential immanent in the music at the time of its being heard, which, in conjunction with the listener's own predisposition, determines his response to the musical reality. For this reason, if a person listens to music neither composed nor rendered by him, he may be confronted with feelings that do not correspond to nor arise out of his own immediate emotional condition. Such a listener, if he is cheerfully inclined at the outset, may become overwhelmed with sadness upon hearing the music, resulting from sorrowful sentiments imparted by the composer or performer. Likewise, a mentally balanced listener may suddenly feel aggressiveness if he hears the musical work of an aggressively inclined composer, or if the performer's rendition evinces aggressive strains. Depending upon the strength inherent in the prior emotional potential of the music, the listener either becomes himself affected by the immanent sentiments, or he only notices them but retains his own emotional inclination.

But what happens if music is conceived, played and heard at once by one and the same person? If the composer, music-maker and listener are unified in one person, does music cease to draw on three emotional sources? No, it does not. Music maintains its threefold emotional input even when it emerges from one and the same individual, because the individual himself harbors different emotional currents. Music is

---

[9] ibid.

conceived in the mind out of certain emotional moves, but in the very moment the spiritual spark materializes as sung or played musical sound, the emotional shades in the heart of the music-maker may change their color. Again once the musical sound flashes back on the mind after being heard by the ear, new emotional streams enter the inner spheres of the listener only to give fresh inspiration to the mind of the composer. The process of creating, rendering and perceiving is thus a cyclic and continuous one, and it is this continuity and cyclic nature of the inspiratory progress that brings forward the musical flow and guarantees its reproductive vitality. The procreative cycle is nourished by the constant upsurge of momentary emotions emanating from the current of musical notes, while music itself is drifting on the waves of emotion.

What energies, however, instigate the uprise of music in the first place? Which is the driving force that mobilizes the emotional potential within the heart of the individual and prompts the musical inspiration? From where does the enlivening power of musical creativity originate? No, it is not external, supernatural spheres where man finds the impetus that leads him into the realm of musical imagination. The desire to express oneself in tunes, to vocalize one's inner feelings in an outburst of melodies, is immanent in every human being as an inborn longing of mankind. The spirit of music exists as an omnipresent reality filling the universe with joy, but the mind entangled in everyday affairs remains unaware of the latent beauty of the unsung song: "We haste on without heed, forgetting the flowers on the roadside hedge. Yet they breathe unaware into our forgetfulness, filling it with music"[10]. Musical inspiration is not conceived through an outside spirit - it rests in man himself, born out of the immanent love of the Supreme Soul, and it is activated once man desists from being ignorant of the infinite reality.

It is indeed the primary quest of the human soul to abolish this ignorance of its eternal lover, to overcome the forgetfulness that makes man blind for the all-pervading beauty in which the Supreme Being manifests himself - a beauty which derives its fascinating charm not from perfection of form, but from the life-giving essence of love out of which it is born. For man, the infinite presence in its ever-changing

---

[10] Rabindranath Tagore, *Lover's Gift*, XLII

outer shapes signifies the very source of being, yet the human mind loses its awareness throughout the transmigratory cycles: "You have moved from my world, to take seat at the root of my life, and therefore is this forgetting - remembrance lost in its own depth"[11]. Once the consciousness of this forgetfulness is raised, once the ignorance of the root of existence is abolished, man becomes painfully aware of his separation from the object of his yearning: "Life, like a child, laughs, shaking its rattle of death as it runs; it beckons me on; but you stand there, where you stopped behind that dust and those stars; and you are a mere picture"[12]. The human mind is naturally inclined towards rationally comprehensible realities, hence the outcry for the sensually perceptible manifestation, and the seeker recalls the time when the infinite revealed itself in the beauty of the finite: "The day was when you walked with me, your breath warm, your limbs singing of life. My world found its speech in your voice, and touched my heart with your face. You suddenly stopped in your walk, in the shadow-side of the Forever, and I went on alone"[13]. And his forgetfulness raises the doubts, because the immaterial infinity withdraws itself from the sphere of rational thought: "Are you not a mere picture, and not as true as those stars, true as this dust? They throb with the pulse of things, but you are immensely aloof in your stillness, painted form"[14].

Accepting the ultimateness of the finite, however, means to give in to an apparent dead end on the spiritual path. But can man's ultimate object of search ever be fake? Is it possible that the supreme energy of love fades from the core of the universe only because it ceases to be apparent in visible form? - "No, it cannot be. Had the life flood utterly stopped in you, it would stop the river in its flow, and the foot-fall of dawn in her cadence of colours. Had the glimmering dusk of your hair vanished in the hopeless dark, the woodland shade of summer would die with its dreams"[15]. In the depth of his heart, the spiritual seeker knows that the true passage cannot terminate in a closed end, and therefore he refuses to acknowledge the obvious futility of his striving for a seemingly non-existent reality. That means he is aware of his

---

[11] ibid.
[12] ibid.
[13] ibid.
[14] ibid.
[15] ibid.

ignorance, of his forgetfulness that hinders him from seeing the infinite truth in its unrestful manifestations, and he recognizes that only once he liberates himself from this ignorance, once he wakes up from his sleep of neglectfulness, only then he will be able to comprehend the ultimate object of his search beyond its immediate material presence. It is once man has shaken off the veil of obliviousness that he realizes the Supreme Being has not deserted him, but appears before him in a different revelation: "You are no longer before my songs, but one with them"[16]. But the inspiration for these songs - it is no more drawn from the outer realm of an alien god. The capacity to voice the soul's yearning for union with the divine rests in man himself, in the human heart where the Supreme Soul has taken his eternal abode. And ultimately, the singer discerns the timeless truth and realizes that he has lost his finite treasure only to be rewarded with the essence of infinite love:

> You came to me with the first ray of dawn. I lost you with the last gold of evening. Ever since I am always finding you through the dark. No, you are no mere picture.[17]

---

16 ibid.
17 ibid.

2

Offering and blessing: the dialectics of music

If we think of music as a sounding reality, the phenomenon that springs to mind reveals itself in a multicolored harmonic arrangement of notes produced from the musician's song or play, and perceived by the listener who chances upon the opportunity to catch the emerging tune. In its physical occurrence, music always involves these two: the one who plays and the one who hears, the music-maker and the music-recipient, the originator and the respondent. Like two opposite poles of one and the same actuality, both individuals demarcate the sphere within which the music spreads - the sphere that stretches from the source of origin to the final destination, from the musician to the music-listener, and between them the music expands like a carpet woven of a continuous chain of melodious sounds. This sphere of musical interaction is not primarily spacial, nor is it temporal, though time and space become relevant as variable and temporary factors as long as the musical presentation continues - represented by the duration of the performance and by the physical distance between the player and the listener, provided that the two of them are embodied in two independent individuals, in two different persons.

What happens, however, if only the musician himself is present to listen to his music - if music is absorbed by the very source from which it emerges without reaching out to an outside listener? The spacial expansion of the sphere of musical interaction becomes reduced to a minimum, confined within the one who plays and hears at the same time. The spacial factor is thus variable in its dimensions, while the time factor, on the other hand, remains of momentary relevance as it arises only with the first note and vanishes as soon as the last sound dies away. If not space or time, what then is it that can be regarded as the essence of that metaphysical sphere filled with music all over? Which is the substance at its basis, the fabric of which the musical carpet is made? It is subtle emotional vibrations, aroused through the musical sound, but inspirited by the flow of sentiments that instigates the music in the first place. It is the emotional intention of the music that establishes the mystical bond between the player and the listener, thereby creating a sphere of active interlink, a sphere of reciprocal giving and taking between two dialectic poles.

What does the necessary existence of the two aspects, of the creative and perceptive elements imply for the process of musical interaction? Music is always conceived from somewhere, and at the same time it is always directed somewhere. But wherefrom is music conceived, and whereat is it directed? On the simplest level, we have the constellation of music-maker and music-listener, both personified in human beings. The musician directs his song or play at the audience in front of him, and once he finds the listeners positively responding, the feedback gives fresh inspiration to his tunes. This is how the recreative process works on the primeval, most primitive level. Then, however, the question arises as to wherefrom the musician derives his creative energy in the first place, before he can possibly receive any reaction whatsoever from his human audience. Or is it only for him to give without taking anything in return, while the listener only takes without giving? Is thus the creative-perceptive process not a reciprocal one, based on mutual taking and giving, but rather a one-sided course of action in which the listener perceives what the music-maker creates, without either of them responding to the other?

No, it is not, because music can never be created out of a spiritual vacuum. There needs to be an emotional substance from which the music springs up. And music, once it has emerged, ripened and finally settled in the heart of the listener, is bound to extricate an emotional response. Therefore, no musician however talented will be able to create and shape his music without the spiritual spark having been conceived in his mind, and none of those listening, however indifferently inclined, can remain fully unaffected by the tune. To understand the basic nature of this dialectic relationship, however, we need to detach ourselves from that just too earthly metaphor of the concert performance, in which a musician unfolds his creative and artistic skills in front of a more or less appreciative audience. If they were to represent the two poles of the dialectic constellation - the musician on the one hand and his audience on the other -, then what happens to the musician who performs on his own, who practices in his lonely corner of the room, readying himself to present his music before the connoisseurs? Would not his creative energy vanish for lack of the perceptive couterpart? Would he not sit there silently, unable to utter the slightest tune, powerless to strike even the least note on his instrument? Yes, it were so if the metaphor would work - but it does not. There are countless instances of musicians rendering most beautiful melodies, enunciating most delicate songs while sitting all alone without even the trace of a human audience. Yet their music is being perceived, appreciated and again reflected upon them as musical inspiration. Their music is being heard, but the listener does not reveal himself in visible form.

So who is that real 'audience', the invisible listener whose apprehensive response becomes the musician's prime source of inspiration? At whom is the music directed? The 'listener', is he always necessarily a person and the 'audience' an assembly of human beings, each equiped with a pair of ears fit to perceive the surrounding waves of sound? No, it is not like this. The one who takes and gives at the same time, who hears and creates music in one single act does not depend on a human sense organ to sensitize him to the vibrations of the heart. Because he himself is the music that reveals itself in a colorful array of harmonious sounds, thus becoming accessible to sense of hearing. The true listener is not the one who listens with the ear, he is not the human being in his physical essence who perceives the music as a mere entity of organized sounds. He - that transcendental listener to whom the musician directs his tune, and from whom he likewise derives his musical inspiration - is the one who listens with the heart, and who creates within the heart. He, the supreme transcendental energy, is the one who becomes manifest in the heart of the music-maker, filling it with ever fresh inspiration while at the same time rejoicing in his own creative beauty. He is the inner listener and also the creator, the core of the dialectic mechanism unified in one and the same reality.

But if the ultimate transcendental reality as such represents already the essence of the dialectic constellation, if both dialectic poles rest in one and the same entity, then where is the need for the musician? Where does the musician stand if the dialectic requirement is fulfilled even without him? With the musician, the human being on the one side, and the Supreme Reality on the other, how can the dialectic construction be put together if the one component is complete in itself while the other is not? Yes, it is true that the Supreme Being carries both the creative and the perceptive elements in himself, inspiration and ensuent excitement, but how can these energies be released, how can they freely interact if they are confined within one single entity? How can the dialectic process become effective if its active parts are strangulated in a stagnant union?

The dialectic relationship will function only where there is the freedom of action enabling both dialectic components to unfold their distinct qualities. It is for this very reason that the Creator himself, in spite of all his inborn perfection, cannot accomplish the procreation of beauty without shattering the ties of inert completeness. So in order to enjoy the dialectic play, he turns towards man as his interacting counterpart and divides the rôles of the play between himself and his human co-player. Why? Because the mere static existence of two energetic forces cannot incite the creative progress. The inspiratory flow of creation is set in motion only once the play, the active dialectic interplay between the two forces becomes effective.

What consequences does this bear on the creative-perceptive process of music? The Supreme Being interacts with the musician in order to instigate the musical current. But in the play of music-making, who is the player and who is the listener? If the infinite one were to take the rôle of the listener, of the one who hears and responds, then how could the musician, the human being assume the rôle of the creator and present his music before Him who is the essence of all music? From where would he derive his musical inspiration unless the Supreme One has given it to him? This is indeed the core principle of the imaginative play between the finite and the infinite, between the created and the Creator, between man and God: the Supreme Being holds the strings of the play in his hands - it is Him who distributes the rôles, and it is Him who bestows upon man the capacity to enact his proper part. And since the play is a dialectic one, it is played with interchangeable rôles. At times it is the musician who plays, the poet who sings while the transcendental listener silently revels in the beauty of his own melodies. Again at times, the poet becomes reticent and the instrument abandons its tune in the halting hands of the musician, and both become listeners absorbed in the infinite music of the universe.

It is this silent listening, the ultimate experience of all-pervading sweetness concealed in the vibrations of sound, that turns into the music-maker's prime source of inspiration. If the creative game were to be played with fixed rôles, if the musician were only to produce tunes and never to listen to the Creator's charming cadences, his imaginative energies were soon exhausted and his voice would fade. Interchange, mutual enrichment is therefore vital to keep the dialectic play going; it is essential to ensure the continuity of the musical flow. The procreative process gains its driving force from the alternation of sound and silence, vocalizing and listening, creating and perceiving. While listening, the listener's part is to observe silence lest he will not hear the music-maker's tune. The silence of the one makes the music of the other audible, hence the poet says: "I know not how thou singest, my master! I ever listen in silent amazement"[1]. Once his heart has been tuned to the music of the infinite, the silent listener begins to make out the unparalleled dignity of this music, artfully shaped yet furnished with unsuspected emotional powers: "The light of thy music illumines the world. The life breath of thy music runs from sky to sky. The holy stream of thy music breaks through all stony obstacles and rushes on"[2].

Now that he has taken his first glimpse of the greatness of his master's music, the astounded listener feels instantly inspired and wishes to express his newly gained excitement in tunes of his own: "My heart longs to join thy song..."[3] - but he cannot. He remains paralyzed at the overwhelming impact of beauty, and his captivated heart "vainly struggles for a voice"[4], leaving him utterly confused and frustrated: "I would speak, but speech breaks not into song, and I cry out baffled. Ah, thou hast made my heart captive in the endless meshes of thy music, my master!"[5]. Yet he remains voiceless only in initial astonishment. His silence will last only for as long as it is his part to listen. Once the play continues with reversed rôles, once he is no more the listener but himself the one who renders the tune, his muteness gives way to sounding eloquence nourished by the joy arising from the ultimate transcendental experience. It is now the humble musician's turn to manifest in melodies his inspiration conceived through the vision of the eternal music-maker, and it is now his turn to captivate his master's heart with his own music.

Listening to the music of the Supreme One, the musician had been delighted and his creative spirit had become refreshed. But now that he assumes the active rôle within the play, now that he delivers the music himself, what is his gain? Having tasted the ultimate sweetness

---

[1] Rabindranath Tagore, *Gītāñjali*, III
[2] ibid.
[3] ibid.
[4] ibid.
[5] ibid.

enveloped in the rays of music sent out by the lord of the universe, what else remains to be experienced which is sweeter even then that music? Having relished the essence of essences, which is the quintessence yet to be tried? Now, sweeter than the substance is the source from which it emerges, hence sweeter than the music of the infinite is He who creates it in his continuous play of sound and silence. And the musician who renders his tune before the eternal listener will experience this ultimate reality, for now he attains to the lord himself. Immersed in his song, he suddenly becomes aware of the divine presence evoked by the notes: "You came down from your throne and stood at my cottage door. I was singing all alone in a corner, and the melody caught your ear. You came down and stood at my cottage door"[6]. And himself bewildered at the effect of his humble melody, he exclaims: "Masters are many in your hall, and songs are sung there at all hours. But the simple carol of this novice struck at your love"[7].

What is it that makes even the slightest tune eligible to bring about ultimate fulfilment? What energy possesses the capacity to enrapture the heart of the Supreme Being and to lure Him away from his abode of divine aloofness to delight in union with the human soul? The singer remains puzzled and excited once he realizes that "one plaintive little strain mingled with the great music of the world, and with a flower for a prize you came down and stopped at my cottage door"[8], but he does not seek an explanation. Yet the motive is clear and the reason at hand. If the singer were just to utter his melody, aimlessly and without direction, the dialectic mechanism would not work and the sound would vainly die away. Likewise if the listener were only to absorb the music, indifferently and unsympathetically, the dialectic relationship could not be established and the dialectic game not be played. But this is not the case in the dialectic dramaturgy of creation, for the music-maker consciously directs his tune at the listener, while the listener wilfully responds to it. Addressing his master, the lord of the world, the singer matches his simple melody "with the great music of the world", and it is the sheer sincerity of emotion conveyed by this melody that enchants the heart of the infinite. Apprehending the love concealed in the musical

---

6 Rabindranath Tagore, *Gītāñjali*, XLIX
7 ibid.
8 ibid.

notes, the Divine Listener responsively reveals himself to his singer, and he comes down from the throne of royal greatness to lose himself in the simplicity of human affection.

While the dialectic mechanism enables the effective interchange of sound and silence, the interaction of creative and perceptive spirits, music as such is always produced out of a prior intention and is aimed at a specific purpose to fulfil. In the universal play of music-making, the object of music is defined by the direction the musical current takes. Depending upon the way in which the rôles are distributed among the participants in the dialectic game, music emanates from either the phenomenal or the transcendental plane, and is received on either the human or the divine level. As long as it remains the musician's part to voice his song or to strike his instrument before the Eternal Listener, the flow of notes makes its way from the realm of physical concreteness towards the sphere of spiritual consciousness. Once rôles are exchanged and it is the musician's turn to listen to the music of the Eternal Music-maker, the musical stream too reverses its course and runs from the transcendental level to the mundane realm. Since the dialectic game is one of continuous rôle reversal, the current of musical sounds constantly alters its direction, resulting in an everlasting cycle between origin and destination, destination and origin.

The circular concept at the basis of the dialectic flow is of essential relevance for the effectiveness of the procreative energy that incites the musical progression. If music were to develop in a linear direction, the rays of sound would be swallowed up in the hollow emptiness of infinity, and the emotional essence of the tune remains wasted in universal non-responsiveness. The musician who time and again delivers his song before an indifferent listener vainly exhausts his resources, and unable to attain the love he strives for, finally "in tears, dies of regret and pain"[9]. And likewise, music itself would die if the melody of the infinite remained entirely unheard in the realm of heedless worldly beings. Mutual respondency is crucial to establish the generative cycle that instigates all evolution, development and advancement. Therefore the music-maker and the listener are bound to interact.

---

[9] Madan Bāul, quoted in Deben Bhattacharya, *The mirror of the sky* (London: Allen & Unwin, 1969), p.93

Creation and perception can form a dialectic constellation only as long as they inspire each other mutually. The cyclic motion of the musical flow represents the vital cause for its continuity, because it ensures mutuality, while a linear movement implies one-sidedness, hence deadly stagnation.

Seeking out for his listener's response, what is the musicians prime intent in rendering his tune? Is it idle self-interest, the search for mere amusement in a multicolored chain of notes? No, certainly not, or else there would be no need for even an abstract, transcendental listener. The singer who gives voice to his inner feelings in well-shaped sounding artefacts pursues a higher goal than enjoyment of his own. He vocalizes the emotional strains hidden in the depth of his heart in order to communicate them to the Divine Listener. Through musical cadences he discloses the secret of his soul and offers its innate treasure to his master, and he says "my songs contain my prayers"[10]. It is an indelible opening up of his innermost emotive spheres arising out of the unsuppressable desire to share his experiences with the one who is dearest to him, which inspires the musician to put forth his sentiments in melodious phrases. Hence the poet exclaims: "Even if you forbid, / dear friend, / I am helpless. / My songs contain / my prayers"[11]. The offering is unasked for, yet the one who offers expects a response. He therefore transforms the sounding expression of emotions into prayer and calls upon his friend and listener, hoping that the unexplained yearning of his heart be fulfilled.

But is the song offering truly an unsought one, made by the poet out of an impulsive strain without being invited by the one to whom it is directed? No, it is not. For if it were so, if the musical prayer would come as an unwelcomed intrusion, the singer would never have found his voice to utter a single melody. Why? Because He who listens is at the same time the one who creates the tune, the stimulative source from which all music emerges. Because He who receives the offering is also the one who bestows the ability to offer. It is Him who shapes the offering according to his own imaginative will: "Some flowers pray / through the glamour of colours / and others, being dark / with fragrance.

---

[10] ibid.
[11] ibid.

/ As the *vīṇā* prays / with its vibrating strings, / do I with my songs"[12]. It is the transcendental listener himself who flashes the spark of inspiration on the musician's mind and causes his accumulated emotional potential to burst out in a downpour of melodies. Yet the singer is not aware of this divine blessing, exclaiming "I am helpless" as he fears that the lord will reject his offering. Engrossed in his own music he fails to recognize that the Supreme Being is listening, and seeks to justify his seemingly immodest song.

Why does the musician remain impercipient of the very source from which he is drawing? Why is he uncertain about the reception of his offering, about the effectiveness of his prayer, while the offering has already been accepted, the prayer been heard? His incomprehension is only temporary, and it is part of the dialectic hide-and-seek played by the one who controls the strings of the game. The Divine Listener wisely keeps himself hidden from the musician's consciousness, thereby stimulating him ever again to continue his song in order to provoke the listener to come out of his concealment. The musician, on the other hand, senses his listener's presence, but he is not able to recognize whether his music is prompting a response, hence he keeps the musical current afloat. It is at the discretion of the Supreme One to end the hiding-game, appearing before the musician and thus giving him the highest reward for his offering of tunes. But the very instant the singer discerns the object of his search, the very moment his awareness is raised, his music breaks off and he stands in silence before the infinite reality. Now that he knows the lord to have accepted his offering, why should he continue to strive for something which has been fulfilled, why should he repeat his prayer which has already been responded to? The turning-point has come when the dialectic play continues with rôles reversely distributed, and the musician quiets down to be open to the music of the divine.

If music directed from the phenomenal towards the transcendental level, from man to God takes the form of an offering, then what is the intent of music flowing into the opposite direction, from the spiritual sphere towards the human realm? For what motive does the Supreme Being reverse the rôles in the play, silencing the human singer to deluge him in the pure current of supernal melodies? Music emitted by the

---

[12] ibid.

divinity, which takes the course from the infinite towards the finite, is born out of the sympathetic reaction to the musical offering made by man, but at the same time it is also the driving force which establishes the prior capacity to make the offering. Thus, the two musical currents mutually effect each other in accordance with the cyclic nature of the dialectic mechanism. But while the human being produces his music out of an immanent desire to express his inner emotions, what is it that inspires the transcendental reality to send out its radiating sound of musical cadences? Once the lord is rendering his own tune, what secret is it that He wishes to tell his human listener? Is the Infinite One not free from emotional strains, is He not unaffected by the sentiments of the human heart, unsusceptible to pleasure and pain?

Yes, he is. And yet no, he is not. He remains the neutral energy only as long as he keeps himself passively aloof from his own play of creation. But for the very sake of maintaining that play, he needs to abandon his unconcern and to indulge in the joys and sorrows of the world. And thus the human singer's tune strikes at the heart of the Supreme One and elicits an emotional response. Listening to the human musician's melodious phrases, the Divine Being instantly wishes to reciprocate the love rendered in the guise of the musical notes. Having received the offering, he communicates his message of acceptance through the medium of his own music. How does this transcendental music come to the human being? It comes in the likeness of a blessing, of divine grace bestowed upon the human listener to fulfil the longing of his heart voiced in the prayer conveyed by his song. The dialectic process of giving and taking, offering and receiving, singing and listening progresses in a continuous cycle of mutual responsiveness. The Supreme Soul interacts with the human soul in order to achieve his own perfection, for God's love finds fulfilment only in the love of man. The Eternal Music-maker thus seeks out for his human listener to share the sweetness of his tune, and the Eternal Listener reaches for the human musician to partake of the great music of the universe.

According to the dialectic principle, music is offered and received, emitted and discerned, "played and heard in one single act"[13]. Offering and blessing represent the two aspects, the two interacting poles of the

---

[13] Lālan Bāul, quoted in Deben Bhattacharya, op.cit., pp.86f.

dialectic constellation that cause the two-fold direction of the musical current: offered music in the form of song-prayer flowing from the human towards the divine level, and musical blessing bearing the shape of spiritual inspiration streaming from the transcendental towards the human realm. In a wider sense, however, the offering is at the same time also blessing, and the blessing is offering likewise. How is this explained? The musician who voices his prayer in tunes presents it as an offering at the altar of the Divine Listener, but how is the offering taken, how is it received by the Supreme Being? - as blessing. The Infinite One accepts the simple string of notes as the sacred garland of love, and for Him, the humble song-offering turns into unbounded grace manifest in the perfect beauty of the musical sound. In return for the blessing thus received from his human singer, the lord of the universe offers a melody of his own, and again the offering turns into blessing once it reaches its destination. Why? Because offering and blessing are the two sides of one and the same coin, their concrete appearance depending upon the side on which the coin is turned: the blessing is sent out as offering from the dispatching end, and the offering is conceived as blessing at the receiving end.

Both offered and received music, like music "played and heard in one single act", arise and unfold in one single instance, because the current of musical sounds cannot flow unless its full circular course is established. The stream of music, therefore, is set in motion only once both its directions are activated. But given the cyclic nature and the dual direction of the musical flow, resulting from the dialectic mechanism that works at the core of musical creativity, the question arises as to the deeper significance of this mechanism. Is the dialectic principle not merely a purpose in its own end, a meaningless cycle that flows without destination? No, it is not, because the musical current takes its prime course between two points, between creator and recipient, between music-maker and listener, between origin and destination. Why, however, does this seemingly linear movement between source and merging-point ultimately become cyclic? The reason is the dialectic relationship that exists between the two points. Once the musical flow has reached its destination, the merging-point automatically transforms into the turning-point where the current changes its direction and flows back to the source of its origin, which is now no more origin but itself destination. Since the process of transformation is a continuous one, the change of direction too occurs as an ongoing phenomenon causing the cyclic progression of the musical current.

In the dialectic play of music-making, the dual direction of the musical flow signifies not merely an interaction between two poles, but symbolizes the living exchange between the phenomenal and the transcendental realms. The reciprocity of the two spheres becomes effective because origin and destination of the musical sound are located on different levels, because singer and listener are settled on different planes. Music is either directed from the mundane to the divine, or from the divine to the mundane realms, but following the rules of the dialectic game, music can never remain confined to a single sphere, it can never take course towards its destination without transgressing the boundary of the plane from which it emanates. Why? The answer is grounded on the unequal predisposition of the two levels of perception, the finite and the infinite, the perfect and the imperfect, the complete and the incomplete. While the Supreme Being on the one end of the dialectic constellation carries both the creative and the perceptive elements in himself, man on the other end can draw only on the potential the Creator has given to him. But how is that potential conferred upon him? - through the active interchange between the human and the divine spheres in the process of mutual giving and taking. If this interaction would not involve both levels, there could be no exchange of potencies. The constructive energies that instigate the creative-perceptive process of music-making would therefore remain confined to the source in which they rest - imprisoned at the core of the Supreme Reality and unable to be released from within the one who is complete in himself. Confinement, however, means unability to act, hence the human being is left empty-hearted and unfruitful because the energetic forces do not reach him on the phenomenal level and thus cannot bear effect upon him. It is for this very reason that the two poles of the dialectic constellation need to be established on different perceptual planes: to ensure that the driving energies are set free from their source in order to incite the creative current.

The progenitive process of music-making is characterized by the existence of two dialectic poles located on the spiritual and phenomenal levels respectively, but what happens if a human musician presents his music before a human audience? Does the demand for reciprocity between the two spheres in the universal process of creation rule out a small-scale reciprocity between two poles located on one and the same sphere? No, it does not, because fundamental principles are always applicable to both maximized and minimized planes of action. It is therefore legitimate to transfer the larger principle of mutual exchange onto the limited terrain of human interplay. The musician who plays or sings before his assembled listeners surely interacts with them, communicating his sentiments to them according to his momentary mood, and in turn taking up the flashes of inspiration transmitted through the responsive attitude of the audience. It is only once the configuration of music-maker and listener is conveyed onto the universal plane, once the dialectic link between creator and recipient is related to the universal flow of music, that the constellation changes and that human singer and human audience no more embody two opposite poles of the dialectic construction, but merge to form a single side in a larger dialectic process.

What is it that enables the coalescence of two reciprocally interacting parties into an homogenous entity? Does the transformation of the active dialectics of musician and listener into a passive co-existence not contradict the dialectic principle of mutuality? Yes, it does - so what happens to the dialectic process? Nothing. The process continues as before, but the perspective from which it is evaluated changes. The two human parties - singer and listener - remain interacting from the perspective of the phenomenal sphere, but from the universal perspective, they are settled on one and the same side of the dialectic constellation, because in the universal context, the dialectic exchange takes place between the phenomenal and the spiritual realms. In the universal course of music-making, the two dialectic poles are formed by the Supreme Being on the one side and humankind on the other, the latter incorporating both musicians and listeners in the same way as the Infinite is himself at once listener and music-maker.

Determined by its dialectic disposition, music lives from the active interplay between source and destination, between the one who produces and emits it and the one who absorbs it. Music hence moves in a continuous current between the point from which it is sent out and the point where it is received. Like the direction of its flow, the intent of music too is two-fold: music is dispatched as offering and accepted as blessing. This dual intention, however, becomes effective only when the exchange takes place between different levels of existence, and both the transcendental and the phenomenal realms form part of the dialectic constellation. Why? Because the definition of musical offering and musical blessing, the way in which the two acts are perceived, is fixed upon the sphere from which music emanates in the first place. In the concrete, that means that on the phenomenal plane, man is most likely to regard his own music as an offering while he takes the musical inspiration received from the spiritual plane as a blessing. The universal view, however, acknowledges offered music to effect as blessing at the receiving end, be that on the phenomenal plane or on the spiritual plane, and likewise it acknowledges that the primary intent of any music sent out from either plane is offering.

What accounts for the perceptual difference between the human view and the universal view? The answer lies in man's own attitude towards the Supreme Reality, in the way he perceives his relationship with the infinite. As long as man approaches the Divine Being with awe due to a supramundane presence, he will not be able to place himself on one and the same level with his eternal lover, but remains evaluating his feat from the position of self-imposed inferiority. It is only once man realizes that both him and his divine counterpart, though settled on different planes, are acting on one and the same level defined by the all-unifying bond of love, that he recognizes that his own musical offering blesses the Supreme One, and that the lord of the universe could not utter his melodies unless he is inspired by the humble human singer's tune. It is the realization of this very fact of reciprocity, of equally shared potencies that emboldens the poet to call out to his god: "your lips can have their smile, and your flute its music, only in your delight in my love"[14]. Acknowledging the cosmic law of mutuality at the basis of the dialectic principle, the poet knows that "my longing is to meet you in play of love, my Lover; but this longing is not only mine, but also yours"[15], and when he consequently concludes that "therefore you are importunate, even as I am"[16], the simple village singer expresses nothing

---

[14] Bāul song, quoted in Rabindranath Tagore, *Creative Unity* (New Delhi: Macmillan India Ltd., reprint 1995), p.81

[15] ibid.

[16] ibid.

but the universal truth of dialectic interchange between giver and taker, between lover and beloved, between music-maker and listener.

Music is presented as an offering and received as a blessing, but does partaking of offering and blessing always necessarily imply active participation in the act of music-making? No, it does not - for else how could the passive human listener be part of the dialectic process on the universal level, forming one single pole of the dialectic constellation together with the human musician? How does that constellation work, with human singers and audience on the one side, and the Divine Listener on the other? The song offering directed towards the transcendental realm is presented by humankind as such, but is this offering not actually made by the musician only, who actively renders the tune? No - the listener too partakes of it. The listener who, immersed in the sound of the musical notes, directs his mind at the Divine Being and weaves the silent prayer of his heart into the melodious current that makes its way towards the sphere of the infinite, that listener, though outwardly passive, is inwardly as actively engaged in the offering as is the musician himself. Consequently, both singer and listener partake likewise of the blessing once the Supreme One has accepted their offering, because the principle of reciprocity knows no distinction between exterior and interior involvement.

What is the significance of music received in the form of divine blessing, or blessing received in the form of divine music, for the human being thus graced? For man, the musical blessing sent out from the realm of ultimate sweetness represents the very source of life. Without the mellow sounds of the music that originates in the unknown depth of the infinite, without the stimulating touch of tuneful inspiration arising from the living experience of the unseen reality, the world of earthly beings remains despondent and perturbed. "The young and the aged / are constantly joyless, / longing to be at your precious feet. / The animals and the birds / are restless, fitful / not hearing your flute sing"[17] - in these words, the mendicant poet describes the woeful state of the Legendary Land after the parting of its presiding divinity. Received music, thus, is an utter necessity for its human recipients in order to stay alive. But is there any need for the Divine Being on the other end of the

---

[17] Lālan Bāul, quoted in Deben Bhattacharya, op.cit., p.86

dialectic constellation to be given the musical offering from the realm of man? Is He not the illimitable, imperishable reality existing in its own right without recourse to the phenomenal world? Yes, he is, but at the same time he is not, because the infinite turns real only when it manifests itself in finite form, and the perfect appears truly consummate only once it is accomplished in the imperfect. Therefore the Supreme Being, instead of keeping himself imperiously aloof, is constantly in search for his human companion, knowing that his own yearning will be fulfilled only when he meets the human soul that longs for union. The poet says "your flute can have its music only in your delight in my love" - the ultimate reality is there, eternally and immutably, but that same supreme transcendental reality finds its sweetness only in the love of man, hence finds its music only in the music of man.

Once he receives the blessing disguised as divine music, how does the listener respond? What sentiments does the sounding manifestation of love arouse in him? The primary and primeval emotion stirred up in the heart of man upon perceiving the cosmic melody is the feeling of infinite bliss, the feeling of overwhelming joy - a joy just being there without beginning or end, an all-pervading joy which with its own rays of excellence covers up the very source from which it emerges: "Sailing through the night I came to life's feast, and the morning's golden goblet was filled with light for me. I sang in joy"[18] - bewildered at the sudden omnipresence of overflowing delight, the human heart wishes to voice its happiness and bursts out in tunes of its own. In that first moment of stunning amazement, the singer is not concerned about the originator of his joy: "I knew not who was the giver, and I forgot to ask his name"[19]. He only knows the emerging delight as such, as a living experience of colorful tunes, and it is the impact of this very experience which keeps its arouser in the unseen: "I ask his name, but I only see his light through the silence and feel his smile filling the darkness"[20].

The reciprocal action of offering and receiving music signifies at the same time the mutual interplay of sound and silence: it is in silence

---

[18] Rabindranath Tagore, *Crossing*, XXXVI
[19] ibid.
[20] ibid.

that the blessing is received, but its response is given in sounding musical cadences. Once quietness enters the listener's mind, he readies himself for the arrival of the joy-bearing tune: "I wait for thy shower to come down in the night when I open my breast and receive it in silence"[21]. As soon as delight descends upon his heart, his desire rises to vocalize the bliss thus attained. But this desire does not come merely as a selfish quest for one's own expression; it rather represents the inborn yearning for reciprocal return, inspired by the dialectic principle of active interchange. Hence the listener, the recipient of divine bliss confesses: "I long to give thee in return my songs and flowers"[22]. Yet his melody may not break forth immediately, and he remains silent, voiceless under the overpowering force of the emotional impact, even as he grumbles out disappointedly, "empty is my store, and only the deep sigh rises from my heart..."[23]. The moment, however, will come when emotions have settled, when the poet regains his speech and the singer finds his tune anew, so he declares confidently, "I know that thou wilt wait for the morning when my hours will brim with their riches"[24].

Beyond alternate sound and silence, the dialectics of offering and receiving implies yet another reciprocity: the interplay of emotional light and shadow, reflected in the mutual exchange of yearning and inspiration, pain and bliss. The silent listener who, filled with bliss born out of the cosmic melody, vainly struggles for his voice desparate for an inspiratory strain - what does he feel in the depth of his heart? Pain, immense pain at his own ineptness to repay his debt to the generous giver of joy. It is only once this state of momentary incapability dissolves, once his creative energy brings the music back to his instrument and loosens the tune imprisoned in it, that distress will turn into delight and the pain gives way to happiness. But what happens on the other hand to the music-maker who keeps on rendering his song, striking his instrument with not even the least response emerging from his secretive audience? Would he derive any joy from his offering directed to an uncommunicative recipient? No, certainly not. He languishes under the pain of indifference inflicted upon him by the non-responsiveness of his listener, a pain which can be removed only once

---

[21] Rabindranath Tagore, *Crossing*, XXVII
[22] ibid.
[23] ibid.
[24] ibid.

the listener abandons his passive attitude and allows mutuality to enter his relationship with the musician, for both of them can find perfect delight only once one-sidedness turns into mutuality, action into interaction.

Bliss and pain, however, are not always clearly distinguishable and their borderline remains fluent. Excessive bliss always carries the essence of pain, while excessive pain has nowhere to go but to merge into the stream of bliss. Why? Because He who is the motivator of all dialectic interchanges, the initiator of all creative forces, the source of all musical currents, bears both bliss and pain in his own heart, and reveals the two opposite poles as the core substance of his love. Startled at love's two-fold reality, the poet ponders over the nature of his emotions, asking himself whether they be joy or sorrow: "Someone has secretly left in my hand a flower of love. Someone has stolen my heart and scattered it abroad in the sky. I know not if I have found him or I am seeking him everywhere, if it is a pang of bliss or of pain"[25]. Once the emotional moves translate into music, however, the question of bliss and pain as such becomes redundant. What is the reason? As soon as the musical flow in its dual determination is activated, the painful struggle for emotional articulation finds its fulfilment in tunes, and the distress of searching is no more perceived as discomfort but gives way to delight: "I knew not when your doors opened and I stood surprised at my own heart's music"[26]. Yet the newly gained joy cannot at once completely erase the signs of the pain lived through, hence an uncertainty remains: "are there still traces of tears in my eyes though the bed is made, the lamp is lit, and we are alone, you and I?"[27].

How is this last doubt resolved? It loses itself in the colorful sweetness of melodies, of music received time and again as the highest gift from a loving soul, of music offered time and again as the ultimate sacrifice of a loving heart. The music-maker says: "when I come to my King's house I have only this single song to offer it for his wreath"[28]. But is that song truly his own? The musician's answer is simple yet clear:

---

[25] Rabindranath Tagore, *Crossing*, XXXIII
[26] Rabindranath Tagore, *Crossing*, L
[27] ibid.
[28] Rabindranath Tagore, *Crossing*, LXIV

> My songs are the same as are the spring flowers,
> they come from you.
> Yet I bring these to you as my own.
> You smile and accept them, and you are glad at
> my joy of pride.
> If my song flowers are frail and they fade and
> drop in the dust, I shall never grieve.
> For absence is not loss in your hand, and the
> fugitive moments that blossom in beauty are
> kept ever fresh in your wreath.[29]

No, the musical offering can never be the offerer's own make. It is not possible, because man can have his music only when the Creator strikes the notes on his instrument, and the Divine Music-maker finds his tune only in the love of man. Dependent on each other, the two thus persistently seek to meet, and it is out of their union that music is born.

---

[29] Rabindranath Tagore, *Crossing*, LXV

3

The infinity of music

Thou hast made me endless, such is thy pleasure.
This frail vessel thou emptiest again and
again, and fillest it ever with fresh life.
This little flute of reed thou hast carried over hills
and dales, and hast breathed through it
melodies eternally new.
At the immortal touch of thy hands my little heart
loses its limits in joy and gives birth to
utterance ineffable.
Thy infinite gifts come to me only on these very
small hands of mine. Ages pass, and still
thou pourest, and still there is room to fill.

Rabindranath Tagore, *Gītāñjali*, I

What is music? Ostensibly music takes the concrete shape of a combination of physical sounds arrayed harmoniously to create beauty of features and emotional satisfaction. Thus it appears that the inner essence of music is sound, an organized construction built up of audible sensations emerging from the oscillating air, a succession of sound waves which poses as the fundamental material truth at the core of music. The sounding phenomenon is finite by nature and linear in its character: it begins when the vibration of the surrounding medium is instigated and ends as soon as this vibration stops, and it stretches in a straight line between the source of its origin and the sensor by which it is perceived. But what is the meaning of music? Finiteness and utter linearity are not apt to generate beauty or emotional pleasure, hence the bare facts about its physical occurence contradict the very purpose of music. Sound, therefore, though it determines the outer appearance of music, cannot be the ultimate reality. There has to be a deeper meaning concealed behind the material cover of sound fabrics. What is this substance that forms the quintessence of music? Which is the fluid that runs through the veins of the musical construction, filling it with life? What is music actually made of?

Facts, produced by logic and reason, will not lead to an answer. Why? Because the key to the mystery of musical potency is kept beyond the reach of rationality. Rabindranath Tagore, one of the greatest thinkers of the present century, illustrates this simple truth with a demonstrative example:

> Let us suppose that the Man from the Moon comes to the earth and listens to some music in a gramophone. He seeks for the origin of the delight produced in his mind. The facts before him are a cabinet made of wood and a revolving disc producing sound; but the one thing which is neither seen nor can be explained is the truth of the music, which his personality must immediately acknowledge as a personal message. It is neither in the wood, nor in the disc, nor in the sound of the notes...The facts of the gramophone make us aware of the laws of sound, but the music gives us personal companionship[1].

We may take this example as the most drastic of all cases, but even if the music were not produced by an inanimate machine but by a living musician, we wonder why the music appeals to us personally even though the musician may not have addressed it explicitly to us. It is the music as such that allures us, and not the device of the gramophon or the person of the musician. Of course music as a physical reality needs its material originator in order to emerge, but the technical source of the sound and the metaphysical source of the music are two different things.

What is it that makes music exist as an incorporeal entity in its own right independent of its material sound-base? What is it that accounts for the emotional appeal music possesses but mere sound is lacking? How come that music carries a personal message to the listener while the musician remains anonymous, sometimes even hidden behind a lifeless sound-producing object? The secret of musical attractiveness lies in the inherent oneness of music - spiritual oneness which allows the musical reality to transgress the limits of physical sound and to expand its rays into the infinite strata of the universe, just as oneness itself represents the very source of infinity. Sound is finite in time and space, but music is not: music springs up as inspiration before the first note is

---

[1] *Creative Unity* (New Delhi: Macmillan India Ltd., reprint 1995), pp.11-12

uttered, and it lasts as memory long after the last sound has died away. Music is born out of the alliance of sound and imagination, hence it embodies the quintessence of universal integrity, unifying at its core the elements of finiteness and infinity, of duality and oneness, of material manifestation and spiritual substance.

If we want to identify the meaning of music, to return to our initial question, we have to go beyond the act of the musical performance, for the musical performance in its concrete appearance is nothing but an exposition of musical sounds, hence of perishable finitude. Sounds, melodies composed of note-strings, emerge and disappear into the unknown spheres of the infinite, giving way to the dark veil of silence. Why else would the disappointed poet lament: "My songs were like milk and honey and wine, they were held in the rhythm of my beating heart, but they spread their wings and fled away, the darlings of idle hours, and my heart beats in silence"[2]? The music presented in the musical performance is finite, it comes and goes with the sound. But music as such, music which is not bound by the immediate implication of 'musical performance', is endless in its scope. It is there as the vibrations of the universe; it is there as the music of beauty, of love, of harmony. It is there as the music that manifests itself in sound, but whose essence is silence - the silent yearning of the soul to express its fulness in tunes. It is this music that conveys the message from the other shore of the cosmic stream; it is this music which is itself the river and also the vehicle that takes across. It is the infinite truth of music taking different shapes and appearances only to reveal itself as the fundamental oneness of emotional fluids, the merging-point where all emotional currents dissolve into one single ocean of joy.

What unifying energy accounts for the inherent integrity of music? From which stimulating potency does music derive its capacity of infinite expansiveness? How is it possible that music time and again pours out to the full its accumulated emotional potential without ever exhausting itself? Which is the reproductive force assuring that the vessel of music be filled ever anew with fresh melodies? It is love - the invisible procreative power of love, for "love is the positive quality of the Infinite, and love's sacrifice accordingly does not lead to emptiness,

---

2 Rabindranath Tagore, *Lover's Gift*, XXXI

but to fulfilment"[3]. Love for whom? - for the one to whom the music is addressed; love for that one into whose direction the musical flow makes its way. Because this very love represents the stimulus that arouses the music in the first place. Out of love, out of the loving soul's urgent desire to communicate its feelings to the object of its love and to reach out to the heart of the beloved, the musical current is motivated, and out of the same love that current is kept in motion. It is love which acts as the very cause of infinity, of never-endingness, of continuity. For the sake of love, the river remains flowing towards the sea in search of fulfilment, and his love becomes consummate once his waters merge into the waters of the ocean. For the sake of love, the music-maker continues to weave his garland of notes into the great melody of the universe. As long as love persists, the musical stream will not be short of tunes and the river will not be short of water; the currents move on in unbroken consistence. Rivers dry out and singers lose their music only when their love fades, and they become impuissant and reticent for the lack of the vital energy.

If love be the "positive quality of the Infinite", infinity is at the same time the positive quality of love. In fact it is this momentum of infinity which signifies the quintessence of love, and by virtue of its infinity true love is revealed. It is the substance of the infinite at its core that qualifies an emotion as love, and it is the presence or absence of that same substance that tells the difference between pure love and infatuation. Love is by nature infinite whereas infatuation is not. Love is limitless; infatuation remains bound to its immediate object. Love is immeasurable and incalculable; infatuation amounts to varying degrees of intensity calculated along the needs of its self-indulgent purpose. Love is inexhaustibe; infatuation consumes itself in vain pursuits. Love is interminable; infatuation evaporates when its target disappears. Love is the procreative energy of the infinite, whose sacrifice "does not lead to emptiness, but to fulfilment", whereas infatuation opposes the very idea of sacrifice. If it is the acceptance of complete self-sacrifice that endows love with the quality of unending reproductiveness, infatuation remains infertile and dies strangulated by its own selfishness. Infatuation, therefore, can never create music. It can create sounds, but these sounds

---

[3] Rabindranath Tagore, *Creative Unity*, p.75

will never commingle to form music, because they are lacking the imaginative spirit of infinity.

Music arises out of the essence of the infinite, but from where does it originate? Where is the infinite truth settled? Does it dwell in the infinity of expansion symbolized by the universe? Is it drifting alongwith the timeless flow of everlasting continuity? Is it hidden in some abstract, transcendental reality? No, that search through the secret spheres of mystery leads to no ends, because the infinite cannot be embedded in itself: the core of infinity rests in the finite as its inner substance, the Infinite within man. And the music of infinity accordingly emerges from man's heart, from the seat of inward infiniteness where the quintessence of eternity takes its ultimate abode: "Look, look for him / in the temple of your limbs. / He is there / as the lord of the world, / speaking, / singing, / in enchanting tunes"[4]. The poet who formulated these lines belongs to the Bāul sect, a religious community of itinerant mendicants from rural Bengal, whose members have realized the truth of the infinite within the human heart. The Bāuls have therefore personalized their god to an extent few other religions have, and they call the Supreme Being 'the Man of the Heart' who abides in the temple of the human body, seated in the shrine of the heart.

Who is this 'Man of the heart'? Rabindranath Tagore describes the deeper meaning of the inner transcendental reality in terms of divine music: "'The man of my Heart', to the Bāul, is like a divine instrument perfectly tuned. He gives expression to infinite truth in the music of life"[5]. The peculiarity of a perfectly tuned instrument consists in the fact that that the sounds emerging from it produce harmoniousness and beauty, hence music in the purest sense. The 'Man of the Heart', the Supreme Being representing this excellent instrument, is at the same time the originator of that music which is infinite in all its dimensions - in time, in space, in emotional intensity, and in perfection. Significantly, man himself becomes the medium of the unending sounds emitted by the divine instrument, because the transcendental tune rises from the place where the instrument is kept - the human heart. It is this instrument which bestows the quality of the infinite upon man in his limited

---

[4] Jādubindu, quoted in Deben Bhattacharya, *The mirror of the sky* (London: Allen & Unwin, 1969), p.74

[5] *Creative Unity*, pp.78-9

finiteness. It is that 'Man of the Heart', the infinite lord of the universe, who makes the human heart boundless by his unbounded presence.

But how is the infinite presence evoked? If the 'Man of the Heart' dwells eternally in each and every human being's heart, then why is man in constant search for Him? Why is it that many a Bāul song opens with the words, 'where am I to find him, the Man of my Heart', the singer expressing his utter desperation at the apparent absence of the infinite reality from his heart, which makes him even more bitterly aware of his own limitations? No, the Infinite is not truly absent - it cannot be, for else human existence as such were not true -, but man feels the pain of his own incompleteness as long as he remains ignorant of the fact that the supreme transcendental reality reveals itself from within and not through an however much sought after external object. The infinite rests within the finite, but it reveals itself at its own will. That is to say, the Supreme Reality can never be held captive within bounds, and the finite does not transgress its finiteness by chasing the infinite and imprisoning it within its own limits. It is only when the infinite truth comes by itself to find ultimate fulfilment within the bounds of the finite that the desired unity is established and man becomes conscious of the bliss arisinig from his own infinite essence.

Is that to say that any search for realization is futile because it is entirely at the discretion of the Supreme Being to reveal himself as the infinite within man? No, certainly not. Fulfilment is not attained, awareness of the infinite reality not raised through passive vanity, for any achievement on the spiritual plane reqires active involvement of the seeker. The Upaniṣads say, *yadā vai sukhaṃ labhate 'tha karoti* - 'when, verily, one obtains happiness, then one is active'[6], and in order to obtain happiness one has to be active in the first place. Search, therefore, is the necessary prerequisite for man to accomplish his quest for the infinite truth, but it is the direction taken by the search which is essential for its success. The transcendental reality, personified as the 'Man of the Heart', is found *within* the heart, hence man must explore his own interior, the inner emotional spheres of his own heart, if he wants to realize that "the Man of my Heart is in my heart"[7]. Striving for the inner truth in fake

---

[6] Chāndogya Upaniṣad 7.22.1
[7] Rabindranath Tagore, *Gītabitān*, I,216

manifestations on the outer surface remains a vain effort - the music emerging from the divine instrument struck by the vibrations of the heart does not come through the air as tunes audible to the ear: "I wandered everywhere, in search of him - / I would have listened to the words of his mouth, but I did not hear - I could not hear"[8]. Why? Because one cannot find outwardly that which is kept within as the core essence of things. "Today, I returned to my own country..."[9] - the seeker gives up his fruitless hunt for the infinite truth on the external path leading nowhere, and turns towards the mystery that rests in his own soul. What succeeds, now that he listens to the voice of his own heart? - "...and now I hear. I hear his flute in my own songs"[10]. Realizing that the infinite reality emanates from within himself, the seeker attains at once and easily the object of all his previous effortful pursuits. Hence the poet's advice, "Why then do you search, like beggars, from door to door? You will not find him. / But come to me - look into my heart, look unto my two eyes, and you will see him there"[11]. For having captured the infinite truth that dwells in himself, in his own heart, man will find the infinite truth of the universe lying at his feet: "The man of my heart is in my heart; *because of this I see him everywhere*"[12].

Once man's consciousness has been sensitized to the fact that the cosmic music originates from his own heart, from his own infinite core, he naturally comes to identify himself with that music. What is it that enables this self-identification with the melodies sent out by the Supreme Being through the medium of the 'divine instrument perfectly tuned'? The very moment he discerns the infinite truth revealed in his own self, man experiences the ultimate bliss arising from the living touch of the divine, because in this very moment he recognizes his Divine Lover as the 'Man of the Heart' with whom he lives in eternal union. The realization of the infinite reality of the universe and the infinite reality within the human heart being ultimately one causes strains of immense satisfaction in the heart of man; it arouses feelings of complete fulfilment, of boundless happiness, and it is this sentiment of excessive joy that prompts man to identify himself with the very tune that enchants

---

[8] ibid.
[9] ibid.
[10] ibid.
[11] ibid.
[12] ibid.

him. His own life thus having been consecrated by the immediate contact with the divinity, with the 'divine instrument' from which the cosmic cadences emanate, man is fully aware of his own indispensability in the process of creating the infinite music of the universe, and knowing that there were no music without him, he gives himself away in ultimate consummation, and proclaims:

> I am fulfilled / being a blow of your own breath -
> / on your flute.
>
> I am not sad / if I end with one single tune.
> Your flute is the universe / of three different
>   worlds, / of god, demon and man, /
> And I am the blow of your breath.
>
> Tuned to your finger-holes, / right or wrong, / I
>   sound through sleepless nights.
> I sound through the months / of monsoon and the
>   spring, /
> But together with your heart.
>
> I have no sadness at all / if I completely end.
> What more can I wish for me / than being blown
>   away with such melody.[13]

Another Bāul song, quoted by Rabindranath Tagore[14], expresses the same sentiment of ultimate fulfilment found through self-relinquishment in the infinite melody:

> I am poured forth in living notes of joy and
>   sorrow by your breath.
> Morning and evening, in summer and in rains, I
>   am fashioned to music.
> Yet should I be wholly spent in some flight of
>   song,
> I shall not grieve, the tune is so precious to me.

---

[13] Ishān Jugi, quoted in Deben Bhattacharya, op.cit., pp.72-3
[14] in *Creative Unity*, p.87

What does it signify, that infinite music of the universe, to create which man is ready to offer up his all? Is this music merely a harmonious construction of sounding notes to form melodies of beauty that appeal to the senses? No, it is not - although it is harmonious, although it is beautiful and appealing, but the infinite cadences of the cosmic realm will never find their fulfilment in the finite perfectness of features. So what is it that makes this transcendental music so special, what is it that qualifies the cosmic tune beyond the plane of concrete completeness, of material excellence? The poet provides us with the answer when he asks, "Do you not feel a thrill passing through the air with the notes of the far-away song floating from the other shore?"[15]. It is the message from spheres unknown, the call from the other end of the universe conveyed by the music emanating from the divine instrument, which gives this music its distinctive place in the complex arrangement of creation. For man, the music of the universe embodies the sounding wave that carries the vital message from the other shore of the cosmic ocean, and it is this very message which constitutes the essential basis for his life. If the universal flow of music would stop, if the communication between the two shores - the transcendental and the human realms - were blocked, man on the phenomenal bank would be deprived of the vital breath enveloped in the transcendental melody, and his life would come to utter standstill.

The infinite music of the universe carries at its core the message of the supreme transcendental reality, a message addressed from the spiritual plane to the level of mundane existence. The divine instrument which produces the music, however, is settled where? - in the heart of man. Is this not a contradiction? How can the tune emerge from the very point at which it is directed? How can the spiritual essence come forth from the core of humanness, the infinite reality be released from the heart of finitude? Yes, the creative truth about the cosmic music would be self-contradictory if limitation were the quintessence of human existence, if the ultimate statement of the finite were finiteness. But it is not so. Because the finite bears in itself the germ of infinity, and the inner substance of man is not human restrictedness but divine unboundedness. Thus the music that disseminates the message of the infinite emanates from the Infinite within man and finds its response in

---

15 Rabindranath Tagore, *Gītāñjalī*, XXI

the endless call of the universe. Being directed from the spiritual to the mundane level, therefore, does not imply that the infinite music emerges as ethereal sounds from the undetectable depth of the universe to manifest itself as audible harmonious cadences. Rather, the music of infinity is sent out from the transcendental sphere *within* the human heart: produced by the divine instrument that rests in man, the infinite melody reveals itself as musical sound once it materializes and turns into sensually perceptible vibrations.

While music in its infinite essence becomes physical, hence perceptible in the form of sound waves, it is important to remain aware of the fundamental difference between music as a spiritual entity and its material manifestation. How is this difference marked? - by the distinction between infinite and finite qualities. Music as the all-pervading transcendental reality is by nature infinite, whereas its physical embodiment, sound, can be determined in time and space, hence belongs to the realm of finitude. Sound is produced and dies away, but the music remains. The music can still be listened to when the sound is already gone, albeit with the inner ear rather than the external sense organ. It is nothing but this elementary truth about the infinite substance at the core of music which the poet expresses when he addresses his beloved:

> If by chance you think of me, I shall sing to you
> when the rainy evening loosens her shadows
> upon the river, slowly trailing her dim light
> towards the west - when the day's remnant is
> too narrow for work or for play.

> You will sit alone in the balcony of the south,
> and I shall sing from the darkened room. In
> the growing dusk the smell of the wet leaves
> will come through the window; and the
> stormy winds will become clamorous in the
> coconut grove.

> When the lightened lamp is brought into the room
> I shall go. And then, perhaps, you will listen

to the night, *and hear my song when I am silent.*[16]

How is it perceived, the music of silence which is no more discernible by the human ear? Can there be music when there is no sound? Yes, it can be, but not in the realm of phenomenal concreteness. The music that is soundless, the music whose essence is the silent mystery of infinity, lives on in the subtle emotional vibrations of the human heart, and it is heard and perceived by the heart. In its stillness, however, the illimitable musical presence withdraws itself entirely from the reach of physical apprehensibility. The singer says, "I shall sing from the darkened room. ...When the lightened lamp is brought...I shall go" lest the human glance will fall upon him and capture his transcendental melody to bind it with the fetters of sounding definiteness. Taking his leave, the singer thus abandons the sound of his tune, but what remains is his music to be heard through the silence. It is the infinite essence which is left behind for the sake of the listener once the finite cover is removed.

But will the listener instinctively know that he is still listening? Will he be consciously aware of the silent presence of the music whose sound has faded? Yes and no, depending on the degree of his emotional involvement. Intuitively, the listener may be able to make out the soundless musical presence that surrounds him, but he will perceive it knowingly only "if by chance you think of me" - only if his heart has been tuned in to the silent message. Once the sound has vanished, music ceases to exist as a material entity, as a sensually perceptible phenomenon. But even the material reality does not disappear without leaving its traces on the mind of the listener. The sound evanesces when the singer's voice holds back its tune, when the instrument rests in silence, but the emotional effects of the sounding reality persist, and the listener continues to perceive the music in his heart - the music which has become soundless yet remains as lively as it had been in its sounding manifestation. What does this mean on the level of universal communication? The music of infinity conveys the message of the Infinite to the human heart in the form of musical sound. Sound, the messenger from the transcendental shore of the cosmic ocean, retreats upon having despatched his message to the human realm, but the

---

[16] Rabindranath Tagore, *Lover's Gift*, XXVI

message itself is left behind. The message - music - remains as the permanent truth, while the messenger - sound - fulfils only a temporary rôle. It is this permanence, its persistence in the heart of man as an emotional factor, which makes music an infinite presence beyond the limits of the musical sound.

Yet even sound as a physical reality bears in itself the momentum of infinity. From the point of view of science, energies cannot be produced nor can they be destroyed - they are there as the timeless vibrations of the universe; however, manifesting themselves in continually changing shapes. It is this continuous process of transmutation which, from the limited viewpoint of material existence, suggests the impression of constant coming and going. What reveals itself to man as a freshly gained inspirational stimulus is in fact nothing but an eternally persistent radiation having transformed into a concrete potency accessible to the human perceptive sense. Likewise an energy that is lost to man is not lost to universal existence as such, but continues to bear effect in its changed appearance, though no more discernible by human means. Musical sound, resulting from the cosmic vibration, represents an energy that is infinite in its essence but finite in its perceptibility. Music can be heard only once it is emitted by the sound-producing instrument, but the silent spark of inspiration is already there before the first note on the instrument is struck. And what happens when the last note has emerged and its sound passed by the human ear? Where does the sound go? It disappears into the Infinite, into the indeterminable deepness of the universe, leaving behind the tremendous spell of stillness: "My songs...spread their wings and fled away...and my heart beats in silence"[17].

The sound disappears, it becomes inaudible - but it does not cease to exist. Its vibrations continue to penetrate the endless spheres of the universe, losing themselves in the boundlessness of infinity. Likewise the music persists through the silence, and only the one who knows how to listen to the soundless music will be able to truly comprehend the sounding musical reality. Why? Because music is heard with the ear, but listened to and perceived with the heart. Music which is only heard but not listened to is unlikely to cast any lasting emotional effect on the

---

[17] Rabindranath Tagore, *Lover's Gift*, XXXI

uninvolved listener. The music of silent infinity, however, cannot be heard, yet can be listened to, and it is this music, the silence which follows the sounding concreteness, which bears the largest impact on the human heart. Nothing could be more inappropriate than an audience in a concert hall applauding straight into the last note of the musical composition presented before them, not waiting even till the physical sound has become completely inaudible. What is it that makes their impatience so unsuitable? - the ignorance of the infinite nature of the music which extends beyond the immediate sound into the silence that follows afterwards. It is their insensitivity towards the infinite essence of music, towards the musical truth that exists above the sounding manifestation, which reveals the ignorant audience's inaptness.

Sound as the finite embodiment of infinite music is followed by silence once it vanishes, but what anticipates the musical sound before it is produced? Silence, expectant silence. The poet says, "The peace of sadness is in my heart like the brooding silence upon the master's lute before the music begins"[18]. What is the special quality inherent in that mysterious silence which precedes the arrival of the first sounding note? It is not merely empty quietude that characterizes this silence. Rather it is pressing fullness, an urgent accumulation of energies persistently pushing forward to be released. Energies of what? - of music, of musical inspiration longing to assume definite form in the sound of the tune. The music exists in fact even before the first sound emerges, and it is this unmanifest presence calling for materialization which adds a new dimension to the silence, elevating it beyond the mere phenomenon of soundlessness. The silence that prevails in anticipation of the music is loaded with the very music to come, but this silence is real only because the music has already become reality. What does that mean? The water which has gathered into a cloud is really existent, hence the cloud is also existent, but the earth becomes saturated only once the rain breaks loose. Likewise, the music is contained in the cloud of silence but does not yet burst into sound.

How long can the cloud hold back the impending rains? How long can silence restrain the music from resolving into sound? The discharge of accumulated energies can be delayed only until the fruit has

---

[18] Rabindranath Tagore, *Crossing*, V

ripened, until the time of release has come. The concrete moment may be
temporally indefinite, but its arrival is inevitable. In the same way as the
night is bound to give way to daybreak, in the same way as the bud is
designed to open into a flower, silence too is destined to metamorphose
into music, thus setting free its aggregated energetic forces. The
definiteness of the deliverance to.come enables man to endure the
pressing expectation:

> Hold thy faith firm, my heart, the day will dawn.
> The seed of promise is deep in the soil, it will
>   sprout.
> Sleep, like a bud, will open its heart to the light,
>   and the silence will find its voice.
> The day is near when thy burden will become thy
>   gift, and thy sufferings will light up thy
>   path.[19]

Silence will find its voice, hence its termination is predetermined, and it
is this finite disposition which makes the silence bearable. Why?
Because the contracted emotional energies need to be untied to become
constructive, for else they develop uncontrollable destructive powers in
order to break away from their confinement. On the other hand, the
silence is the necessary prerequisite for the emotional potencies to
accumulate. There could be no rains if the water would not have
collected into the cloud, and the musical sound could not arise if not the
musical inspiration would have been condensed in silence.

Silence and sound, on the metaphysical level, stand not only for
the two opposing energies of soundlessness and music, but represent
indeed the basic principle of interaction between stagnancy and flow,
confinement and boundlessness. In silence, the musical current is held
up in the stagnant waters of stillness, and it is released into the infinite
only once the silence is broken and the sounding tune makes its way
through the illimitable spheres of the universe. Music, musical sound is
the active energy that pushes on towards the infinite, hence the poet
says, "The wind is up, I set my sail of songs...the wind is stirred into
the murmur of music at this time of my departure"[20]. It is a departure

---

19 Rabindranath Tagore, *Crossing*, XII
20 Rabindranath Tagore, *Crossing*, III

from silence towards sound, a departure from the realm of limits towards the unbounded perpetuity of cosmic music. And music itself is the vehicle that takes across, from the shore of finite existence to the ocean of infinity, because music as the motivating potency of the infinite involuntarily draws the human soul engrossed in finiteness towards the unbounded strata of eternity.

Again, in the context of infinite existence we cannot narrow down the meaning and signification of music to the mere implication of a musical performance, of a set of notes and melodies delivered by a singer or instrumentalist as an utter material reality. Accepting the quintessence of music to be revealed in the temporally and spacially confined musical performance were just to accept its ultimate finitude. It is however not the music as such which is limited but its perception as a solely physical and sensible musical performance. Music is not only musical performance, but rather it is "the creative impulse which makes songs not only with words and tunes, lines and colors, but with stones and metals, with ideas and men"[21]. Music as an aesthetic reality is omnipresent in the universe as an harmonious vibration of beauty, and it reveals itself time and again in the manifold creations of nature. It is the tune produced and perceived from within, the music of the soul which is sweet in its melodious notes and yet silent to the ear, which symbolizes the emotional moves of the yearning soul longing to express its love for the infinite. It is the outwardly silent music - a music which vibrates with lively sound and yet remains inaudible in the realm of the material -, which conveys the call from the other shore, bringing over a touch of sadness and mystery: "My heart is sad, for it knows not from where comes its call. Does the breeze bring the whisper of the world which I leave behind with its music of tears melting in the sunny silence?"[22].

And still, the music which is silent in its outer appearance, the music which makes its impact on the craving heart, is full of sounding cadences uniting in a tremendous current of musical sounds. This is not the silence which precedes the outbreak of music, loaded with the expectation of repressed sounding melodies. It is rather a music which has already found its fulfilment in sound, which has already been

---

[21] Rabindranath Tagore, *Creative Unity*, p.13
[22] Rabindranath Tagore, *Crossing*, I

consummated in overtly vibrating tunes, and which is now inverted so that its sound turns away from the ear in order to fully settle in the depth of the soul. It is a music which has been deprived of its finite, temporary existence for the sake of unfolding its infinite qualities in the unbounded spheres of emotional sensitivity. At a certain point, music inevitably ceases to be perceptible by the human sense organs once the material presence of the sound waves fades away, but for the emotional sensor of the soul, the musical presence will always remain reality. Music is thus limitable in its finite manifestations, but its spiritual core is illimitable.

It is due to the terminable character of its concrete manifestations that music comes forth in ever changing shapes and appearances. The music of life, reflected in the unsteady play of nature and in the eternal stillness of the universe likewise, assumes endless forms that emerge as a multitude of emotional shades conveyed by the musical reality at the bottom. Amazed at the surprising diversity of musical revelations, the poet calls out to the Divine Music-maker who has staged this astounding play of cadences:

> I have seen thee play thy music in life's dancing
>   hall; in the sudden leaf-burst of spring thy
>   laughter has come to greet me; and lying
>   among field flowers I have heard in the grass
>   thy whisper.
> The child has brought to my house the message
>   of hope, and the woman the music of thy
>   love.
> Now I am waiting on the seashore to feel thee in
>   death, to find life's refrain back again in the
>   star songs of the night.[23]

What is it that makes music so universal in its appearance? We find music hidden in the beauty of flowers; it sounds to us from the immeasurable expanse of the sky, and we taste its sweetness in the intimacy of love. So what is it that accounts for this cosmic appeal of music? It is the inherent quest for harmony which music bears at the core of its existence, the quest for beauty and perfection out of which music is born. At the same time, it is also the quest for infinity, the

---

[23] Rabindranath Tagore, *Crossing*, LXX

search to overcome the boundaries set by the crude reality of material existence which instigates the pursuit of the infinite truth epitomized in the harmonious completeness of music.

Manifestations are many, but how does the infinite, concordant presence of music ultimately reveal itself? Music as the most sublime expression of the supreme transcendental reality is disclosed in the sweetest emotional sensation emitted by that reality: it is revealed in love which is the fundamental and most vital quality of the infinite truth. How is it revealed? - as the embodiment of absolute harmony achieved through the realization of transcendental love. Music attains its infinite attributes through being refined by love, for love itself is the positive quality of infinity, just as love is by nature infinite. But what is infinity? It is the unfathomable presence of the Supreme Being, of the ultimate transcendental truth which cannot be captured by means of material potency or even spiritual pursuits. It is the illimitable energy which reveals itself in the sweetness of love and sends out its rays of beauty concealed in the tunefulness of melodious music. It is the indeterminable yet omnipresent reality for whose inspiring vision the poet prays when he says:

> Stand before my eyes, and let thy glance touch
>   my songs into a flame.
> Stand among thy stars and let me find kindled in
>   their light my own fire of worship.
> The earth is waiting at the world's wayside;
> Stand upon the green mantle she has flung upon
>   thy path; and let me feel in her grass and
>   meadow flowers the spread of my own
>   salutation.
> Stand in my lonely evening where my heart
>   watches alone; fill her cup of solitude, *and let*
>   *me feel in me the infinity of thy love.*[24]

It is the infinite presence within man, the Infinite which rests within the human heart, which brings over to the human realm the cosmic tune of the universe and, touching on the heart of the finite, turns man's music itself into an infinite reality.

---

[24] Rabindranath Tagore, *Crossing*, LIV

4

Music and devotion

Music, there is no doubt, emerges as a living presence of energetic forces instigated by the driving potencies of universal existence and delivered by the subtle vibrations of sound. The essential quality of music, which elevates it above the status of any other sounding reality, is its harmonious appearance, the agreeable nature in which the musical sounds are arranged. Yet music is more than merely a pleasurable sensation of sound waves. Music possesses the capacity to touch the human heart with an intensity no other physically evident phenomenon can achieve. Beauty of form appeals to the aesthetic consciousness of man and gives him a sense of satisfaction, but music, being directed at the emotional consciousness, exceeds the aesthetic delight derived from beauty of features in fervor and depth by refining the beauty in the verve of imaginative feeling. Itself a manifestation of congenial perfectness, music brings the positive aspects of existence to fullest excellence because it links them constructively with the emotional powers settled in the heart of man. Music thus catalyzes the energies of creation and adds to them the distinctive vibration of emotive perspicaciousness.

What is it that animates music in such a way as to expand it beyond a mere lifeless material truth? Which is the soul resting at the core of music, clad in the melodious mantle of sweet-sounding cadences? Of what kind is the driving emotional force that makes music the property of the human heart, the vehicle for the human soul to unite with the great soul of the universe? It is devotion, an immense sense of loving devotion concealed in the innermost layer of the musical reality. It is a devotion coupled with readiness for complete self-sacrifice, a devotion that reaches out beyond even the conception of self only to lead the devoted soul to full mergence with the cosmic stream of love. Devotion is the imaginative spirit of music, the vital truth at the basis of the sounding tune, the existential energy that turns harmoniously organized sounds into musical fabrics. Music as such would not exist if its flow were not carried ahead by the powerful current of devotion. All that could emerge would be an endless chain of empty, soulless sounds - beautiful though, but cold and impersonal, thus contradicting the very idea of music. Music becomes music through its indwelling devotional quality, and it is the momentum of devotion inherent in music which makes the sounding construction appear as a harmonious, pleasing reality. Devoid of devotion, even perfectly arranged sounds would be defeated by meaningless hollowness, and harmoniousness turns into utter discord.

Devotion to whom? As an emotional statement, devotion requires an object at which it is directed, a concrete inspiration by which it is aroused, and a source from which it emanates. Devotion is not a state, but a process which calls for an active relationship between the two parties involved in it, and only a dynamic and constructive interchange can ensure that the process of devotion is fulfilled. But who are these two parties, the emitter and recipient of the devotional flow? From where is devotion sent out, and where is its destination? The rise of devotion presupposes the existence of two separate spiritual entities, and it is the intrinsic desire of these two souls to merge into one, their constant longing for union, which produces the imaginative energies out of which devotion is born. Being a motive process rather than a static condition, devotion lives from its reciprocity without which it could not persist. That is to say, the one to whom devotion is directed does not only receive the gift of devotion, but is at the same time himself devoted to the one who presents the gift. If the exchange of devotion were not made on a mutual basis, devotion would lose its existential ground and vanish. Why? Because no living soul can be devoted to a lifeless object, and a non-respondent spiritual energy is reduced to an inanimate entity by its own indifference, hence cannot obtain devotion.

What is devotion? Dictionary definitions will be of little use in explaining the essence of the term, though all attempts to describe devotion throw in expressions relating to emotionality, spirituality and religiousness. Devotion is at times identified with intense love, then again with prayer and religious worship, and else with passionate attachment. While there is a spark of truth in each of the suggested synonyms inasmuch as they are indeed connected with devotion in one way or another, that truth is shattered by the inconsiderateness of plain equation. Devotion is not love as such; it is the stimulating potency at the core of love which turns the imaginery current of affection into an imaginative stream of reality. Devotion is not itself prayer or worship, but it is the invigorative quality of devotion that makes religious pursuits meaningful. Devotion is not attachment either, nor is it passion, but rather it is the sublimating energy that transforms passionate attachment into the unbounded freedom of refined love. It is true, though, that devotion represents an emotional sensation, and this explains as to why devotion is popularly associated with emotional moves, albeit in shady identifications. It is likewise true that devotion constitutes the quintessence of spirituality which is again the fundament of religiousness, but the intensity of devotion exceeds by far the depth of spiritual perception and resulting concerns of religiosity.

In the Indian tradition, the term to denote devotion is *bhakti*, derived from a Sanskrit verbal root *bhaj-* which bears two primary connotations that may take us closer to a definition of devotion than English language thesauri. The first connotation is 'partaking of', or 'participating in', while the second meaning says 'to serve' and 'to love'. Now what do these two significations tell us? Devotion is partaking, it is participating, but in what? - in unlimited bliss arising from the ultimate experience of union with the divine. It is partaking of the unbounded joy experienced by two souls upon meeting and merging into one single reality. It is participation in the fulfilment found once the highest quest has been accomplished, once the object of intense yearning has become real.

But was it not said earlier that devotion is created by the urge for union rather than by the state of achieved consummation? How then could devotion as such imply attainment without contradicting its very cause of origin? Can devotion truly signify partaking of bliss if its vital basis is the search for bliss? Can devotion denote participating in union if it is born out of the desire to overcome separation? Yes, it can. There is no contradiction between the two intrinsic aspects of devotion, between the quest and its fulfilment, because devotion is the way that leads to fulfilment. For this reason, devotion unites in itself the elements of both the progressive and the static, of search and realization, desire and experience. Devotion is participation, is partaking, for even the seeker already partakes of the bliss he is striving for. How? - by identifying himself with the object of his search. That is to say, by constantly directing his mind at the ultimate destination of his spiritual journey, the devoted individual continuously experiences the Supreme Reality and thereby partakes of it, and it is his devotion which forms the vehicle to take him to his journey's goal.

The second connotation of the verbal root *bhaj-*, 'to serve' and 'to love', shall enable us to delve deeper into the essence of devotion. What is the substance of devotion, what is devotion made of? - love, and what is the quintessence of love? Service. Devotion becomes manifest as a subtle emotional vibration, but this delicate fabric of emotion is saturated with the radiant brilliance of love. If love is absent, emotional sentiments may assume various attributes, but none of them will be devotional. Without devotion, on the other hand, no emotion howsoever affectionate will qualify as love. Devotion and love form an integral entity, inseparable to the extent that the one forms an existential ingredient in the fluid of the other. How is devotion materialized? Devotion takes concrete shape in service, in selfless service rendered by the loving soul to the object of its love. What is it that motivates this service? It is the desire for union with the beloved, the eternal quest of two spirits to overcome their duality in order to be one. Service is essentially inspired by this constant search for oneness, because the act of serving brings the lover, the one who actively serves, closer to the beloved to whom the service is rendered. In service, therefore, devotion finds its proper direction and consummates itself in ultimate self-sacrifice. Service is the essence of devotion, and devotion the essence of service, and the interaction of the two aspects of the transcendental truth - the emotional vibration and its definite manifestation - is again determined by mutual indispensability.

Establishing the spiritual identity of devotion, however, remains a vain effort as long as we ignore the factor that accounts for the realness of all emotional expression, be it inspired by devotion, by love or by service: music. What rôle does music play, what significance does it possess in the context of devotion? If we turn to Indian terminology, the intrinsic link between music and devotion becomes most obvious: *bhakti*, 'devotion', is drawn from the same stem *bhaj-* which produces also another term, *bhajana*, denoting a specific type of music. 'Devotion' and 'music' are thus joined together by a common verbal basis, and their conjunction implies more than a mere linguistic stratagem. The word *bhajana* refers in popular usage to any type of devotional song, with certain regional specifications. In the context of devotion and its meaning on the universal level, however, it is only legitimate to identify '*bhajana*' with music in general. What is that to say? Music is devotional in any case, for devotion represents the vital essence of music, and there would be no music without the life-giving current of devotion. *Bhajana*, therefore, is music *per se*, and music qualifies as music only once it qualifies as *bhajana*.

If the Sanskrit language provides us with an identical verbal origin of both *bhakti* and *bhajana*, devotion and music, Indian spirituality supplies the concept of thought according to which music and devotion form one single metaphysical entity. While it is true that music could not exist, that sound would not convert into melodious musical cadences, if it were not stimulated by the subtle feelings of devotion, devotion *vice versa* depends on music for the sake of its emotional expression. Why? Because music is the means *par excellence*, the primary and most effective way to verbalize - or rather vocalize - devotion. And, if we expand the idea of music beyond the immediate physical reality of the sound, if we resort to music in its universal sense of the motivating transcendental potency that inspires harmonious tunes and meaningful silence likewise, then it is no exaggeration to say that there were no devotion without music.

How come that music, which lives only in the wake of devotion, turns itself vital for the emergence of devotion? No, it is not the sound of music which arouses devotional sentiments in the heart of the listener. The sounding tune, however sweet and satiated with emotion, cannot instigate devotion unless the devotional germ is already there. So what is it that leads to devotion in the first place? It is the music from within, the musical spark that indwells the heart of man, concealed in the accumulated emotional energies of silence. It is the musical current emanating from the human heart and making its way towards the ocean of cosmic music in search of union with the Supreme Reality which gives rise to devotion, for devotion is the only vehicle fit to take the human soul across the stream of temporal existence. Devotion is the boat that takes its course on the river of transcendental tunes, carrying the human soul and the soul of the universe to their merging-point. The boat remains futile without the stream in which it floats, hence the vanity of devotion devoid of music. At the same time, however, devotion is also the source from which the musical river springs forth, hence its vitality for the existence of music.

What is the fluid of devotion made of? Of what kind is the essence of the devotional current, and how does it become apparent once it has settled in the heart of man? If we turn back to the word '*bhakti*', then the answer is already implied in its verbal stem *bhaj-* in the sense of 'to love': devotion is made of love, it is instigated by love and it manifests itself in love. But how does love as such reveal itself? - in the readiness of the one who loves to fully offer up his own self for the sake of the beloved. It is this readiness, resulting from the realization that nothing is lost if only one wins over the object of one's own love, the acceptance of complete self-sacrifice, which enables the pure emotions of loving affection to distil and to emerge on a higher qualitative level as loving devotion. The object of love, the target of devotion could be anyone: it could be a person - a friend, or relative, or it could be God on the religious plane. What matters, however, is not the object at which the emotional current is directed, but the emotion itself, the nature, quality and intensity of the devotional sentiments. Love qualifies as devotional love only if it is coupled with the selflessness that accepts even utter humiliation as grace, and devotion qualifies as loving devotion only if it bears in itself the sweetness of emotional affection.

That is not to say that indignity should ever be allowed to enter into a relationship between lover and beloved, between devotee and object of devotion. But the readiness to accept as gift the humiliation suffered at the hands of the beloved is essential for the truthfulness of tne devotional feelings. The Bāuls of Bengal, who are uncompromising followers of the path of loving devotion, have taken this readiness to its ultimate extreme. The Bāul poet says, "You may hurt me, my lord / go, hurt me / as long as I can bear the pain"[1]. No, it is not pain the singer is asking for, even if he cries out, "you may hurt me". The willingness to accept the pain from the one dearest to us is always coupled with a certainty that the beloved will not deliberately make us suffer. To the contrary, it is the very energy derived from the beloved's affection, the very strength bestowed by the love of the one for whose sake the loving soul is ready to make the supreme sacrifice, which emboldens the poet to call out, "you may hurt me as long as I can bear the pain", and which ultimately enables the lover to truly endure that pain. Why else would

---

[1] Podu, quoted in Deben Bhattacharya, *The mirror of the sky* (London: Allen & Unwin, 1969), p.107

the same Bāul poet admit, "Sorrow weighs down on me / and I bear it bending / in spite of my emasculated limbs..."[2]? It is the energy inherent in unswerving devotion nourished by unconditional love which enhances the potencies of the human soul beyond the physical limitations of the body, and which increases man's capacity to bear both excessive joy and excessive pain.

But does sacrifice, even self-sacrifice, always necessarily imply pain? No, it does not. Rabindranath Tagore says, "the sacrifice, which is in the heart of creation, is both joy and pain at the same moment"[3]. Joy and pain, delight and suffering are eternally there as the driving forces whose dialectic interplay keeps the cosmic cycles of creation in motion. Sacrifice as such tends to be associated with penance, with displeasure of one kind or another, but the sacrifice which is made out of love, the sacrifice which is made for the sake of love is not penance but fulfilment. Why? Because love's sacrifice itself is the supreme expression of devotion, and devotion will never lead to suffering: the ultimate goal of devotion is happiness, excessive bliss in attainment, though the way towards this highest aim certainly includes strains of pain and penance. Yet it is devotion which not only lays out the path that leads to fulfilment, but which also provides man with the energy to proceed on that path. And it is music which motivates the seeking soul, thus endowed with devotional energy, to advance towards its ultimate object.

Hardship is inevitable on the way towards realization, throughout the period of questing, but why? Would it not be easier to follow the course of devotion, would it not be more convenient to indulge in loving sentiments if the road were not obstructed by sufferings? And moreover, does love, does devotion not itself eliminate all pain? Yes, it does, but only subjectively. That is to say, pain is turned into pleasure by the power of loving devotion, by the energy of devoted love - but the pain as such is still there, though the individual immersed in loving devotion will no more perceive as pain the agony that has been purified in the fire of love. But is this pain necessary, and why? Where does it arise from? The suffering which accompanies the seeker for perfection

---

[2] ibid.
[3] *Creative Unity* (New Delhi: Macmillan India Ltd., reprint 1995), p.40

on his way arises from the state of incompleteness that prevails before the desired aim is achieved, it emerges out of the separation of the devoted soul from the object of devotion. Agony will be there as long as the quest is yet to be attained, but once fulfilment is found, all agonies dissolve into one single current of bliss. Yet we remain asking as to why suffering, even if temporary and bound to give way to delight, is needed at all. The question, however, is not simply one of bliss and pain, of perfection and incompleteness, of union and separation, but it leads us much deeper into the elemental workings of the process of devotional interaction. Moreover the answer will take us back to our subject of interest and its immediate relation with the devotional quest: music.

The pain of imperfection, the pangs of separation experienced on the path towards attainment are more than empty agony. What appears as blank suffering to the afflicted individual is actually the source which brings forth the substance that carries on its melodious waves the powerful stream of devotion leading to ultimate fulfilment: out of pain arises music, the sweetest and most sublime expression of devotion, which breaks through the cloudy skies of agony as the radiant ray that illuminates the way towards the highest goal with its charming tunes of love. Music, in order to be born, requires the infinite surroundings of the cosmic current. Music calls for the freedom of the limitless, and this freedom is found on the way rather than at its destination; it is found in the quest itself, not in its fulfilment. It is the unlimited power of loving devotion transcending all pain which carries the procreative freedom that gives rise to music. Music cannot emerge from the bounds of pleasure, because the limited nature of captured delight suffocates the very germ of a tune. A mediaeval Indian poet, quoted by Rabindranath Tagore in his essay "The Creative Ideal"[4], addresses his query regarding the fundamental truth about music and its infinite expansiveness to the songbird making her way towards the skies:

> Where were your songs, my bird, when you
>   spent your nights in the nest?
> Was not all your pleasure stored therein?

---

[4] in *Creative Unity*, p.41

> What makes you lose your heart to the sky, the
>   sky that is limitless?

The bird's answer expresses the core quest of music as the unbounded reality which finds its inspiration only in the delight of the infinite, not in non-expansive pleasure:

> I had my pleasure while I rested within bounds.
> When I soared into the limitless, I found my
>   songs.

What does this imply for the impact of devotion on the uprise of music? Devotion is the actuating substance whose flow carries the momentum of infinity, of unlimited expansivity that induces the emersion of musical melodies. It is this spark of boundlessness inherent in the devotional fluid, the root of the limitless resulting from the power of devoted love and manifesting itself as the quintessence of devotion, which accounts for the capacity of devotion to transgress all boundaries, to transcend all pain and to safeguard the devoted soul on its way towards the ultimate aim. It is the same element of unboundedness which nourishes the current of musical notes and makes the accumulated potential of emotion merge into one cosmic symphony. The flow of devotion guarantees the continuity of the spiritual search, and for the devoted individual, "the true endeavour is to keep oneself simply afloat in the stream of devotion that flows through the lives of devotees - to mingle one's own devotion with theirs"[5].

The devotional current not only ensures consistent progression in the process of searching for the ultimate spiritual goal; it is also vital for the perseverance of the quest itself. Without the animating flow of devotion, all spiritual pursuits would come to utter stagnation, and religion would turn into a lifeless institution of meaningless rituals. While the devotional seed, the germ of *bhakti* is indeed inherent in all religions because it constitutes the very root from which the religious idea is born, religion as such is not necessarily equatable with devotion. What does that say? It is devotion which gives rise to religion in the first

---

[5] Bāul comment on the *sahaja* ('simple') way, quoted by Kshitimohan Sen in his essay "The Bāul singers of Bengal", in Rabindranath Tagore, *The Religion of Man* (London: Allen & Unwin, 1931), appendix 1, p.214

place, but religion becomes devotional only if its practices are inspired by devotion. Religion, if sustained by merely theoretical tenets devoid of devotional imaginativeness, if nurtured by merely mechanical rites deprived of devotional fervor, remains an empty and desolate illusion. What are the consequences? Faith itself dies in the dryness of the delusive desert for the lack of the live-giving devotional fluid. Stagnation means death - spiritual death, for stagnation brings to standstill the advancement on the path towards realization. Realization can be accomplished only in the wake of the devotional flow, because its object, the supreme transcendental reality, can be accessed only through devotion. The desired aim is real only if devotion is real and not otherwise. Why? Because the Supreme Being, who embodies the core aspect of the sought-after truth, withdraws his presence from the joyless void where devotion has ceased to well forth: "God is deserting your temple / as you amuse yourself / by blowing conch-shells / and ringing bells..."[6].

It is this state of lack of devotion, the state of ignorance covering up even the last sight of the divine truth, which hurts the devoted soul most. Routinized ritual practices and dogmatized ideological precepts leave no space for the devotional spirit, and the current of devotion cannot break through to proceed towards the ultimate aim. Therefore the poet cries out in distress, "The road to you is blocked / by temples and mosques. / I hear your call, my lord, / but I cannot advance - / prophets and teachers bar my way"[7]. Obstacles on the way to fulfilment that are erected in the name of religion are indeed more fatal for devotional aspirations than are any other, ordinary hindrances, because such dogmatic barriers steal away the very idea of devotion to replace it with empty solemnities. Hence our Bāul poet's moan, "Since I can wish for burning the world / with that which cools my limbs, / my devotion to unity / is dying divided"[8]. Deprived of devotion, deprived of love, deprived even of the elemental musical cadence that indwells the devoted heart, he resigns in utter disappointment: "Doors of love bear many locks - / scriptures and beads. / Madan, in tears, / dies of regret and pain"[9].

---

[6] Padmalochan, quoted in Deben Bhattacharya, op.cit., p.102

[7] Madan, quoted in Deben Bhattacharya, op.cit., p.93

[8] ibid.

[9] ibid.

In order that the devoted soul may never yield to such resignation, the Bāul religion completely renounces any form of institutionalized establishment of faith, and Bāul philosophy does not seek support in theoretical and scriptural fundamentals. The core essence of Bāul thought is devotion *per se*, and religious rites and modes of worship are valued according to their effectiveness on the way of fulfilling the highest quest of the devoted individual. The Bāul, therefore, does not follow the path of prescribed ritual conventions and observances lest these mount up to gather into a firm barrier that separates the seeker from the goal, the devotee from the object of devotion, the lover from the beloved. Having realized the superiority of devotion over meaningless ceremonies, acknowledging that his ultimate aim becomes accomplishable only through the devotional power of unconditional love, the Bāul's advice to his fellow wayfarer on the road towards attainment is to turn away from the dead-end route of established rules and to meet the object of all aspirations on the path of devotion. Rabindranath Tagore expresses but the same thought in his admonition to the searching heart:

> Leave this chanting and singing and telling of beads! Whom dost thou worship in this lonely dark corner of a temple with doors all shut? Open thine eyes and see thy God is not before thee!
>
> He is there where the tiller is tilling the hard ground and where the pathmaker is breaking stones. He is with them in sun and in shower, and his garment is covered with dust. Put off thy holy mantle and even like him come down on the dusty soil!
>
> Deliverance? Where is this deliverance to be found? Our master himself has joyfully taken upon him the bonds of creation; he is bound with us all for ever.
>
> Come out of thy meditations and leave aside thy flowers and incense! What harm is there if thy clothes become tattered and stained? Meet

him and stand by him in toil and in sweat of
thy brow.[10]

So what does the Bāul do instead of performing rites and
observing ceremonial practices? What does he do instead of casting
flowers and burning incenses, instead of blowing conches and telling
beads, instead of keeping fasts and going on pilgrimages? He sings! He
sings, plays his one-stringed instrument and dances to give voice to the
feelings of devotion that have accumulated in his heart and are pushing
to be released from the inner confinement of the soul. Instead of killing
the emotional seed with sanctioned rites yet before it can grow and
mature, the Bāul throws away all permissible conventions to make way
for the gushing flood of devotional sentiments breaking forth in an all-
overpowering outburst of notes that sweeps aside even the last remnants
of ignorant routinism. His devotion takes refuge in music, in the
sounding cadences of joy, in order not to be strangulated by the rigid
strings of ritualism. It is music that liberates the devoted heart from the
bondage of convention, from the restrictive network of formalities, and
ensures the liveliness of the emotional fluid which is essential for the
emancipation of the loving soul. Music becomes thus the vital factor for
the continuity of the devotional flow without which devotion were at
risk of becoming juiceless.

The Bāul sings for the sake of his devotion, but is there not also
the poet's warning to "leave this chanting and singing and telling of
beads" in the very interest of saving devotion from being caught in the
meshes of idle ritual? Is not singing, is not music a likewise useless
sacramental formality? Yes, at times it is, because musical melodies are
surely employed as ceremonial tools in devotionless ritual routine. And
yet no, it is not, because music thus misused is bound to die - its
devotional soul vanishes, and what remains is nothing but the empty
shell of sounds, a dead body made of ringing notes. Music devoid of
devotion is sound, not music, just as ritual lacking devotion is platitude,
not worship. Platitude will never produce music - it may produce sound,
but such sounds cannot arouse the delight called forth by music, even if
they were perfect in their aesthetic harmoniousness. Why? Because
delight is not inspired by neutral completeness but by the devotional

---

[10] *Gītāñjalī*, XI

essence at the core of the sounding reality, by the emotional fluid that touches the human heart and stirs up a feeling of unbounded excitement rising from the depth of the craving soul.

What then happens to music misappropriated as a sacral utensil of ritual mechanicalism? It becomes dogmatized in the same way the religious tenets have been dogmatized. Once faith remains frozen in rigid codes, the flowing stream of devotion halts and music stands deprived of its vital substance. The sounding construction survives, but the musical creation disappears upon losing its elementary purpose of instigating and expressing the devotional sentiments. It is thus that one and the same song, one and the same musical composition, rendered even of one and the same artistic standard but once drenched in devotion and once devoid of all devotion, will not bear the same effect upon the human soul. How is it different? Without being inspired by the fluid of devotion, the tune howsoever beautiful still lacks sweetness, and the sound howsoever well-arranged still lacks the harmonious completeness of music, hence fails to arouse that sense of all-pervading bliss in the heart of man which is carried over by even the least melody saturated with devotion. When devotion is absent, the soul of music is lost and the sound remains empty and meaningless. For want of devotion, the sounding tune itself becomes an embarrassment to the music, and the ritual chant shames the song-worshiper, hence the poet's stern advice, "leave this chanting and singing" - give up this naught repetition of futile formulae and find the true song in the creative current of devotional fulness.

Music is the motivating energy that inspires devotion, and at the same time it is the expressive force which is inspired by devotion. Devotion, however, is not a neutral quality; its arousal calls for the presence of an object towards which devotion turns. Being the principal stimulative potency of devotion as well as the primary manifestation of devotional sentiments, music is obviously tied to the same object out of whose spirit devotion is born. Of what kind is this object of devotion? Who is it to whom all musical tunes are addressed? Well, if we separate the pure essence of devotion from mundane feelings of infatuation, devotion is always ultimately directed at the highest goal of the spiritual quest, at the Divine Being, the supreme transcendental reality - but in what appearance does this most sublime truth reveal itself to the human soul? The Supreme Divinity bears the character of a very personal friend, a close companion to the human heart who takes definite shape in the persona of a concrete being so as to make the devotional quest a feasible one. Why this personalization? The human mind may be equiped with the capacity to interact with an abstract, impersonal spiritual presence, but not so the human heart. Regardless of all his rational excellence, man is still unable to establish an emotional relation with a neutral energy unless it is made accessible in personal form. It is the emotional bond, however, which is vital for the rise of devotion, hence the necessity to personalize the object.

What are the consequences of the intrinsically personal attitude of devotion on music, on the elemental form of devotional expression? Music as a primarily emotional force springs up only if its destination is an emotionally comprehensible, personal entity. Personalization is therefore imperative for the inception of music. At the same time, however, music is the essential prerequisite to establish the personal bond between the devoted individual and the object of devotion. For what reason is it so? The connecting flow of emotions is primally instigated by the stimulating potency inherent in music, and it is the stream of emotion-laden musical notes which bears at its core the linking force that carries the two souls to confluence. Music thus requires a personal inclination in order to rise and flourish, but it is the selfsame music which brings about the personal association in the first place.

Given the inseparability and mutual requisitioning of music and the personal approach devotion asserts, what would be more logical than the fact that those who have most plainly personalized their God are also most excellent singers? For the Bāuls of Bengal, the ultimate transcendental truth is none else than a human being, a fellow living soul: the Man of the Heart. Kshitimohan Sen, a Bengali scholar and Bāul expert of the early 20th century, characterizes the Bāul attitude to the point when he says that "our wise and learned ones were content with finding in Brahma the *tat* (lit. 'that' - the ultimate substance). The Bāuls, not being Pandits, do not profess to understand all this fuss about *thatness*, they want a Person. So their God is the Man of the Heart..."[11].

----

[11] "The Bāul singers of Bengal", in Rabindranath Tagore, *The Religion of Man*, appendix 1, p.216

Not being intellectuals, the Bāuls have nevertheless realized the quintessence of existence, the universal principle of loving devotion scholars are striving for in vain, and it is for the sake of their devotion, for the sake of their love that the Bāuls' way of life has become a constant outburst of song, of music.

It is the human aspect - the man within man and not the scholar - which accounts for the origination of the musical melody. Rational thought can only explain the phenomenon of sound, but it cannot enter into the creative depth of musical inspiration. Discovering the melodious sweetness of music requires an emotional effort, and this emotional effort is aimed at the devotional substance called forth by the soul's personal interest in the object of its love. If this personal stimulus is absent, the devotional energies cannot be released and the spiritual quest remains an unfulfilled - and unfulfillable - search for an impersonal truth. But, as Rabindranath Tagore emphasizes, "this impersonal law is not our God...the God who is God and man at the same time; and if this faith be blamed for being anthropomorphic, then Man is to be blamed for being Man, and the lover for loving his dear one as a person instead of as a principle of psychology"[12]. The Bāul singers are not only musicians *par excellence*; they are at the same time devotees of exceptional emotional profundity, and it is this sincere longing for personal closeness, their intense love for the *ādhāra puruṣa*, the Unattainable Man who is the intimate friend of the human heart and the lord of the universe both in one, which gives the Bāuls' songs their distinctive charm.

Music is the supreme expression of devotion, but why? - because music, being non-material in its inner essence yet material in its outer manifestation, is the only transformative medium capable of converting the creative energy of emotion into a rationally perceptible concreteness. Devotion is however itself an expression. An expression of what? Of love - of pure, spiritual love aroused by the all-pervading touch of the sublime transcendental presence which materializes in the concrete embodiment of the beloved person. Who is this beloved person? He is the companion of the human soul - the Ideal Man who is God without the aloofness of an impersonal divinity, who is man without the inherent

---

[12] *The Religion of Man*, p.114

weaknesses of human existence. It is for Him, for the Divine Man or the human God, that man is prepared to make the supreme sacrifice of self-surrender in unconditional love, and it is for Him that the devoted individual remains no more the silent spectator to the great drama on the cosmic stage, but takes on the rôle of its singer finding his tunes in the stimulating currents of devotion. Rajjab, a mediaeval Indian poet-saint, says about this Supreme Reality which is inborn in man, about the ultimate transcendental truth in personalized form:

> God-man (*nara-nārāyaṇa*) is thy definition, it is
> not a delusion but truth. In thee the infinite seeks
> the finite, the perfect knowledge seeks love, and
> when the form and the Formless (the individual
> and the universal) are united *love is fulfilled in
> devotion*[13].

Love is fulfilled in devotion, but devotion becomes fully consummate only once its imaginative energies are set free in the tuneful current of musical cadences, because it is the motive, the emotive stream of music that carries the two lovers to their meeting-place, and the delight of union is relished in the sweetness of the musical flow.

---

[13] quoted by Rabindranath Tagore, *The Religion of Man*, p.112

5

Music and beauty
(The aesthetics of music)

My soul cries out,
Caught in the snare of beauty
Of the formless one.
As I cry by myself,
Night and day,
Beauty amassed before my eyes
Surpasses numerous moons and suns.
If I look at the clouds in the sky,
I see his beauty afloat;
As I see him walk on the stars
Blazing my heart…

Fikirchānd[1]

Which is the overwhelming emotional power that makes the human soul cry? Which is the overpowering force of brilliance, the luminous beam of delight that sets the human heart aflame? It is beauty - beauty which inherits the capacity to conquer the heart of man in an instant, and "caught in the snare of beauty of the formless one", the human soul dissolves in tears of joy. If we believe the words of our Bāul poet, the one who has encountered this beauty as a living experience, it is the indescribable beauty of eternity whose radiance surpasses the light of "numerous moons and suns". What is the essence carried by this beauty at its core, making its impact on the human heart so substantial and irrevocable? Beauty is revealed in form, yet its essence is formlessness. Beauty assumes a multitude of shapes, yet its essence is unity. Beauty is momentary in its outer appearances, yet its inner truth is permanence. Beauty comes forth as a silent manifestation of joy, yet its quintessence is music. So what then is beauty? Of what kind is the sound of the music of beauty?

Beauty is essentially a spirit, an energy of light to illumine the deep spheres of the soul. At the same time, beauty is also a mode of expression through which the cosmic vibrations are crystallized and made perceptible for the emotional sensor of the phenomenal world.

---

[1] quoted in Deben Bhattacharya, *The mirror of the sky* (London: Allen & Unwin, 1969), p.58

Therefore, the supreme transcendental reality manifests itself in beauty. The principal quality of beauty is its realness: things become beautiful by virtue of the truth contained in them, not by virtue of exterior features. Illusion cannot be beauty, and beauty can never be an illusion. Why? Because the spirit of untruth contradicts the very idea of beauty. Beauty is a revelation of universal energies, and energies can only be revealed if they are real. Music is real, hence music is beauty. Music is the cosmic force of motion pressing to be released into the freedom of infinity. Finding its definite articulation in the expressive manifoldness of beauty, the infinite current of music becomes channelized within the finitude of form.

Whose beauty is it that possesses the power to enrapture the universe? Whose is the beauty of which the poet says, "He who has seen the beauty / of the beloved friend, / can never forget it"[2]? Who is this 'beloved friend', the closest companion of the human heart? It is Him, the Supreme Lover, the Divine Soul immanent in all beings, who is the essence of all truth, hence of all beauty. It is Him, the Formless One, whose beauty of form ensnares the heart of man. But this beauty cannot be comprehended by human means, for the mere reason that the divine appearance of formless excellence exceeds the capacities of rationality. Therefore the poet's reminder, "the form is for seeing / but not for discourse, / as beauty has no comparison"[3]. What does that say? Beauty, the form-bound manifestation of formlessness, withdraws itself from the reach of the human mind, hence it is not fit as an object of discussion guided by reason. Yet beauty does not remain altogether inaccessible from the human level: the spirit of beauty can be conceived by the human heart. Beauty, like music, requires an emotional sensor in order to be captured. "The form is for seeing" - for seeing not with the eyes, not with the sense organ that passes on its information to the brain, but for seeing through the inner receptor connected to the emotional sensor of the human soul.

Seeing the beauty of the formless and listening to the music of the infinite thus signify but one and the same thing in terms of their designation as processes of emotional perception: beauty is not seen by

---

[2] Pāñja Shāh, quoted in Deben Bhattacharya, op.cit., p105
[3] ibid.

looking at material features, and music is not heard by exposing the ear to physical sounds. Why? Because beauty is not a mere amassment of features, and music is not a mere accumulation of sounds. If it were so, wherefrom would beauty, wherefrom would music derive its energy to inspire man and to furnish him with the capacity to live beyond the limits of his physical existence? The Bāul poet's heart has been illuminated by the spark of beauty, emboldening him to take on the invincible powers of the cosmos:

> He who has seen that form
> flashing on the mirror,
> the darkness of his heart is gone.
> He lives with his eyes
> focussed on the form,
> careless of the river between life and death.
>
> His heart forever devoted to beauty
> dares the gods. ...[4]

In the same way music, being the sounding articulation of silent beauty, elevates the human soul above the level of rational finiteness and thereby brings about its delivery from the bonds of materiality.

But if the realization of beauty requires more than a descriptive assessment of aesthetic features, if the comprehension of music calls for more than an analytical investigation into the technical structuralities of organized sounds, then what is the decisive criterion for the true understanding of music, of beauty? It is the realization, the acknowledgement of the inner kinship between man and the cosmic truth of the universe - the formless truth that reveals itself in the silent shapes of beauty and in the sounding notes of music likewise. The same melodious sweetness inhabits this truth whether it comes forth as the silent beauty of cosmic music, or as the ringing sound of universal beauty. Man becomes aware of this music, of this beauty only once he realizes that he is himself intrinsically linked with the eternal truth of existence through an invisible bond of love.

---

[4] ibid. (p.106)

What does this mean? Which are the consequences implied in man's emotional kinship with the universal truth? Being conscious of his part in this truth, man becomes able to recognize a reflection of his own in that which gives him delight. Why? Related to the truth as such, man is also related to its manifestations. His joy in beauty, therefore, is the joy in his own self, and his delight in music is the delight in his own soul's tunes. If there would not be this organic relationship between man and the cosmic truth, if man could not establish his direct link with the beauty and music of the universe, there would be no enjoyment, no delight. Beauty, however perfect, would remain a bare fact of dry aesthetic completeness, and music, however harmonius, were no more than a well-arranged but soulless succession of sounds.

Beauty becomes beautiful because of the fundamental kinship that conjoins man and the truth at the core of beauty. But how are the chords of relation tied? - through love. Love is essential for the emancipation of beauty in the same way as it is vital for the unfolding of the musical melody. Why? The reason is the urgence of love to bring its emotional spirit to perfection in the concrete manifestation of form. Where is this manifestation found? - in beauty, in which the formless and the form melt into one single expression of bliss. "A creation of beauty suggests a fulfilment, which is the fulfilment of love"[5], and therefore the creation of beauty turns into a source of delight - the delight of fulfilment, of attainment of the most sublime bliss that arises out of the consummation of divine love. Music, being a creation of beauty, should naturally arouse the same sensation of overwhelming joy awakened through a revelation of beauty. Yet music at times stirs up sentiments of sadness, of distress, of pain - sentiments reflecting the agony of unfulfilled love.

How is that? Music represents not only the state of perfection, but also the way that leads towards it. Music embodies not only bliss itself, but also the search for bliss. Therefore music is more than merely a completed creation of beauty in which love has come to sheer fulfilment. Music does indwell creation as its vital soul, but at the same time, music represents the process of creating - a process characterized by momentary incompleteness, by perfection yet to be worked out, by

---

5 Rabindranath Tagore, *Creative Unity* (New Delhi: Macmillan India Ltd., reprint 1995), p.19

consummation yet to be attained. It is the aspect of imperfection immanent in the process of searching which gives rise to dissatisfaction, even pain, because an unfinished creation of beauty does not emit the same radiance as does a perfected manifestation of harmonious brilliance. And still it is the process of finishing the unfinished, of perfecting the imperfect, which inherits a special beauty derived from the truth that carries the search to its completion. The same truth inherent in both the process and the finished creation adds beauty to that which is yet imperfect, to that which possesses the capacity to delight in the dignity of ephemeral pain. Music is thus always an expression of fulfilled beauty no matter whether or not it is perfect as a work of art, whether or not the love embodied in it is consummate, whether the tune arouses agony or bliss.

Beauty suggests the fulfilment of love because "beauty is the self-offering of the One to the other One"[6], and love becomes complete in offering, in sacrifice. As an expression of love, beauty is permanent in its nature, but as an expression of love's fulfilment, the concrete forms of manifest beauty are momentary and perishable. To illustrate this idea of impermanence that affects the physical incarnations of beauty, Rabindranath Tagore, in his essay "The Poet's Religion"[7], quotes from an English poem, explaining that

> in the first part of his 'Hymn to Intellectual Beauty', Shelley dwells on the inconstancy and evanescence of the manifestation of beauty, which imparts to it an appearance of frailty and unreality: *'Like hues and harmonies of evening, / like clouds in starlight widely spread, / like memory of music fled'.*

Music, like all phenomenal expressions of beauty, is inconsistent in its presence: it originates, grows, matures and vanishes. But the musical idea, the spirit of musical imagination, is permanent in the same way as the creative spirit of beauty is constantly existent. It is the permanent aspect inherent in music, the omnipresent stimulative energy, that inspires the birth of the sounding creation, carries ahead its productive

---

[6] ibid.
[7] *Creative Unity*, p.19

progression, and lives on as memory once the sound of the melody has faded.

What is it that accounts for the capacity of beauty to maintain its constancy as an emotional value even though its outer manifestations are temporary, short-lived aesthetic phenomena? A flower is finite in its material integrity: it assumes shape once the bud opens, and it dies when its leaves have dried and fallen out. But the beauty of the flower and the sweetness of its fragrance are permanent values in spite of their temporally limited perceptibility. Why? Because beauty is inspired by the great sacrifice of love, the "self-offering of the One for the other One", which bears at its core the essence of eternity but comes forth in an endless variety of forms. For what purpose are these forms designed? - for the sake of offering them to the beloved of the heart. Beauty takes many forms, and form takes many aspects, but the final destination for all these is ultimately the same: to be presented to the one from whom all beauty originates, the intimate companion of the loving soul who embodies the quintessence of love. How is the offering of beauty made? - through music: "My songs are the same as are the spring flowers, they come from you. / Yet I bring these to you as my own. / You smile and accept them, and you are glad at my joy of pride"[8]. The singer-worshiper is well aware of the impermanence of his song-offering in terms of material existence, but their momentariness does not bother him: "If my song flowers are frail and they fade and drop in the dust, I shall never grieve"[9]. What is the reason for his confidence? It is his realization of the plain fact that beauty, which is evanescent as a physical phenomenon, can never be lost as a universal truth: "For absence is not loss in your hand, and the fugitive moments that blossom in beauty are kept ever fresh in your wreath"[10].

The transcendental reality of beauty is unbounded in its expansivity, unlimited in its intensity, and undying in its actuality, and so is music, the most direct expression of cosmic beauty. The infinite, however, cannot obtain fulfilment in infinity, hence it seeks out for the finite where it finds its freedom within bounds. Therefore, limitless

---

[8] Rabindranath Tagore, *Crossing*, LXV
[9] ibid.
[10] ibid.

beauty is brought to perfection only in the limited finitude of form, and the shoreless current of music begins to flow only once it enters the river-bed of definite sounds. Yet the essence within the limits is the essence of infinity: the manifestations may be vanishable as separate entities, but as a sum of realities they are eternal, just as a single drop of water evaporates while the river, the total of billions of water-drops, remains. So then, is that to say that a thing becomes meaningful, becomes effective only if it is part of a large amassment of facts? No, it is not. Every single expression of beauty, however finite and fugitive, carries in itself the dignity of a truth that exceeds all limits of finiteness. It is this dignity of inner excellence which furnishes even the least manifestation of beauty with the ability to send out its rays of bliss and to add a momentum of infinity to even the shortest instant of joy. The poet is fully conscious of his significance in the universal game of beauty when he says -

> My King, thou hast called me to play my flute at
> the roadside, that they who bear the burden of
> voiceless life may stop in their errands for a
> moment and sit and wonder before the
> balcony of thy palace gate; that they may see
> anew the ever old and find afresh what is
> ever about them, and say, 'The flowers are in
> bloom, and the birds sing.'[11]

Beauty, music reveals itself as a momentary, yet live-giving energy because of the vital truth at its bottom. The distinctive characteristic of beauty is inconsistency of features but permanence of substance, and it is the inner essence of love, of emotional sweetness which gives the music of beauty its capacity to arouse permanent delight through impermanent manifestations, and thus to leave lasting traces on the human soul: "He who has seen the beauty / of the beloved friend, / can never forget it".

How does music, how does beauty live on in the spheres of human awareness once it has captivated the heart of man? It assumes transcendental form in the sublime shades of memory. Once spiritualized

---

[11] Rabindranath Tagore, *Crossing*, LXVI

in such a way, the aesthetic reality penetrates the emotional consciousness of man where it instigates an emotional sensation that remains beyond the impact made by the physical sensation of the immediate aesthetic phenomenon. But why does the emotional reaction stay on, even if the arousing agent has disappeared? The poet provides the answer: "He who has seen that form…the darkness of his heart is gone"[12]. The darkness of the heart has given way to the light of fulfilment, of unlimited bliss received upon seeing the form - the transcendental form manifest in the streaks of beauty, the shapeless form whose essence is the truth of existence, hence which is eternal while the material form is not. Beauty stimulates memory only in the mind which comprehends the core substance of infinity, and music is remembered only by the heart that absorbs the inexhaustible sweetness of the transcendental tune. Music, beauty thus becomes unforgettable because the experience of the form, of the sounding melody is brought about by the imperishable essence within the transcendental reality rather than by the transient outer appearance.

The apprehension of beauty as an illimitable, unending truth, however, requires susceptiveness on the part of the individual before whom the creation of beauty opens up. As long as the human mind is not ready to receive the signals of reality beyond immediate, physically perceptible phenomena, the doors of beauty remain locked. The eye that sees the form, the ear that hears the musical sound is concerned only with the external features of the concrete occurence in their restrictive fugaciousness, but the heart has no excuse for being ignorant of the infinite essence concealed in each and every manifestation of finite beauty. The object of the sense organs is to ascertain tangible facts in order that the rational mind may acknowledge their material authenticity, but the ambition of the human heart, of the emotional receptor within man, extends beyond the mere establishment of material actualities. So how does the heart relate to beauty, to music? It responds. The heart being the center of emotional perceptivity, its rôle is not only to discern universal realities, but to react to them and thereby to establish a direct relationship between man and the cosmic creation.

---

[12] cf. footnote 2

But why is it essential to establish such a relation? In reply, we may well return the question: "why is there beauty at all in creation - the beauty whose only meaning is in a call that claims disinterestedness as a response?"[13]. Yes, it is true that beauty would become meaningless if it were to unfold in an emotional vacuum with no response from the other end. It is true that music would become worthless if its cadences were not echoed in the sweetness of love sent out by a responding soul. Why is it so? As an aesthetic presence, beauty is realized only once it enters into dynamic interchange with its object, with the one to whom it is offered. The essential prerequisites to activate this interaction are mutuality of relation and reciprocity of response. What is the reason? We have already observed that beauty embodies the self-offering of the one to the other one, which carries in itself the suggestion of a fulfilment of love. Beauty, therefore, cannot arise without a mutual interest, for offerings require two parties - the one who offers and the one who receives -, and love can only be fulfilled when two entities merge into one.

So what is the essence of beauty? - unity, but unity presupposes a duality in order to be effective. The quest of unity is to overcome duality, hence two entities must be there or else there can be no coalescence, no union. Moreover the two entities have to be mutually responsive, for irresponsiveness on the part of one entity negates its very existence within the interactive process, and the search for unity becomes an irrational quest. Beauty, the aesthetic reality that propounds the fulfilment of love, embodies unity *par excellence*, because the principle of unity, of defeated duality, finds its most sublime and most immediate expression in the mutuality of love. As an aesthetic ideal, beauty represents the creative expression of unity, whose *raison d'être* lies in the creation as such:

> The joy of unity within ourselves, seeking
> expression, becomes creative; whereas our desire
> for the fulfilment of our needs is constructive.
> The water vessel, taken as a vessel only, raises
> the question, 'Why does it exist at all?'. Through
> its fitness of construction, it offers the apology

---

[13] Rabindranath Tagore, *Creative Unity*, p.81

for its existence. But where it is a work of beauty
it has no question to answer; it has nothing to do,
but to be. It reveals in its form a unity to which
all that seems various in it is so related that, in a
mysterious manner, it strikes sympathetic chords
to the music of unity in our own being.[14]

How is the music of unity revealed? - through beauty. Disclosed as
form, beauty is the material expression of transcendental
harmoniousness, whose sounding manifestation is music. Thus, both
music and beauty stand for one and the same aesthetic ideal - the ideal of
creative unity embedded in a stimulative variety of outer shapes.

What is it that makes music and beauty conjoin to form one single
aesthetic truth? It is nothing but the universal quest for unity inherent in
each and every cosmic reality. The quest exists as the driving energy that
dwells in all beings and inspires their search for fulfilment of one kind
or another. Beauty signifies the creative ideal expressed in music, but
music itself finds its most complete expression in beauty. Music is
beauty - it is beauty enlivened and unfolded in the harmonious sequence
of tuneful cadences coming forth in ever-changing melodious shades,
though united by the all-pervading essence of cosmic sweetness. Yet
beauty is music: the music of beauty which is inspirited by the life-
giving essence of unity that seeks expression in the multifariousness of
the concrete in order to prove its inner truth of ultimate oneness. The
music of beauty plays on the chords of universal harmoniousness to
arouse a multitude of emotional strains in the spiritual consciousness of
man, and it is this manifoldness of fleeting emotions which establishes
the permanent truth of unity at the core of things. Therefore beauty, just
as music, claims its aesthetic right of existence without the need of
providing facts about its rational usefulness.

Indeed if beauty were to be judged from the point of view of
constructive applicability, the result would be utter dismissal, as the idea
of beauty contradicts the very concept of material purposefulness. Why?
Because beauty has no purpose to serve; its only object is to represent
the universal principle of unity, of harmony that indwells the supreme

---

[14] Rabindranath Tagore, op.cit., p.5

transcendental reality as its vital essence. What is the consequence in terms of material rationality? Let us take music, the melodious expression of sounding beauty. Evaluated by rational means, music is a most useless, superfluous activity, whose pursuance does not lead to fulfilment of even a single physical need. Guided by constructivism, our rational mind hence tells us to abandon music, and to vest our energies thus liberated from the snares of fruitlessness in purposeful actions that meet our necessities. But what happens? Nothing. The music has vanished but our needs are still not satisfied. How come that our newly-gained energies, withdrawn from music and directed at seemingly meaningful ends, have not helped in achieving our material objects? What is the reason for their failure?

The rational mind has no answer for that which is accessible only to the emotional consciousness of man. Without music, even trivial physical needs remain unfulfilled, because any activity aimed at their accomplishment lacks the driving force of joy concealed in the beauty of music. Music is not itself the action that brings about achievement through a concretely visible undertaking, but rather it is the constructive energy inherent in all action, which guarantees the success of the purposeful move. The mind, however, trained in rationality but devoid of emotional capacities, recognizes only the action as such, not the spirit behind it. The mind hence dismisses that which is beyond the reach of rational comprehension, that which is outside the competence of rational thought. Not so the heart, whose emotional sensor apprehends "the music that teases us out of thought as it fills our being"[15]. What does this music signify? It represents the expression of beauty, material yet spiritual, creative yet stable, rational yet functioning versus rationality. Beauty, because of its illimitable essence that defies all rationality, cannot be captured by means of a rationally inclined, restrictive mind. Owing to its inborn spirit of freedom, beauty cannot be subdued by material intentionality. Beauty emerges as an omnipresent energy of bliss, but it declines to offer reasons for its being there. The music of beauty thus overflows the inner spheres of human existence with its all-pervading sweetness exactly because it is not directed at a mere purpose, for purposefulness with its linear motive contradicts the idea of infinity. Actions of practicality touch the margins of human life to the degree

---

[15] Rabindranath Tagore, op.cit., p.17

determined by their immediate expediency and guided by considerations of rationality, but music as the emotional energy of beauty deeply penetrates the core of being only to "tease us out of thought" for the sake of unbounded bliss irrespective of rational laws.

What is it that bestows upon beauty the capacity to transcend the limits of reason? Beauty is not merely a passive quality imposed upon things by virtue of their exterior characteristics. To the contrary, the essence of beauty never settles in the outer cover of physical entities, but permeates their inner substance. Beauty is the enlivening spirit of creativity, the illuminative energy whose manifestation brings the object of beauty to full radiance. How does this process work? Beauty is revealed in external features, but it is fulfilled through the harmony from within. Thus music as a creation of beauty discloses its aesthetic preciousness in sweet-sounding melodious cadences, but the true essence of beauty at the core of music does not even enter the sound to become manifest in an audible manner. Of what kind is this essence of beauty hidden in the mantle of music? It is the flow of emotion that instigates the musical outburst in the first place, the inherent sentiments that turn the mechanical sound-construction into a living aesthetic reality.

So what then is the criterion for judging the beauty in music? Is it perfection in technical skills, is it flawlessness in the rendition of given sequences of notes? Most certainly not. A presentation of music howsoever faultless and polished in terms of technicalities is still sterile and lacking beauty as long as the imaginative spirit of devotion is absent. Why? Because devotion expresses the emotional readiness for self-offering in its fullest and most sublime pronouncement. Saturated with devotion, music attains true beauty, because beauty represents the fulfilment of the ultimate quest through "the self-offering of the One to the other One", which is accomplished in devotion. The momentum of devotion in music, therefore, is also the momentum of beauty in music. Is that to say that there is no beauty without devotion? Emphatically yes, it is - beauty presupposes devotion in order to be born, for beauty as such is nothing but an aesthetic articulation of devotion. Beauty arises out of devotion, lives forth through devotion, and offers itself up for the sake of devotion. Music is the most immediate expression of beauty, hence music is also the prime manifestation of devotion. And *vice versa*, beauty embodies the material expression of cosmic music, hence beauty is devotion incarnate, for devotion forms the quintessence of both beauty and music.

Beauty expresses devotion, beauty expresses music, but how is beauty itself expressed in the emotional consciousness of man? The beauty perceived by the emotional receptor of the human heart arouses in man an all-pervading sensation of delight, of bliss, inexplicable though, but seeking articulation in spontaneous tunes of joy in order to communicate the overwhelming experience to the invisible transcendental companion of the soul. What has happened? The heart which has encountered the beauty of the infinite remains startled at the immediateness of the cosmic revelation, overpowered by an immense feeling of reality suggested by the divine appearance. Why is it so? The reason is the element of truth that indwells each and every manifestation of beauty - the impetus of the supreme transcendental reality, the "truth [that] reveals itself in beauty. For if beauty were mere accident, a rent in the eternal fabric of things, then it would hurt, would be defeated by the antagonism of facts. Beauty is no phantasy, it has the everlasting meaning of reality"[16].

But beauty does not hurt because it is real. "Beauty is truth, truth beauty", because truth manifests itself in beauty, and the essence of beauty is truth. The human soul, discovering the beauty revealed in a multitude of concrete forms, discerns the truth of unity inherent in the creation of beauty - the unity that joins together the entire spectrum of varied shapes to form one single expression of reality. It is the realness at the core of the aesthetic vision which makes the phenomenon of beauty bearable for the human heart. Why? Realness implies attainableness. Beauty embodies not only an aesthetic ideal, but signifies the object of man's ultimate quest, the supreme transcendental truth, the final destination of all spiritual pursuits. Beauty is real, hence it is attainable, and so is the highest quest, because its ultimate end is beauty. If beauty were fake, if beauty were illusory, the seeker's spiritual goal too would be illusive hence unattainable, and it is the sense of unattainability that gives rise to pain.

---

[16] Rabindranath Tagore, op.cit., p.15

Beauty, however, can never produce pain because its essence of truth rejects the idea of suffering. "All the language of joy is beauty"[17], and all the language of beauty is joy. Beauty is joy manifested in form, and joy is the beauty of the formless. Beauty is the aesthetic expression of joy, and joy is the emotional expression of beauty. What is it that brings forth the joy of beauty? Not truth as such, not realness as a naked actuality, but the intrinsic harmony that constitutes the positive essence of truth. Truth reveals itself in beauty, but this truth is more than a mere accumulation of facts: "truth consists, not in facts, but in harmony of facts"[18]. Beauty thus qualifies as an expression of joy because of its being an expression of harmony - of harmony that inspirits the truth of existence and makes it a manifestation of bliss. Without its inborn harmony, truth would become discordant to be ultimately defeated by its own illusiveness. Truth becomes truth by virtue of its harmoniousness, and beauty becomes beauty on the strength of its joy. Truth finds its supreme expression in beauty because harmony implies joy - the joy of beauty.

So how does music reveal the harmonious essence of beauty, of joy? It is music that transforms the unbounded energies of transcendental joy into a discernible emotional potency accessible to the human heart. In what way? Through the subtlety of its vibrations, music activates the emotional consciousness of man in order to receive the spiritual message of joy concealed in the folds of beauty. Music thus channelizes the cosmic flow of emotions so that its impact becomes endurable by human means. How is this done? - by adding a sense of concreteness to the abstract transcendental reality: the sounding tune, the melodious cadence delivering sublime musical imagination carries at its core the sweetness of universal beauty, the joy of unlimited delight, but in a sensually perceptible manifestation of qualified emotionality. The beauty of music is its harmoniousness, but the music within beauty is the inner essence of joy which is released once transcendental beauty assumes the definite form of a melody.

Inspired by the cosmic energies of love, beauty stretches out its rays of bliss and glows to full radiance in the all-penetrating sweetness

[17] Rabindranath Tagore, op.cit., p.36
[18] Rabindranath Tagore, op.cit., p.32

of music. Yet beauty withdraws itself from the reach of mundanity, and its light remains invisible for ordinary spirits:

> The evening was lonely for me, and I was reading a book till my heart became dry, and it seemed to me that beauty was a thing fashioned by the traders in words. Tired I shut the book and snuffed the candle. In a moment the room was flooded with moonlight.
>
> Spirit of Beauty, how could you, whose radiance overbrims the sky, stand hidden behind a candle's tiny flame? How could a few vain words from a book rise like a mist, and veil her whose voice has hushed the heart of earth into ineffable calm?[19]

No, it is not the candle's dimension that enables it to cover up the brilliance of immeasurable beauty. It is the soul's own closeness to the finite candle rather than to the illimitable reality of beauty which makes the shade of the trivial rise beyond the light of divine truth. It is the listener's proximity to the discordant noise of the insignificant that makes him turn a deaf ear to the harmonious-sounding music of the universe. The radiance of the infinite is overshadowed by fhe veil of ignorance, but the capacity to tear off the shroud rests within the human soul. Music, the sounding manifestation of beauty, is the motivating energy that activates this capacity and thereby effects the soul's delivery, unwrapping the treasure of universal beauty before the inner eye of man.

The expressions of beauty are of manifold kind, yet music emerges as the elemental, most vital manifestation. Why is it so? What is the special quality that elevates music to such excellence?

> Music is the purest form of arts, and therefore the most direct expression of beauty, with a form and spirit which is one and simple, and least encumbered with anything extraneous. We seem to feel that the manifestation of the

---

[19] Rabindranath Tagore, *Lover's Gift*, LVI

infinite in the finite forms of creation is music
itself, silent and visible. ... Therefore the true
poets, they who are seers, seek to express the
universe in terms of music. ... There is a
perfection in each individual strain of this
music, which is the revelation of completion
in the incomplete. No one of its notes is final,
yet each reflects the infinite.

What does it matter if we fail to derive the exact
meaning of this great harmony? Is it not like
the hand meeting the string and drawing out
at once all its tones at the touch? *It is the
language of beauty*, the caress, that comes
from the heart of the world and straightway
reaches our heart.[20]

Music is the language of beauty, but this language is the language of the
heart, not that of the mind, and therefore the human mind with its
rational inclination will never be competent to decode the message of
beauty concealed in the strains of music - the message of love which is
sent out by the Divine Music-maker, only to convert into boundless
bliss in the heart of the Eternal Listener.

20 Rabindranath Tagore, *Sādhanā* (London: Macmillan and Co. Ltd., 1914), pp.142ff.

6

Music and harmony

When thou commandest me to sing it seems that
my heart would break with pride; and I look
to thy face, and tears come to my eyes.
All that is harsh and dissonant in my life melts
into one sweet harmony - and my adoration
spreads wings like a glad bird on its flight
across the sea.

...

from Rabindranath Tagore, *Gītāñjali*, II

Dissonance dissolves into harmony, ugliness into beauty, harshness into sweetness at one single touch of the magic melody emerging from the strings of the cosmic instrument. One fugitive spark of musical imagination sent out by the Divine Music-maker in a creative strain is sufficient to turn darkness into light, desire into satisfaction, agony into bliss. Such is the power of music that its radiance penetrates the universe and illumines the limitless skies of the world, filling the whole creation with a melodiousness whose intensity is beyond rational comprehensibility - a melodiousness whose essence is harmony, the vital bond that weaves the multiple threads of separate facts into one single, organic fabric called cosmos. Who is the Divine Weaver creating this wonderful array of harmonious brilliance? Whose is the spirit that indwells the great music of the world, instilling the breath of life in each and every of its manifestations? Who is it who commands existence to be, and the singer to sing? Is it the Divine Musician who transforms creation into music, or is it the Creator who on a single flash of music designs the entire universe?

The singer finds his tune once he is inspirited by the living revelation of the Supreme Soul, and it is the immediate emotional experience enveloped in a sensation of all-overwhelming bliss which urges him to express the divine vision just obtained in a spontaneous outburst of tunes. "When thou commandest me to sing it seems that my heart would break" - the impact of the tremendous wave of joy released from the depth of the infinite appears unbearable for the human heart unless it eases itself in musical cadences. "I look to thy face, and tears come to my eyes" - because He who reveals Himself through an inconspicious drift of musical inspiration is indeed the cause of all emotionality, hence the existential energy that instigates the flow of music. But why is this emotional inclination of music so essential? What is it that elevates the music thus enlivened by divine imagination above the level of a mere arrangement of sounds? The singer himself provides the answer when he says, "All that is harsh and dissonant in my life melts into one sweet harmony": music, once inspired by the Supreme Reality, inherits the capacity to dissolve discord and establish the unifying link of harmony, thereby removing the strains of disagreement that conceal the universal truth from the glance of the human soul.

But is not harmoniousness a characteristic feature of music in any case? Is it not the inborn harmony of music that marks the difference between music and mere sound? And does not all music emerge from the emotional touch of the cosmic soul? Would else not music be reduced to a bare assemblage of ringing notes? Yes, music is intrinsically harmonious, but the potency to bestow harmoniousness surpasses the quality of being harmonious. It is true that music arises out of the creative union between the human soul and the infinite spirit of the universe, but the capacity to establish union excels the state of unity. Where does this capacity rest? - in the music stimulated by the singer's direct contact with the Supreme Soul, in the music wilfully created by the Divine Being and expressed in the tunes of the Creator's appointed musician. The human singer is well aware of the command that makes him sing, but why is this command at all given? The singer answers,

> I know thou takest pleasure in my singing. I
> know that only as a singer I come before thy
> presence.[1]

Why is it so? Taking pleasure in his singer's tunes, the Infinite One but rejoices in the delight of his own melodies. It is this very music, the transcendental music of joy, which bears in itself the essence of harmony that generates the energetic force of consonance. It is this music which, inspired by the divinity, creates the great harmony of the

---

[1] Rabindranath Tagore, *Gītāñjali*, II

universe, because the sweetness of its tunes is nothing but the sounding manifestation of cosmic harmoniousness.

What is more, the tune is presented to the human singer as a gift of divine imagination, an expression of the Supreme One's infinite love for the human soul. Why else would the Eternal Music-maker part with his own melody to have it unfolded at the hands of his human musician? Why would He deliberately give away the illimitable treasure of melodious cadences resting within the divine instrument to have it delivered to the world through a humble human's song? The reason is love - an intense love that unites the boundless with the finite, the formless with the form, God with man. The music of the universe may retain its transcendental excellence as long as the Creator keeps it for himself, but it lacks the joy of fulfilled love, which is born only once the tune is handed over to the human singer as an offering of love. Music existing merely as a transcendental reality may be perfect in its intrinsic harmoniousness, yet falls short of the power to create harmony, which is acquired only once the musical melody has been consecrated by the sacrifice of love. Why? Because harmoniousness is an inert quality, a state of relation between things, but harmony is the relationship itself, the active, continuous process of establishing the state of harmoniousness ever again. Music as an aesthetic presence of static harmoniousness is therefore nothing but a sounding manifestation of well-arranged completeness, beautiful but neutral. However, once the musical reality evolves beyond the limits of empty prettiness, once music becomes an expression of the powerful bond of love that unites the human heart with the soul of the world, the sounding embodiment of harmoniousness is endowed with the potential to not only represent the principle of harmony, but to arouse harmony as an all-overwhelming emotional experience.

It is the inherent generative energy of harmony that makes the Supreme Being take pleasure in the tunes of the human singer. But why is it that "only as a singer I come before thy presence"? Why is it that man can approach his Divine Lover only in the capacity of the musician? What is so special about the singer's place in the universal game plan of creation? It is his oneness with the musical reality, the mergence of music-maker and music, creator and created, which represents the truth of unity, of harmony guised in sweet-sounding cadences:

"...music and the musician are inseparable.
When the singer departs, his singing dies
with him; it is in eternal union with the life
and joy of the master.
This world-song is never for a moment separated
from its singer. It is not fashioned from any
outward material. It is his joy itself taking
never-ending form. It is the great heart
sending the tremor of its thrill over the sky.
There is a perfection in each individual strain of
this music, which is the revelation of
completion in the incomplete. No one of its
notes is final, yet each reflects the infinite.[2]

Indeed music as a sounding phenomenon ceases to exist when the musician withdraws his presence from the stage of world-music. Even though the memory of the tune may last in the mind of the listener, the tune itself cannot be separated from the imaginative spirit out of which it is born. The sounding melody remains a silent secret buried in the depth of the musical instrument if not the musician's skilful fingers lure it away from its toneless confinement. The pressing emotional energies of love, urging to be released in musical outflows, stay back as a painful longing if not the singer voices them in song. Music and musician, song and singer thus form one single, inseparable entity - a harmonious entity moreover, in which the unity of cosmic creation finds its highest and most delightful articulation.

Music, through its inherent principle of unity, of harmony, grows into one with the musician, with the creative force by which it is brought forth. The musician thus becomes one with his song, but is the tune truly his own? No, it is not - it belongs to the one who is the originator of all music, who offers the melody to his human friend as a gift of love. And yet yes, it is, because having been entrusted with the treasure of music, the human singer makes the tunes his own only to present them to the Infinite Musician to reciprocate his love. Moreover, the act of returning the affection shown by the Supreme Soul brings the human musician closer to his transcendental lover. What is the reason? Music

---

2 Rabindranath Tagore, *Sādhanā* (London: Macmillan and Co. Ltd., 1914), pp.143f.

extends the emotional capacities of the human heart by transgressing the limits of bodily finitude. It is through the sounding tune, through the explicit musical melody that the bond between man and the divinity is protracted and intensified. Through music, man becomes able to accomplish what he could never achieve by rational means:

> I touch by the edge of the far-spreading wing of
> my song thy feet which I could never aspire
> to reach.[3]

Music embodies the supreme sacrifice - the sacrifice of love for the sake of love. The offering of music, therefore, signifies at the same time the musician's surrender to the one to whom the music is offered. In the universal process of music-making, this surrender is of two-fold nature: it is the Divine Music-maker's surrender to his human singer, and it is the human musician's surrender to the Supreme Soul. How is it done? - in music. The Eternal Musician hands over his tunes of cosmic sweetness to the human singer, but it is not only the tune which is given away - the Infinite One surrenders himself to his human companion to find fulfilment in union with the finite. But how could the human soul bear the immensity of this union without surrendering herself to the infinite reality? Therefore, man responds to the transcendental melody with cadences of his own, and offers his own self to the illimitable truth. Because the finite can own the infinite only by being ready to lose itself in boundlessness, and the infinite becomes free only by accepting the bounds of the finite.

But why is it music which instigates and establishes this mutual self-sacrifice? Why is music at all needed in the process of reciprocal responsiveness? The reason lies in the capacity of music to inspire and establish the harmony of contrary forces. Harmony is the necessary prerequisite without which there can be no surrender, no union. Why? - because the principle of harmony implies the mutual desire to unite, and where there is no such desire, attainment in union remains a vain illusion. The quest for harmony represents the driving energy that unifies contradictory, even antagonistic forces, and it is the emotional potencies of music through which this universal energy is channelized

---

[3] Rabindranath Tagore, *Gītāñjali*, II

and thereby made effective. Without harmony, without even the quest for harmony inherent in the cosmic reality, there can be no union, and the soul's readiness for surrender passes off unanswered, leaving behind a deep sense of pain as the Bāul poet woefully observes: "How the days drag / before my union / with the man of my heart! / Round the hours / of the day and night / as the rain-bird, *chātaka*, / watches the clouds, / I gaze at the black moon / hoping to surrender myself / at his feet - in vain".[4]

What has happened? Where is the measureless harmony of the infinite gone? How come that the world-song has lost its harmoniousness? No, it is not the harmony of the boundless which as vanished. It is not the strain of universal music that has been deprived of its sweetness. The root of discord does not rest in the realm of infinity, but in the human heart. The cosmic melody retains its eternal charm, but it becomes harmonious only once it finds its reverberation in the heart of man, because harmony can be established only on the basis of a duality. What does this mean? Harmony is not a state, but the quest for a state, namely the quest for the state of abolished antagonism reflected in unity within the duality. It is the quest for unity without conquest - the constructive intent to melt the duality by mergence rather than suppression. The precondition for harmonious unity to be achieved, however, is mutuality of intention, reciprocal responsiveness. So who then is to blame when union cannot be established, when the devoted soul is barred from surrendering to the object of aspiration?

If the Supreme Soul were nothing but a neutral, impersonal energy of cosmic excellence, the answer were easy to be given. But it is not so. The Infinite One responds to the human soul reciprocally, that is to say in the same way He is being approached. If the human heart is ready to surrender, yet held back by some inexplicable force of disharmony, then it is from within the human soul that the dissonance arises. Which is the cause? It is the doubtfulness of the human mind, of the rational mind not capable of comprehending the infinite essence of the cosmic reality, hence not willing to accept the emotional necessity for the sacrifice of love. The mind, inclined towards reason, judges things

---

4 Lālan, quoted in Deben Bhattacharya, *The mirror of the sky* (London: Allen & Unwin, 1969), p.92

according to their immediate perceptibiliy, refusing to see their permanent essence. Since the Supreme Being manifests himself in a variety of transient incarnations, the rational mind apprehends these embodiments in their finite momentariness and takes their evanescent forms for the ultimate truth: "Like lightning / flashing through the clouds / and hiding in the clouds / never to be found again, / I saw his beauty / flashing through my dream / and I lost Krishna"[5].

But loss can never be the last word in the great poem of creation. For if it were so, there would be no harmony at all in the world, and the universe were nothing more than a single stream of tears. The very idea of loss as a definite, unchangeable reality contradicts the spirit of unity that indwells each and every particle of cosmic existence. If loss were final, no music could ever arise from the depth of the infinite, and the human soul would eternally wander about in agony, "hoping to surrender herself at his feet - in vain". Yet it is not so. The cosmic music is very much there as a living presence in its full sweetness and harmony, and the quest for union with the Supreme Lover, for attainment in complete self-surrender is a very much real, feasible quest. What does that say? The conclusiveness of loss, the finality of discord is but an illusion of the rational mind, caused by the limited perspective of reason. However, it is this very illusion which arouses the feeling of disharmony, of resignation in the heart of man once the supreme spiritual goal is not obtained in an instant, once the desired union with the divine is not immediately achieved, or is achieved but not sustained. It is the sense of doubt, raised in the heart which has fallen victim to the deceit of the mind, that prevents the human soul from her self-offering in spite of all readiness. It is the disbelief in the eternal truth behind the finite form - the disbelief which is instigated by misleading arguments of reason - that negates the harmonious essence of the world-music and elevates discord to the superior rank.

Yet the human soul resists the trickery of rationality, and her inborn sense of harmony is ultimately stronger than the artificial promotion of disunity. At the bottom of all spiritual pursuits, there is always an intense longing for harmonious unity, which is given voice in the profound prayer of the human heart, "Let all my songs gather

---

[5] ibid.

together their diverse strains into a single current and flow to a sea of silence in one salutation to thee"[6]. It is the eternal prayer of the human soul for union with the soul of the world, for surrender to the Supreme Soul in order to find her fulfilment in complete mergence with the universal flow of cosmic music in its full melodiousness. It is the permanent prayer of the heart that knows the quintessence of harmony embodied in music, the quintessence of music expressed in harmony. But how is harmony itself expressed? - in tunes of delight, in joy:

> Drunk with the joy of singing I forget myself
> and call thee friend who art my lord.[7]

It is through music that man attains to the divine, it is through music that man unites with the Supreme Being - but through joy he obtains the music. Joy is the vitalizing force of harmoniousness concealed in the folds of beauty, and it is the potency of joy that incites the melodious outbreak of universal harmony. Music is essentially a product of harmony, an expression of the all-pervading energy of harmoniousness, but joy is the stimulative power that inspires the cosmic harmony in the first place.

How does the energy of joy become effective in the expansive network of creation? In what way does joy instigate the constructive workings of harmony? Harmoniousness is enlivened by the mutual delight of opposite energetic forces, by the bliss reciprocated in the union of different emotional entities. That is to say, the joy of the infinite within the limits of finitude, and the delight of the finite within infinity, represents the intrinsic harmony between the finite and infinite energies. It is this inborn harmony which gives rise to the joy, and which is at the same time expressed in joy. Harmoniousness means closeness, and harmony is the unifying agent that brings the two entities together in a relationship of joy. What is the place of music in this relation? Music is the medium through which the state of union, the condition of harmoniousness is brought about. It is in music that the quest of harmony, the desire for fulfilment in union finds its fullest and most melodious expression, and it is by virtue of its motivating capacity that music ultimately succeeds in accomplishing the search for attainment.

---

[6] Rabindranath Tagore, *Gītāñjalī*, CIII
[7] Rabindranath Tagore, *Gītāñjalī*, II

So how does the threefold mechanism of joy, harmony and music practically function? Which are the rôles assigned to the three components? Music, harmony and joy are the inseparable and indispensable energetic forces whose unity represents the supreme transcendental reality. Harmony, the metaphysical manifestation of cosmic music, becomes explicit in joy, but at the same time, this harmony is stimulated by joy. There can be no joy without an intrinsic harmony of things, but how could harmony arise if the universe were not permeated by joy? And without joy there would be no music, yet joy is born of music: "Drunk with the joy of singing I forget myself...". What is it that explains this mutual requirement of music, joy and harmony? Why is it that the one arouses, yet at the same time expresses the other? Is it not a paradox that an energetic force could not exist without another force brought forth by its very own capacities?

No, it is not, because none of the three energetic forces is in itself the ultimate truth, but all of them share their portion of that quintessential truth: the constituents of the harmonious trinity are nourished by one and the same emotional essence, which is the essence of love. It is love that generates the all-pervading harmony of the universe. It is love that instigates the cosmic flow of music. It is love that sends out the all-overpowering joy that fills the entire creation with its rays of bliss. And it is love that emboldens the human soul to surrender, yet unite with the soul of the world on an equal level: "Drunk with the joy of singing I forget myself *and call thee friend who art my lord*". Self-offering yet intimacy between two souls on a coequal level is possible only once a state of complete harmony has been reached. How is this state of absolute harmony attained? - through music, through the joy of music, "the joy of singing" as our poet proclaims. The Bāul sings, "Even if you forbid, / dear friend, / I am helpless. / My songs contain / my prayers"[8]. Having made the Supreme Being the property of his heart by surrendering to the Man of the Heart, the Bāul poet has established a perfect harmony between himself and the Supreme Soul, hence has no need to be shy of calling the lord of the universe 'friend'.

---

[8] Madan, quoted in Deben Bhattacharya, op.cit., p.93

What is more, by winning over the Eternal Music-maker, the giver of divine music, the human singer - through the self-sacrifice clad in the tunes of his song - acquires the music as well, for the one who owns the giver owns also the gift. Thus making the gift of music his own, the human musician is now able to mould the cosmic tune into a melody that belongs to himself, a melody fit for offering to the Divine Being to renew the human soul's surrender to the Supreme One. Thereby, the intrinsic harmony at the core of the relationship between man and the infinite reality is yet intensified, giving rise to a refreshed sense of bliss whose response becomes manifest in yet more cosmic cadences. The creative circuit of mutually stimulating energies unites the currents of music, harmony and joy into a single, organic whole which is continually inspired by the imaginative spirit of love. There is no music without harmony, no joy without music, no harmony without joy, yet none of them without love.

Which is the most immediate quality implied in the state of harmoniousness? - intimacy. Harmony signifies intimacy - intimacy between two opposite forces longing for union, intimacy between two souls, between two spheres of existence, between two levels of perception: intimacy between humanity and divinity in the broadest sense. Harmony is the positive quality of joy whose constructive energy possesses the capacity to establish an intense closenesss between emotional entities searching for one another. Yet this closeness, the intimacy between loving hearts, remains intelligible only for the spirits involved, but withdraws itself from the understanding of the outside world. The uninitiated eye sees the form, but not the formless essence; the unknowing ear hears the sound but not the music; the oblivious heart comprehends the facts but not the harmony of facts, and no rational explanation will gratify the offshoots of ignorance:

> I boasted among men that I had known you.
> They see your pictures in all works of mine.
> They come and ask me, 'Who is he?' I know
> not how to answer them. I say, 'Indeed, I
> cannot tell.' They blame me and they go away
> in scorn. And you sit there smiling.
> I put my tales of you in lasting songs. The secret
> gushes out from my heart. They come and

ask me, 'Tell me all your meanings.' I know
not how to answer them. I say, 'Ah, who
knows what they mean!' They smile and go
away in utter scorn. And you sit there
smiling.[9]

Who is this outside world, the embodiment of mundane thought, of ignorance? Whose is the petty spirit vainly seeking to define in words the undescribable transcendental reality? It is the rational mind, the faculty of reason that lives in permanent discord with the emotional potential of the heart. Why this dissonance? Because rationality, in its continuous search to interpret the uninterpretable, constantly questions the ultimate transcendental truth. With its persistent demand for logical explanations, the rational mind thus qualifies as the most fruitful source of doubt, and doubt signifies nothing but disharmony. Once the indisputable truth of harmony is called into question, discordance is predestined. Doubt rejects the fundamental unity of things only to impose an artificial conflict nourished by suspicion. According to the laws of rationality, the antagonism raised by suspiciousness can be dissolved only upon elucidation of facts. The truth of harmony, however, exceeds the explanatory capacity of language, hence cannot be defined in words only to satisfy the desire of the rational mind.

But why should it be impracticable to explain harmony in terms of logic? Does not philosophy provide us with adequate rational and rhetorical potential to express the metaphysical workings of existence? Yes, it does, but all that can be explicated by means of reasoned arguments is facts as outer manifestations, not realities as embodiments of the most sublime transcendental truth. What does that say? Harmony can be described as a phenomenon of harmoniousness, as a state of concordant relation between different entities, but the inner substance of harmony disclosed in the intimate nature of that relationship can only be experienced, not explained. For what reason? Harmoniousness is a rationally comprehensible condition, but harmony is essentially an emotional experience, whose intensity reaches beyond the realm of physical perceptiveness. More than that, harmony, because of its implicit intimacy, is understood in its immediate manifestation only by the

---

[9] Rabindranath Tagore, *Gītāñjali*, CII

emotional entities involved in the harmonious process. It is the two souls entering into a relation of harmony who are open for the subtle emotional vibrations, and not the outside interferer, hence the knowing soul alone, the one who lives harmony as an active experience, is truly conversant with the transcendental reality: "they go away in utter scorn. And you sit there smiling...".

What does the experience of harmony imply? - joy, and music. Is joy, is music explicable in rational words? Yes, to the extent of the visible, audible, sensually perceptible phenomenon it is. What cannot be communicated through verbal expressions is the emotional essence of music, which is joy, and the spiritual experience of joy, which is music. Music, however, incorporates more than the mere experience of joy, of harmony: music is at the same time the primary manifestation of transcendental bliss. Enabled by its expressive force, music becomes competent of articulating the sublime feelings arising from the ultimate transcendental experience. That is to say the emotional essence of harmony, withdrawing itself from verbal reach, can partly be communicated through music. How is it communicated? - as the living emotional experience enveloped in the melodious sounds of musical cadences. Music thus inherits the momentum of intimate twofoldness implicit in harmoniousness, represented by the reciprocal interaction between the music-maker and the listener. At the same time, music contains the momentum of unity implied in harmony and carried forth by the intrinsic oneness of the interacting duality.

In the cosmic play of creation, music emerges as the most immediate, most lively and most sublime embodiment of the all-pervading, omnipresent vibration of harmony. Yet music suggests not only the revelation of that harmony, but is also the driving energy which motivates the universal harmony in the first place. Why else would the distressed poet pray for the divine blessing that comes in the guise of a simple melody: "When the heart is hard and parched up, come upon me with a shower of mercy. *When grace is lost from my life, come with a burst of song*"[10]? It is music which incarnates, yet more significantly establishes the live-giving harmony of forces, hence music is the most effective remedy to cure the human heart from strains of dissonance.

---

[10] Rabindranath Tagore, *Gītāñjalī*, XXXIX

Therefore, "when tumultuous work raises its din on all sides shutting me out from beyond, come to me, my lord of silence, with thy peace and rest"[11] - and with thy music. Which is the powerful energy that furnishes music with the capacity to instigate the cosmic harmony in spite of all discordances? It is the all-permeating essence of love, the quintessence of existence enveloped in the tuneful sweetness of the melodious creations. Love manifests itself in harmony, and harmony in music, but it is music as the living substance of cosmic delight which inspires the supreme transcendental truth to break through the clouds of darkness and to enlighten the searching soul with its rays of harmonious brilliance.

Harmony is expressed in music, harmony is born of music, but the essence of all music is harmony. Music is the imaginative energy of harmony whose effects function against the destructive forces of disorder, of disharmony. As a universal principle, harmony belongs to the sphere of the infinite, settled on the plane of transcendental unity. Yet harmony as the all-penetrating energy of the infinite cannot stay aloof from the world of material existence, for whose very sake it strives to manifest itself in a sensually perceptible appearance: harmony is realized in tunes, it enters the world in the likeness of music - "...the world with its dust, doubts, and disorder - and with its music"[12]. What quest, what intent is it that stimulates the musical revelation of cosmic harmony? It is the ultimate quest behind all spiritual pursuits - the quest for unity against dissention, for harmony against disorder, for consonance against discord. But why is there disorder, why is there discord at all in the world if their state is only to be abolished?

What is the sensation of harmony? - delight. How is disharmony experienced? It hurts. It causes an intense feeling of pain. Why is it so? Because disharmony represents the unreal and revolts agains the eternal truth of harmony. The painfulness of dissonance is caused by the element of disunity that indwells discord, by the refusal of the one to acknowledge its ultimate unity with the other. It is the negation of the intrinsic oneness of opposing emotional entities which arouses the agony of separation, of disunion. But why is this agony in any way

---

[11] ibid.

[12] Rabindranath Tagore, *Crossing*, LVIII

needed? Disharmony exists in opposition to harmony, but its only purpose is to establish the ultimate truth of harmony, hence agony is there only to prove the final truth of delight. Rebelliousness against the supreme transcendental truth only results in pain for the rebel, but it does not affect the state of truth as such:

> I came nearest to you, though I did not know it
> when I came to hurt you.
> I owned you at last as my master when I fought
> against you to be defeated.
> I merely made my debt to you burdensome when
> I robbed you in secret.
> I struggled in my pride against your current only
> to feel all your force in my breast.
> Rebelliously I put out the light in my house and
> your sky surprised me with its stars.[13]

Disharmony does not always necessarily arise out of disunion - more often it is born out of disunity within union. How is that? Union is achieved in two ways determined by the "two fundamental divisions of human nature. The one contained in it the spirit of conquest and the other the spirit of harmony"[14]. Only that union which is attained through harmony carries at its core the essence of unity, hence can be maintained. Where union is achieved through conquest, the intrinsic element of unity is lacking, and union becomes unsustainable due to its innate disunity. The spirit of conquest signifies possessiveness: "I owned you at last as my master when I fought against you to be defeated", and it is out of possessiveness that disharmony springs up even in a seemingly harmonious union.

Yet disharmony is ultimately to give way to harmony, disorder to unity, dissonance to music. In the complex arrangement of cosmic existence, the spirit of conquest with its possessive greed cannot be the final answer to the universal quest for union, which is the quest for harmony, for unity. For if it were so, the entire system of creation were prone to collapse, because

---

[13] Rabindranath Tagore, *Crossing*, XXIII

[14] Rabindranath Tagore, *Creative Unity* (New Delhi: Macmillan India Ltd., reprint 1995), p.64

creation is the harmony of contrary forces - the forces of attraction and repulsion. When they join hands, all the fire and fight are changed into the smile of flowers and the songs of birds. When there is only one triumphant and the other defeated, then either there is the death of cold rigidity or that of suicidal explosion[15].

The power of disharmony is the power of conquest, of possessiveness, but the power of harmony is the power of love. Love can never be conquest, because true love is not possessive. The essence of love is selflessness and, more than that, self-sacrifice. Therefore the quest of love is harmony, is unity - the very quality disowned by the covetous intent of conquest.

And music? Conquest cannot produce music, because its inherent possessiveness contradicts the spirit of music. Music is an act of giving, of offering, of surrender - an expression of selfless harmony free from the avaricious motive of conquest. In its emotional substance, music is inclined towards unity, towards the harmony of the manifold, towards the essence of oneness within duality. Harmoniousness reflects not a state of lifeless uniformity, but rather the entire spectrum of forms and appearances in their full variety *linked by proportion*, and harmony is the active energy of proportionality. Music is the connecting flow of emotional dynamism that establishes proportion, hence unity - unity between differing entities, that is to say an active unity based on proportional balance within the variety, not a passive unity accomplished in the stagnant boredom of sameness. "Truth consists, not in facts, but in harmony of facts"[16], and this harmony is embodied in the proportion between facts. The principle of duality, therefore, is not there to oppose the principle of unity, but to prove the ultimate truth of unity which is represented by the concordant mergence of the two poles of the duality into one single, harmonious whole. The quest for union, for repeal of the duality is inborn in all beings as an instinctive longing for unity, for harmony, for proportionality. Once union is attained, once the dual forces have mingled into one, which is the energy born out of this

---

[15] Rabindranath Tagore, op.cit., p.65
[16] Rabindranath Tagore, op.cit., p.32

cohabitation? It is music, the living incorporation of harmony, the melodious manifestation of unity, the creative potency of proportionality.

Music arises out of unity, but unity is established through music. Why? - because music inherits the spirit of surrender which is the essential prerequisite for harmony to unfold. Music embodies the self-sacrifice of the loving soul for her transcendental lover in the most sublime way, for music is offering and attainment both in one. Music is the soul's prayer to forsake her own self at the feet of the lover -

> In one salutation to thee, my God, let all my senses spread out and touch this world at thy feet.
> Like a rain-cloud of July hung low with its burden of unshed showers let all my mind bend down at thy door in one salutation to thee.
> Let all my songs gather together their diverse strains into a single current and flow to a sea of silence in one salutation to thee.
> Like a flock of homesick cranes flying night and day back to their mountain nests let all my life take its voyage to its eternal home in one salutation to thee.[17]

- and music is the prayer's fulfilment: "I touch by the edge of the far-spreading wing of my song thy feet which I could never aspire to reach"[18]. It is in music that harmony finds its fullest and most direct expression, but it is music which, in the tuneful perfection of its delightful melodies, reflects nothing but the eternal sweetness of cosmic unity.

[17] Rabindranath Tagore, *Gītāñjalī*, CIII
[18] Rabindranath Tagore, *Gītāñjalī*, II

7

Music and love

Let thy love play upon my voice and rest on my
silence.
Let it pass through my heart into all my
movements.
Let thy love like stars shine in the darkness of
my sleep and dawn in my awakening.
Let it burn in the flame of my desires.
And flow in all currents of my own love.
Let me carry thy love in my life as a harp does its
music, and give it back to thee at last with my
life.

Rabindranath Tagore, *Crossing*, LV

How does the music of joy enter the spheres of human perception
and settle in the heart of man as an all-overpowering sensation of bliss?
How is the tune of delight conveyed to the realm of emotional
awareness? It flows in the powerful currents of love brought along by
an all-pervading energy of sweetness - of transcendental sweetness
whose intensity exceeds the limits of imagination. It comes over as the
melodious manifestation of the omnimpresent vibrations of love, the
subtle yet live-giving rays of joy: from love all beings are born, by love
they are sustained, and in love they merge in ultimate fulfilment. There
would be no music if the universe were not penetrated by love, and
without the music of love, the cosmic mechanism would come to
standstill, for not even a single creature could exist without the vital
breath of life - of love. Whose love? - the love of the infinite one who is
the essence of all sweetness, the quintessence of joy, the living
embodiment of bliss. The love of Him who is at once the Supreme
Lover and the supreme energy of love, who reveals Himself as both the
giver and the gift of love. Through love He creates the universe, and His
creation is a sheer expression of bliss - a work of music, of harmonious-
sounding sweetness, of joy reflected in the delightful cadences of the
great world-song. Love finds its most complete consummation in music,
but it is out of love that music emerges in the first place.

Love is essentially an energy, a force of motion which, through its
stimulating potencies, inspires an existing duality to fuse into a dynamic

unity. At the same time, however, love is also the expression of that energy, which is unity *per se*. What does this imply? Love, in order to become effective as a vitalizing factor, presupposes a duality. Without the presence of "pairs of opposing forces", love cannot fulfil in union. Yet in order to make union feasible, these forces must not be antagonistic: "These forces, like the left and the right hands of the creator, are acting in absolute harmony, yet acting from opposite directions"[1]. The opposing yet complementary powers represent in their interplay more than a dull mechanism of dialectic functionings: "they are a rhythmic dance. Rhythm can never be born of the haphazard struggle of combat. Its underlying principle must be unity, not opposition"[2]. Therefore the opposing forces striving to unite in perfect harmony need to be linked by an intrinsic unity from within, or else their union remains an unattainable object. It is this indwelling unity, the absence of a spirit of conquest, which qualifies the energy that motivates the merging of the two forces as an energy of love.

The prerequisite for the emancipation of love is a duality, but love's quest is to overcome the duality. To overcome the duality in what way? - by coalescence, not by combat. The poet voices his prayer, "Let thy love…flow in all currents of my own love", because he is well aware that only a harmonious confluence can melt the two entities into one. If the one devours the other, the duality is outwardly dissolved only to increase the inward antagonism of contradictory forces. If union is achieved by conquest, it is devoid of love - but can there be union without love? No, it cannot be, for the mere reason that union is a state of fulfilment which is the fulfilment of love. And without love, there can be no music, because it is fulfilled love that finds its most complete expression in music. Conquest goes along with discord - but discord cannot produce music, and love does not enter the tuneless realm of disharmony.

What is more, conquest is a one-sided initiative on the part of the active force to take possession of its resenting opponent, and the victory of the one is the pain of the other. Love presupposes a mutual interest, a concordant effort from both sides of the duality for the realization of a

---

[1] Rabindranath Tagore, *Sādhanā* (London: Macmillan and Co. Ltd., 1914), p.96
[2] ibid. (p.97)

shared goal - a reciprocal longing for union whose attainment is joy, not pain. Conquest finds its expression in dissonant noise, love in sweet-sounding music, because it is the joy of love that gives rise to music. Joy is the essence of love, pain the essence of conquest; yet the most intense agony is brought forth by love - by pure love, and not by defeat in combat. How is that? The pain of defeat is an imposed suffering caused by an artificial union in which one force thrusts its mastery on the other. In love, however, agony is aroused not by an arbitrary union, but by disunion. The pain of separation results from the profound yearning of two souls to transcend their duality and to merge into one. There will be pain as long as the desired object is not attained, but once separateness gives way to unity, separation to union, all pain fades and dissolves into bliss.

Yet the question remains, why is there pain at all? What is the implication of agony caused by love? Is such pain inescapable, and what is the reason? Yes, the pain of love is inevitable - inevitable in the same way as is the preliminary existence of a duality -, but more than that it is meaningful. The duality creates the required constellation of two spiritual entities striving for each other, which is essential to instigate the interactive dynamism of love. It is that same duality, however, from which pain springs up, because the very state of a duality represents the condition of love not fulfilled, hence pain. Once the unfulfilled longing is satisfied, the pain is transcended by bliss, but what is it that instigates this transformation from pain to bliss, from agony to joy? It is the desire to abolish the state of suffering. The pain of love, therefore, is needed as the driving energy that stimulates the quest for fulfilment in the first place. Without that pain, love becomes stagnant in a rigid union, and the joy of consummation loses its intensity ultimately to turn into discontent.

Pain is unavoidable, even necessary to guarantee the dynamic interchange of mutual love, of love directed at attainment in union. The pain emerging from unfulfilled love is real, yet its only object is to defy that realness and to establish the truth of joy - just as the duality at the core of the relationship derives its sole right of existence from the quest for unity. That is to say -

> The joy, whose other name is love, must by its
> very nature have duality for its realization. When

the singer has his inspiration he makes himself
into two; he has within him his other self as the
hearer, and the outside audience is merely an
extension of this other self of his. The lover
seeks his other self in the beloved. It is joy that
creates this separation, in order to realize through
obstacles the union.[3]

It is joy that creates this separation - the very separation from which pain
is produced. Thus it is the joy of union that results in pain in order to
confirm its ultimate truth through the pangs of separation. How is this
explained? Love can unfold its full energy only if the way towards
consummation is obstructed by obstacles derived from the duality.
Within unity, within oneness, where is the joy of union? Where is the
bliss experienced by two merging into one? Where is the singer's joy
without the hearer, where the lover's joy without the beloved? "Let thy
love...flow in all currents of my own love" - where is the confluence if
not the two rivers, the two currents of love are there? How can there be
commingling in love if there is only one entity? For love to emerge, for
love to reach out, and to fulfil, the dualism is imperative; it must be two:
two entities, two souls - two lovers.

For this very reason, the Creator divides himself into two in
whatever creation he brings forth. In music, he manifests himself as the
singer and the listener. In beauty, he invents the form and the one who
sees the form. In the realization of love, he creates the lover and the
beloved to make their union truly blissful. And to raise the awareness of
that bliss in the human consciousness, he arouses pain - the agony felt
by two lovers in disunion, a pain whose essence is lack of peace:

> Dear Love,
> You who share my pain,
> Can tell me why my heart
> Is lost to listlessness
> And walks on its own
> Towards its own self,

---

[3] Rabindranath Tagore, *Sādhanā*, p.104

With no hue and cry.[4]

What is the cause of such indolence? What is it that makes the soul weak and spiritless? It is the absence of the vital duality without which the stream of love cannot be set in motion. It is the lack of an opposite pole in which the lover's own self finds its response, the need for a destination towards which the emotional current can flow. More than that, it is the constellation of a stagnant, hence unfruitful harmoniousness that grows weary for want of its stimulating energy - like silent music losing its imaginative sweetness for lack of the sounding tune:

> There is no patience
> In the core of my heart -
> Shivering with tears
> It cries with the eyes,
> *And in the silence of lovely sound*
> *Forever calls:*
> *Come, please come.*[5]

Can the call of love remain forever unheard? Is it possible that love misses out on the essential duality, depriving itself of its indwelling energetic power? Could it be that the accumulated forces of musical creativity are permanently held back in the clouds of silence? No, it cannot be lest the universe should burst of unreleased potencies. But what does the absence of a constructive duality, the imposition of an unproductive oneness signify? Separation. Why else would the pained heart "walk on its own towards its own self" if not in search for its loving counterpart? And what else does this search imply if not the quest for the one lost through separation? But separation as such cannot be the ultimate end - it is bound to give way to union, because its only object is to verify the realness of union. Silence likewise cannot last as the final condition, for silence is but to dissolve into music. What is the meaning of this outbreak of music from inspiration-laden silence? The emergence of the tune symbolizes the fulfilment of love - a fulfilment in which the contracted energies of bliss are completely discharged, a

---

4 Anon, quoted in Deben Bhattacharya, *The mirror of the sky* (London: Allen & Unwin, 1969), p.49

5 ibid.

fulfilment in which the force of unity finds its most perfect expression in the duality while at the same time the quest to melt the duality is realized in union.

What factor enables the identification of love with music to such a degree that the manifestation of the one embodies the perfection of the other? Why is it the "silence of lovely sound" which carries the timeless call of unfulfilled love? And why is there "no patience in the core of the heart" as long as the lover thus being called remains inconsiderate? The answer needs to be sought in the intrinsic unity of seemingly opposite things: silence appears contrary to sound, separation contrary to union, though in reality the one is but an aspect of the other. Why is it so? Because the dynamism of love works only through the interplay of union and separation; that of music through the alternation of sound and silence. If silence is regarded merely as an expression of soundlessness, separation merely as an obstacle to union, the core tenor is negativity. If, however, the signification of silence is perceived beyond the immediate phenomenon of stillness, the emotional sensor recognizes the germ of the tune contained in the soundless manifestation waiting for its time to come forth and burst into song. Separation, if understood as the necessary prerequisite that makes union meaningful, will then be comprehended in its full significance as the momentary state that is to be overcome.

But which is the energy that makes the opposites lose their antagonism and fuse into a single whole within a larger dialectic machinery? It is love:

> In love all the contradictions of existence merge themselves and are lost. Only in love are unity and duality not a variance. Love must be one and two at the same time.
>
> Only love is motion and rest in one. Our heart ever changes its place till it finds love, and then it has its rest. But this rest itself is an intense form of activity where utter quiescence and unceasing energy meet at the same point in love.[6]

---

[6] Rabindranath Tagore, *Sādhanā*, p.114

Only love is motion and rest in one, and only love is silence and music in one. Without love, there can be no music, because sound and silence resist each other in stern opposition. It is the liquefying potency of love which melts the inherent antagonistic forces and establishes unity within the duality. If "there is no patience in the core of the heart" and the "silence of lovely sound" still contradicts the tuneful melodiousness of music, the reason is that love is yet to be found, that the call of love is yet to be answered, since the loving heart can rest only when its inborn longing finds a response in the longing of the beloved soul. Through the response the music of love is born, the music which represents the sweetest and most artful expression of bliss, for once a mutual reaction is instigated, once the one soul finds its own sentiments echoed in the feelings of the other, the ultimate truth of union emerges in transparent form from the tangle of separation.

There is no definite answer as to when the emotional outcry will be heard, but the response is to come for sure. Why? Because the separation that causes the heart's suffering is relative, hence temporary. In love, separation cannot be absolute, for

> if this separation were absolute, then there would have been absolute misery and unmitigated evil in this world. Then from untruth we never could reach truth, and from sin we never could hope to attain purity of heart; then all opposites would remain opposites, and we could never find a medium through which our differences could ever tend to meet. Then we could have no language, no understanding, no blending of hearts, no co-operation in life[7].

Then we could have no music, for sound and silence would never find together to form a harmonious whole. But it is not so, because the universe is not sustained by indifference, and obliviousness is not the final answer to the call of love. The sufferings brought forth by love are more than mere obstacles on the way towards the ultimate object; they are a challenge to pursue the quest of love yet more eagerly and to obtain

---

[7] Rabindranath Tagore, *Sādhanā*, p.105

bliss through the dignity of pain. What is more, the human soul herself has been given the power to transcend those sufferings, and this power rests in the intrinsic oneness of the human soul with the Supreme Lover - a oneness that reveals itself even and especially in separation:

> Yes, our individual soul has been separated from the supreme soul, but this has not been from alienation but from the fulness of love. It is for that reason that untruths, sufferings, and evils are not at a standstill; the human soul can defy them, can overcome them, nay, can altogether transform them into new power and beauty.[8]

Of what kind is this new power and beauty? It is music - music in its purest form, music distilled from the most sublime vibrations of love. Distilled in what way? - by transforming the creative energy of love into the sounding sweetness of a tune: love is offered through music, love is received through music, love is realized through music, and manifests itself in music. The singer prays, "Let thy love play upon my voice and rest on my silence" because he is aware that only the love of the Divine Musician can provide him with the inspiration needed to produce even the least streak of a melody. But at the same time he knows that he is ultimately to return the divine gift: "Let me carry thy love in my life as a harp does its music, and give it back to thee at last with my life". What is the gift made of? - love, and music. Love is the principal imaginative force that instigates the emergence of music, hence music qualifies as the prime expression of love. As an audible phenomenon, music embodies the material manifestation of the transcendental energies of love, yet music is a transcendental reality in its very own nature. Music represents love because it represents beauty, and love becomes apparent in beauty.

If love comes forth from the spheres of the invisible as the sounding tune, as the creation of aesthetic beauty, it is because some motivating factor has inspired the conversion of the abstract truth into a concrete, sensually perceptible presence. Which is the motivating factor that results in the birth of music, of form? It is the joy that arises from the creative union between the Supreme Soul and his human lover,

---

[8] ibid.

between the human soul and her Divine Lover. It is the joy aroused by the fulfilment of love on the highest level of cosmic creation - a joy which is echoed in a multitude of instants of consummation on each and every level of existence, a joy which finds its most spontaneous expression in the cadences of universal music, in the ethereal melodies of the world-song. The lover finds his tune through the offering to his beloved, an offering of love which indelibly turns into music once it is translated into terms of emotional delivery. The offering of music is thus always an offering of love, for without love there can be no music. Having received his lover's affection through music, the beloved returns his own love in the guise of tunes - of musical melodies if he is a singer, or else of transcendental cadences reflecting the intensity of soundless music, of unspoken love.

What does that say? Music is not always sound, love not always articulated in visible actions. True love in its full fervency extends beyond all expression, just as the most intense tune is that which lives forth in the mind of the singer before it emerges from his mouth. So how then is the music of silence, how is the beauty of the formless, how the love of the unspeakable revealed?

> Love's play is stilled into worship, life's stream
> touches the deep, and the world of forms comes
> to its nest in the beauty beyond all forms.[9]

It is revealed in worship. The lover's song-offering, the gift of music received by the beloved - they signify nothing but mutual worship, reciprocal giving and taking. Love is the highest form of worship, because only in love is it that worship becomes truly interactive. That is to say, only in love the worshiper finds his response, hence worship turns into a meaningful act. Without mutual responsiveness there can be no communication, and without communication, love is bound to never fulfil. Nourished by the energies of love, worship is fulfilment and quest for fulfilment both in one: it is through worship that the lover reaches out to his beloved, and it is in worship that the two of them unite.

---

[9] Rabindranath Tagore, *Crossing*, XIV

Active worship presupposes more than mere affection. Worship through love requires readiness for complete self-surrender: that is, the loving soul's surrender to the beloved, the worshiper's surrender to the object of worship. Surrender of one's own self to another is the essential quality and at the same time the most intense expression of love. Yet the sacrifice which is made out of love distinguishes itself from an ordinary act of surrendering in both attitude and effects. How is it different? Sacrifice implies forfeit, but the sacrifice brought for the sake of love only leads to gain, not loss. Surrender signifies relinquishment, but surrender of the loving soul to the lover means deliverance, not defeat. The lover's readiness for self-sacrifice constitutes the quintessence of love; without this readiness, love is powerless and fake. In its true essence, however, love indicates not merely the longing of two hearts for union - it rather represents the vital principle of creation by which the progression of the universe is sustained:

> In this wonderful festival of creation, this great
> ceremony of self-sacrifice of God, the lover
> constantly gives himself up to gain himself in
> love. Indeed, love is what brings together and
> inseparably connects both the act of abandoning
> and that of receiving.[10]

It is the capacity of love to unite contradicting forces which accounts for the differentness of love's sacrifice. In love, forfeiture is not loss, suffering not pain, because love inherits the potency to transcend the latent aspect of negativity. The apprehensive lover, therefore, is ready to accept agony and bliss likewise, because he knows that "the sacrifice, which is in the heart of creation, is both joy and pain at the same moment"[11]. The duality of agony and bliss, pain and joy, suffering and delight is there, but love alone is competent to overcome that duality and to consolidate its inborn tendencies of contrariness, thereby melting all attributes into one single expression of bliss. Of bliss which is not attained by utter negation of the pain, but by accepting the pain as the sacrifice made for the sake of the lover, sanctified by the living touch of love.

---

[10] Rabindranath Tagore, *Sādhanā*, p.114

[11] Rabindranath Tagore, *Creative Unity* (New Delhi: Macmillan India Ltd., reprint 1995), p.40

But truly, whose is the worship that is performed through love? For whose benefit is the sacrifice of love, the surrender in love? The offering of love enriches the worshiper, but what profit does he gain? What gift, what favor is the lover striving for? The poet provides us with the answer when he voices his cry, "That I want thee, only thee - let my heart repeat without end"[12]. It is the call of love - the call for the lover:

> Much have you given to me,
> Yet I ask for more -
> I come to you not merely for the draught of
> water, but for the spring;
> Not for guidance to the door alone, but to the
> Master's hall; *not only for the gift of love, but*
> *for the lover himself.*[13]

The call of love is indeed more than solely a call for love; it extends beyond the mere request for a response. The lover's self-surrender to the beloved signifies at the same time the longing for reciprocity, for return of the surrender. "Not only for the gift of love" does the poet raise his voice - not only for the energy that conveys the bliss, but for bliss incarnate: "for the lover himself". Not only for the inspiration that carries the tune does the musician strike his instrument, but for the tune itself. Surrender to the lover is the highest expression of love, but the gift of love is complete only once the giver offers up his own self: "I am only waiting for love to give myself up at last into his hands"[14]. The intensity of unconditional love, though, remains outside the reach of conventional perception, hence "those who came to call me in vain have gone back in anger. I am only waiting for love to give myself up at last into his hands"[15]. Yet the quest of love represents the intrinsic desire of all beings, because it expresses the indwelling search for unity, for harmony - for union with the supreme energy of love.

---

[12] Rabindranath Tagore, *Gītāñjali*, XXXVIII

[13] Rabindranath Tagore, *Crossing*, LII

[14] Rabindranath Tagore, *Crossing*, XVII

[15] ibid.

Why is it that the call of love becomes essentially the call for the lover rather than the quest for love alone? Because love finds its sweetest embodiment, its most sublime manifestation in the person of the lover: "Could I ever forget him / since I delivered my heart / at his feet?"[16]. The act of surrender ties the worshiper to his master, the lover to his beloved in an irreversible union. That is to say, the one who has delivered his heart at the feet of the lover will not get away from the supreme manifestation of love. What is the reason? The Divine Lover reveals himself in beauty, and beauty is by nature unforgettable: "His beauty enchants my eyes / round the compass / wherever I steer myself"[17]. This beauty, that delights the eyes and captivates the heart of the beloved, is not the beauty of form: it is the beauty which comes forth through the dignity of love, the beauty whose essence is absorbed by the heart and transformed into ever fresh energies of bliss. It is the beauty radiant in the form of the formless lover, the shapeless beauty revealed in cadences of joy. It is the beauty that emerges from divine love, a beauty which is too subtle to assume definite appearance, because the lover's own beauty withdraws itself from the realm of form: "Though not cast / in any shape, / the man is evidenced / in the ways of love"[18].

The Supreme Soul manifests himself in beauty which is the beauty of love, but in what way does this beauty diverge from the beauty of form? Love represents unity, whereas form incorporates the duality that instigates the quest of love. Form, therefore, proceeds towards the formless solely to lose itself in the currents of love: "Love springs / as feelings merge - / divided forms / assume a single way. / A pair of hearts / running in parallel streams, / long to reach the god of loving"[19]. It is the duality seeking unity, the core quest of love embodied in the formless essence of the transcendental lover. Who is he, that transcendental lover? He is more than the impersonator of an abstract energy, more even than the representative through whom that energy is revealed. The Supreme Lover is love itself, he is love's voice:

Follow him where he marches, keeping step to
the rhythm of his drum-beats. ...

---

[16] Lālan, quoted in Deben Bhattacharya, op.cit., p.90
[17] ibid.
[18] Haridās, quoted in Deben Bhattacharya, op.cit., p.67 (2)
[19] Haridās, quoted in Deben Bhattacharya, op.cit., p.67 (1)

> For his call sounds at every step and we know
> that he is love's voice.[20]

The identification of the lover with love, of love with the lover is self-evident from the manifestation of bliss that comes forth through the call of love - through the call of love which is the call of the lover. The lover is the voice of love, but love's voice is what? It is music! How can it be music? The essential quality of love is surrender - the lover's self-offering to his beloved, and music is the activity which represents this attitude of surrender to the fullest degree. Every presentation of music is at the same time an act of self-sacrifice: the musician's surrender to his listener - to the Invisible Listener from whom all musical inspiration is received. What is this inspiration made of? - love. The call of love is not a hoarse cry of speech, it is the tuneful sweetness of a musical melody: "The flute of love / enters my ears - / the flute of the lord of love"[21]. The Divine Lover is at the same time the Divine Musician, and the Divine Musician the Divine Lover. Because from love alone is it that music emerges; where love cannot unfold between two souls, the inherent energies of music cannot be set free to dissolve into tunes. In music, the surrender of the one to the other finds its most melodious expression, hence music qualifies as the subtlest embodiment of love's quest.

What is more, music and love form one single emotional entity, and their unity is imperative for the effectiveness of the emotional mechanism that guides the search for spiritual perfection. Without that unity, music loses its expressive power and turns into a neutral aesthetic phenomenon, and love is blocked on its way towards fulfilment. Knowing the intrinsic oneness of music and love, love and music, the singer declares, "My songs are one with my love, like the murmur of a stream, that sings with all its waves and currents"[22]. What is the essence of that oneness? It is joy - the joy that brings forth love's consummation, the joy from which music is born. "Joy is the realisation of the truth of oneness, the oneness of our soul with the world and of the world-soul with the supreme lover"[23]. Joy, bliss is the fulfilment of love, and love is fulfilled in joy. The singer's music is one with his love, for if it were

---

[20] Rabindranath Tagore, *Crossing*, LXI
[21] Padmalochan (Podo), quoted in Deben Bhattacharya, op.cit., p.99
[22] Rabindranath Tagore, *Lover's Gift*, IV
[23] Rabindranath Tagore, *Sādhanā*, p.116

not, how could the tune emerge without the joy of love? Love manifests itself in beauty, and beauty finds its fullest expression in music, hence music is nothing but love concealed in the mantle of tunes.

Yet love, in order to be realized, requires the apprehension of the lover lest the energies of love remain unused. The core quest of love is sacrifice, but love's sacrifice is complete only once it receives a reciprocal response, and this is why the Supreme Soul's love finds fulfilment only in the love of man:

> Thus it is that thy joy in me is so full. Thus it is
> that thou hast come down to me. O thou lord
> of all heavens, *where would be thy love if I
> were not?*[24]

Realizing his own value in his relation with the Supreme One, man feels emboldened to address the lord of the universe on an equal level, knowing though that his own life is but a reflection of the divine lord's love:

> Thou hast taken me as thy partner of all this
> wealth. In my heart is the endless play of thy
> delight. In my life thy will is ever taking
> shape.
> And for this, thou who art the King of kings hast
> decked thyself in beauty to captivate my
> heart. And for this thy love loses itself in the
> love of thy lover, and there art thou seen in
> the perfect union of two.[25]

The poet proclaims, "if I call not thee in my prayers, if I keep not thee in my heart, thy love for me still waits for my love"[26] in full consciousness that his own love will always find its response in the love of the infinite one, because without the love of the human soul, the cosmic stream of love cannot flow. Without the love of the human singer, the music of the universe cannot unfold its full melodiousness, and creation remains

---

[24] Rabindranath Tagore, *Gītāñjalī*, LVI
[25] ibid.
[26] Rabindranath Tagore, *Gītāñjalī*, XXXII

deprived of its vigor: "When my heart did not kiss thee in love, O world, thy light missed its full splendour and thy sky watched through the long night with its lighted lamp"[27].

Why is it so? Because the Creator's own love alone is not sufficient to vitalize the spheres of being unless it has been refined through the love of man, unless the two levels of existence have met in perfect union. How does that union come? - as music: "My heart came with her songs to thy side, whispers were exchanged, and she put her wreath on thy neck"[28]. And it is music - the music of love, the music of love in union, of mutual love between the transcendental and the phenomenal worlds, which makes the whole difference in the spirit of creation: "I know that she has given thee something which will be treasured by the stars"[29].

But why is it that God's love is complete only in the love of the human heart? Why does the transcendental tune of cosmic music settle in the sweetness of sound only once the human singer raises his voice? Why is creation perfect only once the imaginative spirit of the universe reverberates in man's own creativity? The reason is the need for the stimulating duality of the finite and the infinite, the bounded and the unbounded, the momentary and the eternal. More so it is the call for the duality of contrary, yet non-antagonistic forces which is realized only through the energies of love, because

> Bondage and liberation are not antagonistic in love. For love is most free and at the same time most bound. If God were absolutely free there would be no creation. The infinite being has assumed unto himself the mystery of finitude. And in him who is love the finite and the infinite are made one.[30]

It is the freedom within bonds, the liberation attained through bondage, which prompts a bird in a mediaeval Indian poem to answer, "I had my

---

[27] Rabindranath Tagore, *Crossing*, LXXII
[28] ibid.
[29] ibid.
[30] Rabindranath Tagore, *Sādhanā*, p.115

pleasure while I rested within bounds. / When I soared into the limitless, I found my songs!"[31]. Without the emancipation of the infinite within finitude, love cannot extend its full energetic force, hence music cannot rise from the spheres of soundlessness. But how can there be creation without love, without the music of love?

Wherever there is music, there is also love, for where there is no love, all music remains reticent. From what source does love come forth? From the ultimate transcendental reality, from the Supreme Being whose love is the vital breath for all beings: "All of us / in our different ways / think of God. / He is the dispenser of love - / beyond senses and feelings"[32]. Yet the Infinite One reveals himself in love alone: "It is only in the essence of loving, / that God is found"[33]. The revelation of love, though, is always at the same time a revelation of music. How is that? "God has bound himself to man, and in that consists the greatest glory of human existence. In the spell of the wonderful rhythm of the finite he fetters himself at every step, and thus *gives his love out in music* in his most perfect lyrics of beauty"[34]. Love is by nature a dialectic process of giving and taking, offering and receiving, and so is music, because music is the gift of love and the offering of love both in one.

Yet love can fulfil only in mutual union, and music can break forth only in mutual delight of the music-maker and the listener. What succeeds once this delight has been attained? What happens to the loving soul once its entire being is filled with the lover's presence? The poet prays, "Let him appear before my sight as the first of all lights and all forms. The first thrill of joy to my awakened soul let it come from his glance"[35]. Once the human soul has tasted the sweetness of divine love, there is no way to satisfy the heart's longing other than by constantly evoking the presence of the infinite: "Ah, my closed eyes that would open their lids only to the light of his smile when he stands before me like a dream emerging from darkness of sleep"[36]. But what is it that causes this obstinacy, what is it that makes the Bāul singer

[31] quoted in Rabindranath Tagore, *Creative Unity*, p.41
[32] Anon, quoted in Deben Bhattacharya, op.cit., p.39
[33] ibid.
[34] Rabindranath Tagore, *Sādhanā*, p.115
[35] Rabindranath Tagore, *Gītāñjali*, XLVII
[36] ibid.

presumptuously declare, "I shall not open my eyes again / if I do not see him at first sight"[37]? It is the persistence of the Divine Lover's own longing, the very fact that the Supreme Soul cannot accomplish his own love without the love of man, an instant which the Bāul poet knows only too well when he asserts that "if your love can be complete without mine, let me turn back from seeing you"[38].

Our Bāul's proclamation doubtlessly carries a spark of rebelliousness, but even the rebel cannot deny the ultimate object of his love:

> That I want thee, only thee - let my heart repeat
> without end. All desires that distract me, day
> and night, are false and empty to the core.
> As the night keeps hidden in its golden gloom
> the petition for light, even thus in the depth of
> my unconsciousness rings the cry - 'I want
> thee, only thee'.
> As the storm still seeks its end in peace when it
> strikes against peace with all its might, even
> thus my rebellion strikes against thy love and
> still its cry is - 'I want thee, only thee'.[39]

Why? Because the divine presence envelopes the resistant lover's heart as well, and the impact of love dissolves any ambition of disharmony into sheer delight. The joy of love is the joy of the truth of love, the joy that arises from the inner awareness that love is the ultimate reality - and it is this joy which absorbs all dissonance to turn rebelliousness into devotion, discord into harmony, combat into concordance. "For love is the ultimate meaning of everything around us. It is not a mere sentiment; it is truth; it is the joy that is at the root of all creation"[40]. Love is truth, and truth is bliss because it is love. What is that to say? Rabindranath Tagore, one of the most excellent advocates of the religion of love, provides the answer when he translates the term *ānanda*, the Sanskrit expression for the supreme, transcendental bliss, as joy and love in one:

---

[37] Madan, quoted in Deben Bhattacharya, op.cit., pp.94f.
[38] Bāul song, quoted in Rabindranath Tagore, *Creative Unity*, p.82
[39] Rabindranath Tagore, *Gītāñjali*, XXXVIII
[40] Rabindranath Tagore, *Sādhanā*, p.107

"Who could have breathed or moved if the sky were not filled with joy, with love"[41]. Bliss is joy, bliss is love, and truth. Love is joy, love is bliss, and truth. Love "is not a mere sentiment" because it is the sum of all emotional vibrations penetrating the realm of cosmic existence. More than that, love is "the power which accomplishes the miracle of creation, by bringing conflicting forces into the harmony of the One", because love "is no passion, but a love which accepts the bonds of self-control from the joy of its own immensity - a love whose sacrifice is the manifestation of its endless wealth within itself"[42]. Love is the all-inspiring energy of creation, the omnipresent force of life precisely because its quintessence is surrender rather than conquest, hence it is love that wins over the world-soul with its sweetness and transforms utter noise in most melodious music.

Love is "not a mere sentiment", yet it is an intense expression of emotionality, a tremendous call from one heart to the other. Love is the truth whose comprehension exceeds the capacity of rationality. Why is that? Love manifests itself in music, and music is an emotional energy that withdraws itself from the faculty of reason. Thus, even a simple melody conveys a deeper truth than does the most sophisticated rational explication, because the melody prompts a response in the heart of the listener - an emotional response which rational intents can never aspire to obtain: "The solicitor does not sing to his client, but the bridegroom sings to his bride. And when our soul is stirred by the song, we know it claims no fees from us; but brings the tribute of love and a call from the bridegroom"[43]. The essence of love contradicts the sense of rationality, because love lives forth as a pure energy for its own sake, independent of its physical manifestations, whereas the rational mind accepts the truth of things only as material facts. The solicitor may claim fees for the service he renders as an act of rationality, but not so the artist, the music-maker: "Between the artist and his art must be that perfect detachment which is the pure medium of love. He must never make use of this love except for its own perfect expression"[44].

---

[41] Rabindranath Tagore's translation of the passage from Taittirīya Upaniṣad 2.7.1 *ko hy evānyāt kaḥ prānyāt, yad eṣa ākāśa ānando na syāt...* ('Who, indeed, could breathe otherwise [if] this bliss in the space would not be'); in *Sādhanā*, p.107

[42] Rabindranath Tagore, *Creative Unity*, p.66

[43] Rabindranath Tagore, op.cit., p.35

[44] Rabindranath Tagore, op.cit., p.39

Since love cannot be captured through the ways of reason, rational means are most inappropriate tools to win over the lover's heart: "Reaching for reality / is lame talk / to describe the goal / of the lover-worshipper"[45]. The message of love cannot be delivered through speech, but through music it can. The same call which, as a verbal expression of rationality, falls on deaf ears, is readily accepted when it comes as a song of love: turned away for once by the skeptical mind, it is received by the responsive heart. But what is the prize for the one who conceives that message of love? "He will attain / the great unattainable, / stare at the face / of the invisible one, / bearing the nectar of love"[46]. Love is the energy that enables the attainment of the unattainable - of that which is unattainable by rational means, hence the Bāul poet's advice, "If you wish to hold / the moon in your hands, / clip the noose / around your neck, / and worship love"[47]. For the one who knows the essence of love, the impossible is not impossible, the unattainable not unattainable. Because impossibility, because unattainableness mounts up to obstruct the way of rationality, but cannot affect the path of love: "It is the high function of love to welcome all limitations and to transcend them. For nothing is more independent than love"[48]. The obstacle is no obstacle to the lover, for love itself is nothing but a continuous act of transcending limits. An act that finds its reverberation in the strains of music constantly surpassing the confines of silence.

What is it that accounts for love's capacity to overcome all obstacles, to transcend all limits, to traverse all boundaries? It is the intrinsic unity of two forces, the lover and the beloved, which multiplies the impact of the imaginative energies of love.

> The singer alone does not make a song, there has
> to be someone who hears:
> One man opens his throat to sing, the other sings
> in his mind.

---

[45] Gosāiñ Gopāl, quoted in Deben Bhattacharya, op.cit., p.65
[46] ibid.
[47] Gosāiñ Gopāl, quoted in Deben Bhattacharya, op.cit., p.63
[48] Rabindranath Tagore, *Sādhanā*, p.115

> Only when waves fall on the shore do they make
>   a harmonious sound;
> Only when breezes shake the woods do we hear
>   a rustling in the leaves.
> Only from a marriage of two forces does music
>   arise in the world.
> *Where there is no love, where listeners are dumb,*
>   *there never can be song.*[49]

From interaction of the two forces, love is advanced to its fulfilment, and at the height of love's fulfilment, music is born: the music of God's love, and the music of man's love. Where the two streams of music merge into one, at the confluence of the cosmic tune and the melody of the human heart, creation emerges from an immense whirlpool of bliss. And it is love alone - love that harmonizes the generative duality and melts all contradictions into one sweet harmony - which empowers the spring of infinity to well forth with music.

---

[49] from Rabindranath Tagore, *Broken Song*

8

Music and creativity

I have come to thee to take thy touch before I
  begin my day.
Let thy eyes rest upon my eyes for awhile.
Let me take to my work the assurance of thy
  comradeship, my friend.
Fill my mind with thy music to last through the
  desert of noise!
Let thy Love's sunshine kiss the peaks of my
  thoughts and linger in my life's valley where
  the harvest ripens.

Rabindranath Tagore, *Crossing*, LIII

Fill my mind with thy music to last through the desert of noise, in order that the imaginative potencies of music may inspire the day's work with their creative force. Music is motivation, music is the driving energy that stimulates creativity, but how is music itself called forth? What is it that instigates the musical impetus in the first place? Which music is so creative as to awaken the creativity of music? Whose is the primeval music of creation? To whom do we thus pray, 'Fill my mind with thy music to last through the desert of noise' lest that noise swallows up all streaks of inspiration, of creativity?

Words are many to name that one supreme transcendental reality from where all imagination emanates, just as the Nameless One plays his great game of creation in countless revelations. Yet He is one and the same reproductive energy immanent in all outer manifestations: He is joy, He is love, He is truth - and He is music. It is the presence of that transcendental energy, the verve of the divinity within, which acts as the prime cause of creativeness. Invoking the infinite truth in the form of the creative spirit, therefore, means to evoke the strains of inspiration gathered up in the motivating fluid of creativity. Imaginative capacities are born out of the awareness of the divine presence, hence the poet's plea, 'Let me take to my work the assurance of thy comradeship, my friend', for creativity can rise only from the heart which is filled with the presence of the infinite. More so, musical creativity springs up when the musician opens his inward senses to the Eternal Music-maker's tune, and it is only once his whole being is penetrated by the cosmic music that he finds a melody of his own. Thus we hear the musician's entreaty echoed in the poet's words, 'Fill my mind with thy music to last through the desert of noise' - that is, to transcend the noise and to make way for music.

What does the core essence of the prayer imply? Music is conceived through divine inspiration, because the divinity manifests itself as musical energy. Without that inspiration, there can be no music, for how would the tune emerge without the vital creative force from which it is produced? How could the singer raise his voice, how the musician strike the chords of his instrument unless he is indwelled by the sound of eternal music? The Bāul poet, the one who weaves his entire life into one single chain of songs, knows only too well to whose creativity he owes his melodies: "Attested by your own heart, / O my master, / lead me the right way / as you play the melody / on the lute. / The lute could never sing / on its own, / without you to play it"[1]. The instrument as such remains inanimate until the musician's fingers instil life in it. But this life, the soul of the tune, does not rest within the fingers - it pours from the heart where it is stored as musical inspiration taking concrete shape in the melody formed by the fingers. Now the human musician, the human singer is but a musical instrument - an instrument which is brought to life at the hands of the Divine Music-maker. It is Him, the Infinite Musician, who makes that human instrument resound, for it is Him who carries in himself the inspiriting tune, the spark of creativity that conveys the essence of music.

So what then is musical inspiration? What is creativity, what is musical creativeness? It is the manifestation of the transcendental energy of love; it is bliss that comes in the guise of a blessing - of a divine blessing. Creativity is an expression of joy - of infinite joy pressing to be released into the imaginative realm of finitude, of formless joy urging to assume definite form in the sweetness of musical cadences. Joy is love, and once love becomes consummate in the fulness of the musical efflux, joy transforms into bliss. That is, in music love culminates, and through music the Divine Lover gives his ultimate testimony of love to his human friend. The gift of music, clad in the garment of creative

---

[1] Anon, quoted in Deben Bhattacharya, *The mirror of the sky* (London: Allen & Unwin, 1969), p.40

energy, is thus the highest gift man can obtain from his divine master, hence it is in musical inspiration, in the exchange of imaginative potencies, that the love between man and God finds its most excellent articulation.

But the effectuation of the creative process calls for more than a plain act of giving, more than simply exchange: being essentially an energy of love, creativity requires mutual exchange, that is, interchange. Acknowledging the Infinite Music-maker as the originator of all melodious strains, one Bāul poet rightly asserts that "the lute could never sing / on its own, / without you to play it". Yet another declares boldly, "your flute [can have] its music, only in your delight in my love"[2], and his claim is no less justified. How is that? Does not all music emanate from the love of the Supreme Being, manifest in the progenitive potencies of musical ideas? Yes, it does - and exactly here lies the crux: love is an interactive communication whose vital basis is reciprocity. Thus it is not insolence but understanding of love's essence that makes our Bāul singer proclaim -

> My longing is to meet you in play of love, my
> Lover;
> But this longing is not only mine, but also yours.
> For your lips can have their smile, and your flute
> its music, only in your delight in my love;
> and therefore you are importunate, even as I am.[3]

His proclamation brings to the point the obvious truth that the Supreme Being needs the love of his human counterpart to give out his gift of love, and that means that the Divine Musician calls for the human musician to share his own overflowing musical energies. Love implies always a mutual interest, hence music as the most sublime expression of love is nourished by an interactive flow of creativity. That is to say, the spark of inspiration flashes from the divine realm to the human level and from the realm of man to the divine level likewise, in the same way as the creative current runs in either direction.

---

[2] Bāul song, quoted in Rabindranath Tagore, *Creative Unity* (New Delhi: Macmillan India Ltd., reprint 1995), p.81
[3] ibid.

How does this cyclic flow become effective? Music is essentially emitted from the transcendental level - so how can there be a backward current moving from the destination to the source? What makes the human musician competent to deliver imaginative potencies of his own to his infinite inspirer? It is the mutuality of love, the principle of reciprocal exchange that prompts the dynamic stream of creativity to reverse its course. The gift of music, of musical inspiration is received by man as a blessing from the divinity, yet the very act of receiving arouses the desire to return the divine favor thus obtained. It is through that same desire that the human singer's creative potential is activated and that he becomes able to transform the transcendental tune into a song of his own to be presented before his master: "My songs are the same as are the spring flowers, they come from you. / Yet I bring these to you as my own"[4]. The blessing is turned into offering, the gift received into the gift extended, and the reversal of the imaginative current signifies the completion of the mutual exchange. Exchange of what? - of creativity. Creativity is revealed as an energy of motion, of emotion, which can unfold its full dynamism only once it enters into a process of reciprocal interaction, hence the establishment of mutuality is vital for the emancipation of the creative potencies.

Yet the question remains as to whether the exchanged energies are truly reciprocal, that is, whether they are equal in their intensity and original in their indwelling spirit. Or is it just one and the same imaginative substance continually shifted from one end to the other, like a ball thrown between two players? No, it is not - for if it were so, the interaction would not be productive and creativity could not arise. Is that to say, though, that inspiration emanates from both sides of the dialectic constellation? Does even the human singer possess the creative capacity to shape a melody which is new for the divine master? Yes, he does. The musical instrument on its own may not be fit to resound without the musician being there to play it, but the musician can call forth his tune from the depth of the musical instrument only because it is a musical instrument and not another thing. That means, the 'thing' must have some inherent characteristic that qualifies it as a musical instrument and thereby enables it to respond to the musician's touch. In the same way, it is the human musician's intrinsic responsiveness to the music of the

---

[4] Rabindranath Tagore, *Crossing*, LXV

Infinite which makes him an adequate partner in the process of universal creation.

Responsiveness, however, implies originality, for mere replication is not responsiveness. Therefore the human musician, in order to be responsive to the inspirational stimulus received from the divinity, has to acquire the necessary creative potential. How is this potential generated? It emerges from the musician's awareness of the source of his inspiration - an awareness that results in the inspirited mind's immediate quest to come forth with its own creations. For what end? - to uncover the invisible imaginative energies through which the transcendental melody is disclosed: "it shall be my endeavour to reveal thee in my actions, knowing it is thy power gives me strength to act"[5]. It is the divine power which gives strength to act in a double way: it induces the musical spark in the first place, and it incites the creative response. The humble singer is conscious of the fact that it is the Divine Music-maker's tune which sounds through his own music, hence he fully opens his mind to the cosmic song:

> My poet's vanity dies in shame before thy sight.
> O master poet, I have sat down at thy feet. Only
> let me make my life simple and straight, like a
> flute of reed for thee to fill with music.[6]

Like a flute of reed for thee to fill with music - but whence does the Creator's music come? "Your flute can have its music only in your delight in my love" - it emanates from the heart of man, from the love of the human being reverberant in the love of God. The music of the master poet's flute emerges from the heart of his human lover, born out of the delight of the Infinite in the love of man. The modest poet thus voices his prayer,

> Stand before my eyes, and let thy glance touch my
> songs into a flame. ...

---

[5] Rabindranath Tagore, *Gītāñjalī*, IV
[6] Rabindranath Tagore, *Gītāñjalī*, VII

> Stand in my lonely evening where my heart
> watches alone; fill.her cup of solitude, and let
> me feel in me the infinity of thy love.[7]

- but it is the infinity of his own love which makes man feel the immensity of divine love. *Let me feel in me the infinity of thy love*: the infinity of the Supreme Soul's love which is the source of all inspiration, of all creativity - but only in the love of man is it that this infinite love becomes truly creative, because only once the two currents of love come to confluence arises the delight that brings forth music, and the bold poet can still proclaim, "Your flute can have its music only in your delight in my love".

Every creation is a work of music. Music arises from the marriage of two imaginative forces tied together by the bond of love. Love is the prime cause of all creativity; without love, no musical inspiration could ever come to light. Love is the source of joy - of joy which is the root of music:

> What divine drink wouldst thou have, my God,
> from this overflowing cup of my life?
> My poet, is it thy delight to see thy creation
> through my eyes and to stand at the portals of
> my ears silently to listen to thine own eternal
> harmony?
> Thy world is weaving words in my mind *and thy
> joy is adding music to them*. Thou givest
> thyself to me in love and then feelest thine
> own entire sweetness in me.[8]

The Divine Musician listens to his own tune through the ears of the human listener, and the Divine Listener makes the human musician create the melody for his own delight. *Thy joy is adding music* - the Creator's joy, the joy of the infinite reality finds its utmost expression in music, and yet in its essence this music is self-induced: it is "music that should rise on its own joy from the depths of the heart"[9]. But how can music be at the same time attached to the delight of the Supreme Being

---

[7] Rabindranath Tagore, *Crossing*, LIV
[8] Rabindranath Tagore, *Gītāñjali*, LXV
[9] Rabindranath Tagore, *Broken Song*

and self-sustained on its own joy? Does not the one statement contradict the other? No, it does not. Music emerges from the innermost spheres of the human heart, stimulated by its own joy - but how could the human heart emit a single tune if not the Infinite Music-maker had taken his seat there, if not the human heart were penetrated by the joy of the immeasurable? In creation, the supreme divinity reveals himself as a manifestation of joy, as an embodiment of beauty. But what is joy, what is beauty in terms of perceptive articulation? It is music - music which reverberates in the immaterial rays of joy. Without joy there would be no music, and without music, creation would remain an inanimate artefact of sterile perfection.

The creative product, however, is full of life, so what is it that inspirits creation? Which is the energy that fills creation with creativity? How is joy evoked - the vitalizing joy that indwells music as the stimulative power whose impetus makes the tune "rise from the depths of the heart"? The poet says of the Supreme Soul, "thou givest thyself to me in love and then feelest thine own entire sweetness in me" only to delight in that sweetness: it is love's sacrifice, the Supreme Soul's self-offering to the human lover, which creates the joy of the divine and thereby instigates music, instigates the creativity of music. Love, in one single instant, brings forth joy, music, and creativity: the music of love becomes creative through the self-sacrifice of the divinity. Creation is essentially an act of offering, of sacrifice in which the Creator forgoes a part of his own to regain it in refined form through the creative manifestation. Music embodies the fullest sacrifice of creation, because the Divine Music-maker, the creator of transcendental tunes abandons not only an aspect of himself, but parts with his entire self for the sake of a single melody. It is an offering from love, a gift of love which raises the musical strain in the soul of the beloved and brings the sounding reality to full force. It is that same offering through which joy is aroused and expressed at the same time, the sacrifice which rests at the core of all creativity.

But does not sacrifice, in one way or another, imply pain? And if there is pain, how come that this very pain is linked to the source of joy? How come that creativity, that music, that musical creativity emerges from sorrow inspite of its vital basis which is joy? Yet creativity does not arise simply from pain, but from qualified pain:

> It is the pang of separation that spreads
> throughout the world and gives birth to
> shapes innumerable in the infinite sky.
> It is this sorrow of separation that gazes in
> silence all night from star to star and becomes
> lyric among rustling leaves in rainy darkness
> of July.
> It is this overspreading pain that deepens into
> loves and desires, into sufferings and joys in
> human homes; and this it is that ever melts
> and flows in songs through my poet's heart.[10]

The pain which is implicit in joy, the pain which is concealed in the sacrifice of creation and carried along by the endless flow of cosmic music, is more than idle suffering: it is the pain of love, the pain which arises from love, the agony endured by the loving soul in disunion, in separation from the object of its love. If joy is the source of creativity, then pain - the pain of separation - is its essential stimulus. And it is not pain *per se*, not pain as an impartial reality, which motivates the creative current: it is pain whose qualifying momentum is love. Because only where there is love, separation can be felt; only where there is love, the agony of separation can be felt, hence only where there is love, the strains of suffering can unfold their creative power. What is more, the joy that invokes the sense of musical creativity, the joy that awakens the imaginative spirit at the root of creation - that joy is born from the dignity of pain, a dignity which can emerge only from the core substance of love. It is from joy that the creative outflow wells forth, but it is pain which stimulates joy in the first place - because this joy is the joy of love, and love can only be sustained by the interplay of two lovers: in separation and union, agony and bliss.

But still we may ask, why is it pain which acts as a cause of inspiration, of creativity? Why does it have to be pain? Is not pain by itself negatively inclined - then how can it create an immensely constructive potential, contradicting its own adverse disposition? The answer lies in the qualification of pain as an aspect of love: the pain of love, the agony sensed in love can never yield to hopelessness as long as

---

[10] Rabindranath Tagore, *Gītāñjalī*, LXXXIV

love is real, because this pain carries at its core the certitude of its own ending. If pain were an unchangeable condition of finality, it would be unbearable, but the impetus of love within makes the pain of separation endurable through its indwelling assurance of an impending reunion. It is this certainty, the definiteness that the pain will ultimately give way to joy, which raises the creative spirit from the depth of the heart only to announce the joy to come in a melodious outbreak of musical cadences: "Many a song have I sung in many a mood of mind, but all their notes have always proclaimed, 'He comes, comes, ever comes'"[11]. Who is He, the hero of the song, whose coming turns sorrow into joy, pain into bliss? Who is He, the thought of whose presence makes all imaginative strains mingle into one abundant flow of tuneful sweetness? He is the Eternal Lover, the Supreme Soul in his creative aspect of the Infinite Music-maker from whose transcendental melody the universe springs forth. He is the source of all love from whose invisible presence joy is born - the joy which emerges from the shreds of abolished pain: "In sorrow after sorrow it is his steps that press upon my heart, and it is the golden touch of his feet that makes my joy to shine"[12].

From where, however, does the human soul take its confidence that pain is only temporary and that joy will arise for sure? Which is the silent power that enables the heart of man to transcend its agony and to create the music of its own joy yet before the pain is gone? Where is the assurance of the bliss in prospect, and is this assurance at all feasible? Yes, it is - it is there, attested by the vibration of the infinite. It is realistic but not rational, attainable but not seizable within the reach of reason. The assurance that inspires creativity, the promise that sets forth the flow of music exists in its own right without giving records of wherefrom and whereto. The poet does not ask from where: he knows, simply knows that "early in the day it was whispered that we should sail in a boat, only thou and I, and never a soul in the world would know of this our pilgrimage to no country and to no end"[13]. He knows that his waiting is meaningful for he has been given the assurance that pain will dissolve into joy, weariness into creativity, and that his listless singer's mind will burst forth with intensely sweet tunes brought to life at the

---

[11] Rabindranath Tagore, *Gītāñjalī*, XLV
[12] ibid.
[13] Rabindranath Tagore, *Gītāñjalī*, XLII

sanctifying touch of the divine: "In that shoreless ocean, at thy silently listening smile my songs would swell in melodies, free as waves, free from all bondage of words"[14]. He may wonder, "Is the time not come yet?"[15], and still he knows that the time is to come - he knows without asking.

Is that to say that the question, whence comes the assurance of eternal joy, is a futile one? Does this mean that there is no answer? No, it does not. The answer is at hand, but it cannot be pronounced. Why so? Because the limitless reality does not respond to the rational mind which raises the question, and the heart which alone is eligible for a reply from the transcendental level does not query. There is no need to ask, for the heart knows what the mind knows not. The heart, being the center of emotionality, is able to perceive the subtle message from the spheres of infinity, a message which is conveyed in a language of love neither spoken nor understood by the mind. It is the language of music, of the creative current that delivers the melody from the transcendental realm to the world of phenomenal existence, from perpetuity to momentariness, from formlessness to form - from God to man. It is the language of the song which, inspired by the divine presence, "would swell in melodies...free from all bondage of words". It is the language that transcends the limits of language: it is music *per se*, music in its most sublime, most refined form. It is music which responds to the emotional strain within creation, music that withdraws itself from the rude grasp of rationality and evaporates at the imprudent touch of the inquisitive though limited human mind.

Where does this unfathomable music originate from? It is produced in the creative mind of the Divine Music-maker, in the mind which is illimitable hence capable of absorbing the timeless reality in its full unendingness. Yet it is the Divine Listener through whom the musical creation is inspired in its flow: "*at thy silently listening smile* my songs would swell in melodies". The Supreme Soul is giving out his tuneful fabric as an offering of love to bring his own joy to perfection. What is that to say? The Creator assumes his two-fold manifestation as the Eternal Musician and the Eternal Listener in order to instigate the

---

14 ibid.
15 ibid.

response in the human soul which is needed to make the love of the Divine Being complete, hence to bring forth musical creativity. It is only in this dual aspect of the Infinite that music can arise, for only in the duality love can unfold its imaginative play. So truly the transcendental musician is the one who listens, and the transcendental listener is the one who generates the tune in his human lover's instrument through the stimulative power of his apprehensive attendance. Because it is the presence of the divinity, the bliss-giving company of the boundless reality which arouses the joy in the heart of man and fills the human soul with creative delight - and with music.

Music arising from divine inspiration surpasses the limits of rational language, but what is more, the inspiration itself carries man beyond the limits of his human potencies. Why else were the poet taken aback by his own inexplicable strength?

> I thought that my voyage had come to its end at
> the last limit of my power, - that the path
> before me was closed, that provisions were
> exhausted and the time come to take shelter in
> a silent obscurity.
> But I find that thy will knows no end in me. And
> when old words die out on the tongue, new
> melodies break forth from the heart; and
> where the old tracks are lost, new country is
> revealed with its wonders.[16]

Thy will knows no end in me, hence the poem exceeds the capacity of the poet's mastery, and the singer's voice, the musician's instrument delivers tunes unknown to the music-maker's consciousness. It is the Eternal Poet speaking through the verses of his human singer, the Infinite Music-maker manifesting his own joy in the melodies of the human musician. The creative force that emanates from the unbounded flow of cosmic music brings to light the musical sweetness distilled from the imaginative stream of universal creativity. The process of distillation, however, requires both the medium and the distillatory agent. The medium, which is the human soul, cannot produce the desired

---

[16] Rabindranath Tagore, *Gītāñjalī*, XXXVII

subtlety without the agent, but likewise the agent's efforts remain vain without the medium. Only when the two of them meet, only when the human soul meets the soul of the world in a creative union can the melody emerge from the gloomy spheres of cosmic mysteriousness. It is therefore the Creator's own interest to share his unlimited capacities with the creator in man, for if the one is weak and exhausted, the other will not find creative fulfilment.

So what happens once the Infinite Reality settles down as the infinite within man? *New melodies break forth from the heart*: the human soul beams with freshly gained inspiration resounding in novel musical cadences flowing out - from where? - from the heart. It is from the seat of emotionality that music is emitted by the emotive force of creativity, because creativity, being an emotional spirit, can come forth only from the heart. The mind, the constructive abode of rational thought, cannot harbor creativity as the very concept of rationality opposes the quintessence of creativity which is emotion. Rationality creates objective realities, whereas creativity brings realities to perfection. Rationality produces outwardly concordant entities, creativity fulfils these entities in harmonious completeness. Rationality fabricates neutral artefacts, creativity turns artefacts into living works of art. Music is by its very nature a product of creativity:

> A mere procession of notes does not make
> music; it is only when we have in the heart of the
> march of sounds some musical idea that it creates
> song. Our faith in the infinite reality of Perfection
> is that musical idea, and there is that one creative
> force...[17]

The musical idea acts as the decisive factor for the unfolding of creativity. What is this musical idea? It is "our faith in the infinite reality of Perfection": it is the awareness of the Supreme Reality whose imaginative power permeates the core of the universe. It is even more than mere awareness: the musical idea which sustains the creative quest arises from the realization of the instrinsic oneness that unites the individual soul with the cosmic soul; the creative spirit springs up from

[17] Rabindranath Tagore, *Creative Unity*, p.25

the recognition of the fact that the unity of the two souls is not an illusion but is the ultimate truth which is to fulfil expressly. It is the definiteness of this union which animates the singer's tunes to proclaim with "all their notes..., 'He comes, comes, ever comes'".

The musical idea is more than merely an inspirational impetus: it is the emotional idea of creation, the vital soul which elevates creativity beyond the crude reality of rationalism. The 'procession of notes' is the rational phenomenon, a well-organized array of ringing sounds whose material presence alone does not evoke music. Only once the emotional stimulus in the guise of the musical idea enters the chain of notes is it that the lifeless body turns into a soulful personality, that sound becomes music. Creativity is that musical idea, the emotional impulse which transforms meaningless facts into meaningful realities. Creativity is the emotional idea - the emotional ideal whose life-giving force personalizes neutral entities to form embodiments of beauty, for "in a creation of art...the energy of an emotional ideal is necessary; as its unity is not like that of a crystal, passive and inert, but actively expressive"[18]. Actively expressive of what? - of joy. It is joy that becomes manifest in each and every creation of beauty, because beauty is in itself an expression of joy. It is joy that permeates each and every articulation of music, because music is the sounding incarnation of transcendental bliss. It is joy that brings to life inanimate objects of rational thought by defeating the disheartening force of rationality through its emotional appeal to the musical consciousness of existence, that is, through its musical appeal to the emotional consciousness of man.

Musical creativity emerges from the emotional idea carried forward by the imaginative spark that instigates the process of creation. Without this emotional impetus, the work of music remains impersonal, "but when it is the outer body of an inner idea it assumes personality"[19]. Once the musical fabric imbibes the vital spirit of creative emotionality, it becomes creation, and once the musical creation has been born, joy finds its fullest vocalization in the melodious sweetness of the cosmic tune. Creativity is by nature spontaneous because of its underlying emotional spirit, hence the musical creation reveals its own spontaneity in a sudden

---

[18] Rabindranath Tagore, *Creative Unity*, p.33
[19] Rabindranath Tagore, *Creative Unity*, p.34

cloudburst of emotion - of emotion which qualifies music as music, of emotion which elevates music above sound, creativity above rational constructivism. Therefore "we find that the endless rhythms of the world are not merely constructive; *they strike our own heart-strings and produce music*", hence "we feel that this world is a creation; that in its centre there is a living idea which reveals itself in an eternal symphony, played on innumerable instruments, all keeping perfect time"[20].

So what is creation? What is the musical creation? It is the revelation of the one transcendental reality in a multitude of forms tied together by the bond of an instrinsic unity and inspirited with vital breath by the inherent emotional idea. Creation is manifoldness of shapes, yet their variety is but an expression of a single truth. Creation is the unity of proportions within heterogeneity, yet the mere fact of harmoniousness does not make the creative harmony:

> In the world-poem, the discovery of the law of its rhythms, the measurement of its expansion and contraction, movement and pause, the pursuit of its evolution of forms and characters, are true achievements of the mind; but we cannot stop there. It is like a railway station; but the station platform is not our home. Only he has attained the final truth who knows *that the whole world is a creation of joy.*[21]

It is this very creation of joy, the articulation of cosmic delight that accomplishes the "harmony of contrary forces, which give their rhythm to all creation"[22]. It is the emotive energy of creativity which inherits the strength to melt the antagonism of contradicting potencies and to make all adverseness dissolve into an immense stream of bliss - of music.

What does this music of joy imply? Why is it that this music carries the message of universal bliss? Music as a creative reality signifies truth, pure truth, and creativity is the call to reveal the truth from within: "This great world, where it is a creation, an expression of

---

[20] Rabindranath Tagore, *Creative Unity*, p.35

[21] Rabindranath Tagore, *Sādhanā* (London: Macmillan and Co. Ltd., 1914), p.99

[22] Rabindranath Tagore, *Creative Unity*, p.65

the infinite…has its call for us. The call has ever roused the creator in man, and urged him to reveal the truth, to reveal the Infinite in himself"[23]. To reveal the Infinite in himself and thereby to find his freedom within bounds, because creativity is the perfect freedom which fulfils itself in the confinement of definite manifestations. The creative spirit is the spirit of freedom because its quest is the quest for truth, and truth is by its very own nature infinite. What is truth? Truth is joy, truth is love, hence in creativity the realization of infinite joy, the consummation of infinite love becomes verbalized. "True creation is realization of truth"[24] - that is to say, true creativity is realization of the Supreme Reality from which all truth emanates.

More than that, true creativity is realization of the intrinsic truth of union, of spiritual union between the finite and the infinite, of the union which is the prime cause of all joy, of all music, of all creativity. It is for the attainment of that state of ultimate bliss that man becomes creative in the first place, longing to vocalize the desire of the human heart to unite with the great soul of the world. Yet it is the Supreme Soul's own yearning to find fulfilment in the love of man which conveys the imaginative spark to the human mind still before the first strain of creativity breaks forth. How is creativity revealed? Creativity manifests itself as the tuneful expression of beauty, of joy: as music. Music is the most spontaneous, the most immediate response to man's creative mind, for music is the pure emotional essence, the liquid whose flow delivers the quintessence of all creativity. Who instigates the creative flow of music? It is Him, the transcendental musician who dwells in the heart of the human singer, filling his song with music. It is Him to whom the Bāul poet prays, "Attested by your own heart, / o my master, / lead me the right way / as you play the melody / on the lute. // The lute could never sing / on its own, / without you to play it"[25]. It is Him, the source of eternal delight whose radiant being satiates the universe with music, and whose infinite presence shines ever forth with creative joy, joyous creativity.

---

[23] Rabindranath Tagore, *Creative Unity*, pp.26-7

[24] Rabindranath Tagore, *Creative Unity*, p.21

[25] Anon, quoted in Deben Bhattacharya, op.cit., p.40

9

Music and spiritual union

> It is the object of this Oneness in us to realise its
> infinity by perfect union of love with others. All
> obstacles to this union create misery, giving rise
> to the baser passions that are expressions of
> finitude, of that separateness which is
> negative...[1]

What is the meaning of spiritual union? The state of union implies
all those qualities that are essential attributes of joy: infinity as opposed
to the finitude of disunion, oneness as opposed to the dualism of
separation, positivity as opposed to the negativity of separateness.
Infinity, oneness and positivity share one and the same core substance:
love, hence joy, and therefore all three qualities of union are at the same
time attributes of music. Spiritual union is the prime source of these
qualities because it is the union of love: love is by its very nature
infinite, love is the quintessence of oneness, love is the elemental energy
of positiveness. Union of love signifies the perfect condition of ultimate
bliss in which all currents of creative evolvement come to confluence
with the one infinite reality of cosmic existence. Love is the positive
truth that defies the untruth "of that separateness which is negative"
hence illusive. Love is infinity that refutes the limitativeness of
"passions that are expressions of finitude" hence perishable. Love is joy,
the joy of oneness between the individual soul and the Supreme Soul,
the joy of "this Oneness in us" that withstands the pain of separation,
the pain which is an expression of the hurtful split of that oneness into
two. The union of love, therefore, accomplishes the attainment of love
by eliminating the negative, the limitable aspects of delusive
momentariness from the spiritual quest: the union of love is the union
between the finite and the infinite, between the form and the formless,
between creation and the Creator. The union of love is the most sublime
state of spiritual oneness out of which is born all joy, all beauty, all
music.

How is this state of perfect bliss attained? Which is the
stimulating force that instigates the quest for union? Of what kind is the

---

[1] from Rabindranath Tagore, "The poet's religion", in *Creative Unity* (New Delhi:
Macmillan India Ltd., reprint 1995), p.5

liquid that carries forth the flow of emotion, the vital current of love continually progressing in its course towards the ocean of universal joy? The union of love is the union of two souls, but what is it that motivates the yearning of the two to merge into one? In short, which is the procreative energy in the heart of creation that sustains the cosmic stream of life?

The procreant force is love itself - love which bears at its core the essence of its own fulfilment. It is love which stimulates the desire for its own consummation through its inherent momentum of truth. What does that mean? The truth of love manifests itself as love's intrinsic sweetness, and it is this sweetness which arouses the one soul's longing for union with the other. Truth, if perceived solely as a neutral fact, has no appeal to the emotional consciousness of man, just as the bare amassment of ringing sounds conveys no musical meaning to the human heart. Once the reality of truth is inspirited by the fluid of love, however, it rises beyond its mere factual existence and turns into music, into melodiousness in whose essence is enveloped a deeper message for the heart. The emotional message is the call of cosmic sweetness, but at the same time the message is truth itself, and it is the impulse of this very truth which adds the quality of definiteness to the transcendental sweetness. How is truth revealed? It manifests itself in the ultimate experience of bliss evoked through the union of the two souls longing to reach out for each other from different levels of cosmic existence. Spiritual union is pronouncement and at the same time expression of universal truth. Being essentially a revelation of truth, union is real and therefore definite.

What is it that affirms this realness of union? Every union implies the dissolution of an initial duality into one. Union is the mergence of two entities, two souls, two emotional powers. What is more, this union signifies the meeting of two spheres, of two worlds: the human merges with the divine, the phenomenal with the transcendental, the finite with the infinite in order to bring forth that most refined essence of bliss which surfaces at the meeting-point of the cosmic realms. Spiritual union, therefore, is the creative union of progenitive forces whose coalescence acts as the prime cause of universal progression. It is the union whose core reality is truth, hence sweetness, for else the vibrations of the cosmic energies could not find their response in creation. It is the union whose inner substance is music, for music is the supreme expression of transcendental sweetness. It is the union whose actuality, whose definiteness defies all pain and distress on the way towards this ultimate goal. Still more, it is the certainty of this union which not only makes the pain of separation bearable, but transcends that pain altogether by adding an aspect of sweetness to the agony of longing:

> My eyes have lost their sleep in watching; yet if I
> do not meet thee still it is sweet to watch.
> My heart sits in the shadow of the rains waiting
> for thy love; if she is deprived still it is sweet
> to hope.
> They walk away in their different paths leaving
> me behind; if I am alone still it is sweet to
> listen to thy footsteps.
> The wistful face of the earth weaving its autumn
> mists wakens longing in my heart; if it is in
> vain still it is sweet to feel the pain of
> longing.[2]

It is sweet to feel the pain of longing - but what is it that emboldens the human heart to fully appreciate the taste of this sweetness? *If she is deprived still it is sweet to hope* - but wherefrom does hope arise? In the light of its emotional ambition, hope is not vanity: it is the expectation of bliss to come, an expectation which is nourished by the existential longing of the soul for fulfilment, an expectation which is realized through the sureness of its accomplishment. The poet audaciously states, "if it is in vain still it is sweet to feel the pain of longing", only because he is confident that his waiting is not in vain - that it cannot be in vain, for if it were so, if his longing were fruitless, it would take away the very basis of his life. If pain were a wasted emotional effort, there would be no sweetness of longing, and love were doomed to die of its own hollowness. But truth can never be a state of neglect. The deprived heart yet awaits love, for if it were truly deprived, how could it be sweet to hope? How could hope at all persist? If meeting, if union be denied forever, how could it be

---

[2] Rabindranath Tagore, *Crossing*, XI

sweet to watch? If silence were the ultimate answer to the quest for the melody, why then is it that the universe overflows with music in every single moment?

Darkness cannot be conclusive, silence not be the final reply to the spiritual aspiration. Sadness is real in non-fulfilment, but the truth of discontentment is its momentariness, and the silence of pain is to give way to the music of joy: "That the bud has not blossomed in beauty in my life spreads sadness in the heart of creation. When the shroud of darkness will be lifted from my soul it will bring music to thy smile"[3]. What force is it that lifts this shroud of darkness from the soul? Which is the energy that instigates the tuneful smile of music? It is love, the quintessence of existence, the liquid at the core of the flow of life. It is love, the substance from which creation raises the form out of the formless. As a cosmic energy, love is omnipresent, all-penetrating and permanent. As a universal principle, love is truth reverberating with sweetness. Love extends beyond the limits of qualitativeness, yet it is the source of all qualities - positive and negative, sympathetic and averse, bliss-giving and agonizing. How do these qualities arise? They emerge from an emotional bias towards the infinite or the finite, towards the perennial or the fugitive, towards the intense or the shallow. The function of love is to channelize these qualities and to extract their positive essence of unity, for love is oneness - oneness whose intent is "to realise its infinity by perfect union of love with others"[4].

Realizing the infinity of love's oneness, however, requires the realness of love and the feasibility of its fulfilment. The tangibleness of love's consummation is therefore a fundamental principle of cosmic creation, of which each and every being is entitled to partake, or else creation itself comes to standstill:

> If love be denied me then why does the morning
> break its heart in songs, and why are these
> whispers that the south wind scatters among
> the new-born leaves?

---

[3] Rabindranath Tagore, *Crossing*, IX
[4] Rabindranath Tagore, *Creative Unity*, p.5

> If love be denied me then why does the midnight
>   bear in yearning silence the pain of the stars?
>   And why does this foolish heart recklessly
>   launch its hope on the sea whose end it does
>   not know?[5]

If love be denied to even the least creature in the boundless realm of universal life, love would lose its claim to truth and creation were no more than a gigantic lie. If the call for love would remain unheard in even one single instance, the music of joy would forever forfeit its cosmic appeal and the silence of hopelessness would spread its wings of darkness over the barren fields of meaningless life. In such a world of permanent discord, no melody could ever rise from the strings of the broken instrument, and the life-giving spirit of beauty dies in the suffocating stranglehold of ignorance.

But truth is altogether different though. The vital energies of joy cannot be held captive in the snares of defeat, and illusiveness can never maintain its supremacy over truth. The current of transcendental music remains flowing towards the sea of cosmic love even and particularly through the clouds of silence, and more than that, it fills the empty veil of silence with the sweetness of cadences yet to resound. It is this music-charged silence which conveys the longing of unfulfilled love - the longing of a love still immature, yet meaningful: a love in which nothing is complete, yet nothing is lost either:

> I know that this life, missing its ripeness in love,
>   is not altogether lost.
> I know that the flowers that fade in the dawn, the
>   streams that strayed in the desert, are not
>   altogether lost.
> I know that whatever lags behind in this life
>   laden with slowness is not altogether lost.
> I know that my dreams that are still unfulfilled,
>   and my melodies still unstruck, are clinging
>   to some lute-strings of thine, and they are not
>   altogether lost.[6]

---

[5] Rabindranath Tagore, *Crossing*, XXX
[6] Rabindranath Tagore, *Crossing*, XVIII

What is it that makes the poet know? How come the singer's tune is kept safe even in the silence of unsung notes? Which is the distinctive criterion to endow unfulfilled love with a deeper sense?

The driving energy is the expectation of the fulfilment to come: it is the energy of hope derived from the certainty of union as a definite prospect which adds the meaning to the soul's longing. It is the assurance of love as a cosmic truth, and of union as its ultimate state of perfection, which takes away the spell of futility from the pain of separation. Equiped with an emotional sensor, the heart instinctively knows that its agony in disunion is only temporary and that consummation will follow as the logical answer to the call for spiritual union. But does this union come all by itself? No, it does not. The union of love, however unquestionable as an impending reality, needs to be evoked. How is it evoked? - through music. Music is the path that leads towards union, and the musical melody is the vehicle that carries the searching soul ahead on that path. The quest for spiritual union is the core quest of music, and music is the elemental essence of the spiritual quest. Music is search and fulfilment of the search at the same time, for music is both the river and the sea towards which the river flows. Music is at once the call of love and the call for love; it is the message exchanged between the two souls longing to meet, just as much as it is the medium to convey the message.

Owing to its motivating potencies, music acts as the prime stimulative impetus that urges on the seeker's heart to proceed on the way towards the meeting-point where the Eternal Lover is waiting to receive his human friend. But music provides more than the mere incentive: being essentially an expression of beauty, music illumines the path to fulfilment with its indwelling radiance of joy, guiding the human soul towards her ultimate aim:

> Ever in my life have I sought thee with my
> songs. It was they who led me from door to
> door, and with them I have felt about me,
> searching and touching my world.
> It was my songs that taught me all the lessons I
> ever learnt; they showed me secret paths,

they brought before my sight many a star on
the horizon of my heart.
They guided me all the day long to the mysteries
of the country of pleasure and pain, and, at
last, to what palace gate have they brought
me in the evening at the end of my journey?[7]

Music is inhabited by the powerful light of beauty that shines through the obscurity of anticipation, turning the object of union into a feasible reality. But what is it that entitles music itself to become that reality?

The path towards spiritual union lies ahead of the aspiring soul as a beautiful network of musical cadences, with a cart made of melodies to ride on, the way towards love's ultimate end lit up by the resplendent echo of tunes. Yet it is not simply music which leads to spiritual accomplishment. The music must have some deeper purpose in order to become meaningful, hence suitable to evoke the union of souls. Which is this purpose? It is the dedication of the tune to its inciter: to the supreme transcendental reality, to the source of all music and destination of all emotional intents. The music fit for the arousal of ultimate spiritual excitement is the music which is directed to the Infinite Being, because it is in union with the Divine Lover that this music becomes complete as an offering, while at the same time union is accomplished only once the current of music has progressed from spring to merging-point, from origin to destination, from music-maker to listener.

How does this dialectic mechanism function? What is it that qualifies music as the connecting bond through which union is tied, and more than that, as the powerful essence of bliss whose impact demobilizes the negative forces of separateness? The answer lies not within the sounding reality, but within the heart from which the tune comes forth: it is the emotional designation of the musical outflow which is essential for the spiritual capacities of the melodious creation. That is to say, at the core of the music nourished by divine inspiration rests the idea of the offering: the tune is brought to life, shaped and perfected not for its own sake, but for the joy of the one to whom it is ultimately consecrated. The act of offering is thereby an act of selfless

---

[7] Rabindranath Tagore, *Gītāñjali*, CI

giving, of giving away without demanding anything in turn, and yet the offering is not made for no end. The expectation of the giving heart, however, extends beyond mere reciprocation of the gift of love: it aims at the lover himself. But this expectation does not succumb to the limitativeness of desirous demand; it rather manifests itself as a subtle longing of immense emotional profundity, a longing which maintains the full dignity of the loving heart without devaluing the selflessness of its intention.

The expectation raised by the worshiping soul is an expectation of union, of fulfilment, but on what grounds does this expectation come up in the first place? It emerges from the definiteness of union as a cosmic truth. How is this expectation instigated? - through the statement of love made through the act of selfless offering. Offering of what? - of music. Music possesses the intrinsic emotional energy essential to establish a relation between two souls, hence the capacity to tie the emotional bond between the two spiritual entities longing for each other. In other words music, through its primarily emotional appeal, qualifies as the tool *par excellence* to accomplish the union of love. It is the heart searching for this union which takes the active part in the process of aspiration, guiding the mind of the music-maker to the manufactory of tunes. The emergence of the melody from the singer's throat, the harmonious revelation that wells forth from the depth of the musical instrument, are nothing but creative expressions of the loving soul's yearning for union with the object of its love. The offering of music, the offering enveloped in the tuneful sweetness of musical cadences is in reality more than a mere articulation of love: it is the quest for love's fulfilment, the quest for union concealed in the wrap of beauty.

Music raises its melodious voice to pronounce the call for union, but what happens once the call is heard? What succeeds once union turns real?

> Put out the lamps, my heart, the lamps of your
> lonely night.
> The call comes to you to open your doors, for the
> morning light is abroad.
> Leave your lute in the corner, my heart, the lute
> of your lonely life.

The call comes to you to come out in silence, for
the morning sings your own songs.[8]

The morning sings your own songs - for it is reverberant with the tunes
of the one who has been gifted with the musical offering. The quest for
union finds its vocalization in music, but once the quest is accomplished,
music emerges all by itself from the spheres towards which it had been
directed. Why is that? Because in the moment of union, the lover
himself, the one who has thus accepted the musical gift, takes up the
strings to add his own music to the joy of union. The music of bliss thus
conceived embodies the most sublime essence of transcendental joy,
which is born at the culmination of spiritual fulfilment. But how is this
ultimate melody revealed? *The call comes to you to come out in silence* -
music as the most excellent embodiment of universal joy manifests itself
in soundlessness, as its vibrations are too subtle to be captured by the
crude spirit of sound. It is the infinite essence of this ultimate musical
reality which withdraws itself from the grab of the finite immanent in the
sounding presence, and thus the pure substance of transcendental music
gives out its full melodiousness in waves of immensely sweet silence.

What is silence? Is it mere soundlessness, or does silence
encompass a meaning deeper than that? Silence is of two types
characterized by its inclination towards the finite or the infinite, towards
the adverse or the constructive, towards emptiness or excessive fulness
with sound. The phenomenon of silence accordingly moves along these
two denominations - meaningless or meaningful, vain or creative.
Silence as a bare statement of soundlessness is an expression of
finitude, hence futile and negative in its impact. How is this blankness
caused? It is the lack of an emotional content which turns silence into an
aimless stillness. The silence which carries at its core the spark of
transcendental music, however, is of different kind. Loaded with
musical imagination, it is no more the silence of voidness, but of plenty.
It is this silence which is truly meaningful, which bears in its heart the
infinite essence of love - of worship, silent worship whose intensity
exceeds the limits of sound. It is this silence which is intrinsically
positive and life-giving; it is this very silence which defeats the streaks
of soundlessness. It is this silence which emerges from the instance of

---

[8] Rabindranath Tagore, *Crossing*, XL

highest bliss, the silence which is the ultimate response to spiritual union. It is the silence which is the final destination of all song, the merging-point of all musical strains where the current of cosmic melodies finds its freedom in the boundlessness of quietude.

How is this silence attained? It arises out of the supreme transcendental experience evoked through the union of love, through the union in which the mutual longing of two souls culminates and dissolves at the same time. The way towards spiritual union is built on the dialectic interplay of sound and silence, music-making and listening, offering and receiving, but union itself, the ultimate climax, is silence: "They sing, dance, constantly practice (service); attaining supreme bliss, they remain silent"[9]. If song is the anticipation of union, the moment of bliss is revealed in silence, but the transition from anticipation to realization, from vision to union, from joy to bliss is fluent - hence the poet's advice to welcome the utmost instant in tunes and silence likewise:

> My guest has come to my door in this autumn
>   morning.
> Sing, my heart, sing thy welcome!
> Make thy song the song of the sunlit blue, of the
>   dew-damp air, of the lavish gold of harvest
>   fields, of the laughter of the loud water.
> Or stand mute before him for awhile gazing at
>   his face.
> Then leave thy house and go out with him in
>   silence.[10]

And go out with him in silence, for silence is yet the ultimate answer to all tunes. More than that, it is the impact of union itself that leads to speechlessness - the impact of bliss, of universal joy which expands beyond the capacity of man's emotional consciousness. Thus the singer's heart "longs to join in thy song, but vainly struggles for a voice"[11],

---

[9] Bhāgavata Purāṇa 11.3.32 ...*nṛtyanti gāyanty anuśīlayanty ajaṃ bhavanti tūṣṇīm param etya nirvṛtāḥ*

[10] Rabindranath Tagore, *Crossing*, XLVI

[11] Rabindranath Tagore, *Gītāñjali*, III

while "the poet sits speechless in the corner"[12]. For union is not merely a state of fulfilment, of complete spiritual satisfaction - it is at the same time the vision of the eternal truth, enlightenment which is attained through the emotional experience of love, of fully consummate love in its most refined cosmic essence.

But how long can the silence of union persist? How long can the emotional response be held back? Silence is the ultimate reply, yet does not silence prompt itself a reply? Union is the ultimate state, yet union cannot be ultimately static, or else the course of creation would stagnate as "life walks away / together with the days / but with no songs for God"[13]. It is for this very reason, in order to maintain the motion and vitality of cosmic life, that the overwhelming impact of bliss arising from union must be discharged. If the universal current of emotion is held up, its accumulated force turns destructive, threatening to strike at the roots of existence: "From the distance of millions of miles / the sun rays unravel the lotus bloom, / opening its petals" - but without singing to the lord, "Podo is burnt to death / in the field of lotus blooms / by the fire of feelings"[14]. How is the emotional surge released? Destruction arises "with no songs for God" because song, music is the prime substance to set free the aggregated potencies of emotional energy. Silence is the culmination, yet even silence is but an aspect of song, hence calls for liberation in song. For if the discharge does not happen, if the emotional forces are restrained and silence is prevented from melting into music, the constructive energies of silence reverse their impact and bliss turns into pain. It is then that the agonized heart "shivering with tears / …cries with the eyes, / *and in the silence of lovely sound / forever calls: / come, please come*"[15].

What is the reason for this sudden change? Why is it that joy gives way to sorrow even though truth itself attests the supremacy of joy? How can silence expressing the ultimate state of bliss revert to the articulation of utter pain arising from unfulfilled union? How can union return to separation, how perfection lapse back into incompleteness? The

---

[12] Rabindranath Tagore, *Crossing*, XLV

[13] Padmalochan (Podo), quoted in Deben Bhattacharya, *The mirror of the sky* (London: Allen & Unwin, 1969), p.98

[14] ibid.

[15] Anon, quoted in Deben Bhattacharya, op.cit., p.49

fact of reversion is not remarkable as such, for every union is followed by separation as a natural process of creative development - an existential process moreover, whose functioning is vital to sustain the course of universal life. Separation implies pain in any case, hence the interplay of joy and sorrow is likewise but a normal occurence in the current of creation. What is harmful, however, is interruption in the natural flow of evolution - and this is what happens if the amassed energies of cosmic music are held back to artificially retain the state of blissful silence. Why? Because an enforced silence cannot maintain its positive essence unless it dissolves into sound and is born, grows and matures anew. Spiritual union as the most sublime expression of transcendental bliss is by its very nature a process rather than a state, hence its pureness can only be preserved through constant regeneration. That is to say, the quintessence of union is not the mergence at the moment but the mergence ahead - ahead of pain, ahead of separation, ahead of refreshed emotional experience.

Union signifies silence at its culmination-point, yet union implies at the same time the outbreak of music. Union is the commingling of two souls, of two emotional currents - and of two streams of music. What is more, the two currents that come to confluence are not simply flowing towards each other: to the contrary, they are running in parallel direction. It is their parallelism, the sheer unattainableness of union at least in rational terms, which enhances the yearning of the souls for each other. Yet the seemingly infeasible object turns real through the power of love: "A pair of hearts / running in parallel streams, / long to reach the god of loving"[16] - because once they have reached that god, once they have accomplished the quest of love, they have attained to each other. The union of parallel rivers appears unrealistic as long as they remain running within the confines of the river-bed, but once they merge into the boundlessness of the ocean, their confluence materializes all by itself. Love is the sea that unites parallel currents. The union of love is the union with the unattainable, in which the limits of the impossible are unknown. It is the union in which silence becomes music and music silence, the union in which oneness is accomplished through the creation of the duality rather than its neglect.

---

[16] Haridās, quoted in Deben Bhattacharya, op.cit., p.67

Union reveals itself as a state of perfect harmony, but how is union achieved? - through struggle. It is the struggle of love, the struggle between two lovers which ultimately culminates in their union - in a union of equal entities purified through the constructive struggle for rather than against each other. In union, silence resolves into song and song into silence, reflecting the course of the two musical currents constantly longing to meet, yet continuously struggling to repress each other:

> Let my song be simple as the waking in the
>   morning, as the dripping of dew from the
>   leaves,
> Simple as the colours in clouds and showers of
>   rain in the midnight.
> But my lute strings are newly strung and they
>   dart their notes like spears sharp in their
>   newness.
> Thus they miss the spirit of the wind and hurt the
>   light of the sky; and these strains of my
>   songs fight hard to push back thy own
>   music.[17]

These strains of my songs fight hard to push back thy own music - but is this music truly to be pushed back? No, it is not, and even the tune that struggles on the one end desires but to meet with the tune from the other end, and it is this overpowering desire welling up in the one soul that makes it push against the other. Yet the ultimate intent of both is oneness:

> There are numerous strings in your lute, let me
>   add my own among them.
> Then when you smite your chords my heart will
>   break its silence and my life will be one with
>   your song...[18]

It is oneness in which all tunes dissolve into silence, yet silence finds its fulfilment in the discharge of melodies.

---

[17] Rabindranath Tagore, *Crossing*, LXIX
[18] Rabindranath Tagore, *Crossing*, LXVIII

What is important about the struggle of love is the fact that this struggle is not the wrestle of antagonistic opponents as is the struggle of passion. The struggle of love it is not conflict but contest - the contest of two souls establishing mutually responsive statements of love, and its aim is to abandon rather than affirm opposition. Nourished by the infinite essence of love, this contest brings forth the positive energies through which union is induced, while passion as an articulation of finiteness opposes this union and with its negative inclination works towards contrariety, towards separateness, towards separation. How is the adverse effect of passion neutralized? It can be counteracted by love alone. Bare passion

> is fiercely individual and destructive, but dominated by the ideal of love, it has been made to flower into a perfection of beauty, becoming in its best expression symbolical of the spiritual truth in man which is his kinship of love with the Infinite. Thus we find it is the One which expresses itself in creation; and the Many, by giving up opposition, make the revelation of unity perfect.[19]

Love possesses the capacity to counterbalance the destructive impact of passion not by eliminating passion, but by transcending its inherent negativity and transforming the indwelling energies of passion into expressions of infinity. It is thus that the Bāul poet, having realized the pure potencies of love, gives out his warning to the human heart:

> Shut the doors / on the face of lust.
> Attain the greatest, / the unattainable man, / and
>   act / as the lovers act.
> Meet the death / before you die.[20]

Attain...the unattainable man, and...meet the death before you die - the power of love extends beyond merely deactivating adverse forces: love awakens the transcendental energies of joy and stimulates their

---

[19] Rabindranath Tagore, *Creative Unity*, p.8
[20] Gosāiñ Gopāl, quoted in Deben Bhattacharya, op.cit., p.64

creative potential. The driving force of love arouses the spirit of the infinite from within the finite and endows man with the ability to exceed the limits of his own finite existence. It is thus that the human soul becomes eligible to attain the unattainable, that man comes to meet the death before he dies. But how does the expansion of man's capacities function in the concrete? Which is the spiritual impetus, the spark of divinity that instigates the multiplication of human energies? It is the prospect of union, the prospect of love's fulfilment, the prospect of the pain of longing to give way to the bliss of attainment. It is the expectation raised by love's quest and affirmed by its own intrinsic truth. It is the certainty, the definiteness of hope to materialize, which finds its ultimate expression in the revelation of the Infinite: "I knew not when your doors opened and I stood surprised at my own heart's music"[21]. It is the manifestation of love's essence in the ultimate transcendental truth which, at the moment of union, leaves the singer voiceless - or else endowed with an abundant flow of transcendental melodies whose sweetness is beyond human imagination.

What does that mean? Love is the energy that enables the creative spirit to unfold, but in order to effectuate the actual process of creation, the bliss-giving potencies of love need to be released. How are these potencies released? - through fulfilment. That is to say, for love to become truly creative, the union of love must be feasible, because this union, because the joy arising out of this union is the indispensable prerequisite for the accumulation of creative energies. But is it not the quest for union, the quest to overcome an existing state of separation, which inspires creativity in the first place? Yes it is, but not alone: the quest for an unattainable end can never be productive, because it dies of its own limitedness. Creativity springs up when quest and fulfilment meet in active interplay, when union confirms its realness by time and again defeating separation. The call of love therefore is the call for union, and the response to that call is vital to establish the joy out of which creativity is born. Without the joy of union, all creative strains remain strangled, and the strings of the divine instrument are left forever unstruck, burying the cosmic song at the bottom of universal boredom. So then, can the poet's plea be inordinate when he entreats his lord for company? -

---

[21] Rabindranath Tagore, *Crossing*, L

> I ask for a moment's indulgence to sit by thy
> side. The works that I have in hand I will
> finish afterwards.
> Away from the sight of thy face my heart knows
> no rest nor respite, and my work becomes an
> endless toil in a shoreless sea of toil.
> Today the summer has come at my window with
> its sighs and murmurs; and the bees are
> plying their minstrelsy at the court of the
> flowering grove.
> Now it is time to sit quiet, face to face with thee,
> and to sing dedication of life in this silent and
> overflowing leisure.[22]

No, his plea is not inordinate. The quest for spiritual union, for union with the divine, the quest for the union of love can never be inordinate, hence the lover retains his full right to voice his request. But when is this call raised? The singer whose each and every song has been a pronouncement of his aspiration for the Infinite, the musician whose every single tune has been an offering to the Divine Lover - when will he say, "It was my part at this feast to play upon my instrument, and I have done all I could"[23]? When will he take heart to ask, "has the time come at last when I may go in and see thy face and offer my silent salutation?"[24]. The call is voiced when it is no more the part of the searching soul to proceed towards the other. It is raised when the seeker has no further to walk, when the singer has no melodies left, when the lover has exhausted himself in yearning, and union is yet to come. The plea for union is pronounced when the creative mind dwindles for lack of imaginative joy that can only be found in fulfilment. And this plea is not a demand - it is not the giver's insistence on reciprocation of his gift, but rather it is the elemental call for mutuality, for reciprocity of love which is vital to establish union. For spiritual union is not the unqualified mergence with an attributeless reality - it is the qualified attainment of the most sublime emotional quest: it is the fulfiment of love. It is the fulfilment of love which lives even through separation, for

---

[22] Rabindranath Tagore, *Gītāñjali*, V
[23] Rabindranath Tagore, *Gītāñjali*, XVI
[24] ibid.

"in love there's no separation, but commingling always"[25] - in love there is no separation, because even physical separation becomes spiritual union through the awareness of the one in the mind of the other.

The union of love is evoked through music, but what is the essence of this union? What is the essence of love? It is silence, silence in which all music culminates, silence in which the song offering finds its most perfect expression:

> Tell me, my silent master, / O my lord, / What
> worship may open me / to Brahma's lotus
> bloom.
> The stars and the moon eternally move, / with no
> sound at all.
> Each cycle of the universe / in silence prays, /
> welling up with the essence of love.[26]

But what is union? What does it mean, "to sing dedication of life in this silent and overflowing leisure"[27]? Union is surrender. Union is the complete submission of two souls to each other, the unconditional mutual self-offering of two spiritual entities striving to merge into one. Union is bliss - the bliss that is born of the supreme sacrifice of love. And union is music - the music of eternity reverberant in the infinite melody of the cosmos, the music whose sweetest tune is the song of the silent:

> Into the audience hall by the fathomless abyss
> where swells up the music of toneless strings
> I shall take this harp of my life.
> I shall tune it to the notes of forever, and when it
> has sobbed out its last utterance, lay down
> my silent harp at the feet of the silent.[28]

---

[25] Bāul song, quoted in Kshitimohan Sen, "The Bāul singers of Bengal", in Rabindranath Tagore, *The Religion of Man* (London: George Allen and Unwin Ltd., 1931), appendix 1, p.209

[26] Ishān Jugi, quoted in Deben Bhattacharya, op.cit., p.72

[27] Rabindranath Tagore, *Gītāñjalī*, V

[28] from Rabindranath Tagore, *Gītāñjalī*, C

10

Communication through music

No more noisy, loud words from me - such is
my master's will. Henceforth I deal in whispers.
The speech of my heart will be carried on in
murmurings of a song...

from Rabindranath Tagore, *Gītāñjalī*, LXXXIX

*The speech of my heart will be carried on in murmurings of a
song*, because the communicative power of music exceeds the eloquence
of speech. Language, speech draws on the potential of sound alone: the
recited syllable, the pronounced word derives its entire impact from the
inherent force of the sounding vibration. The more the wavelength of the
sound corresponds to the wavelength of the universe, the more intense
is the energetic effect of the recitation. Speech, if properly calculated in
its flow so as to meet with the course of the cosmic current, is therefore
apt to develop spiritual energies of immeasurable fervency able to
motivate even most static facts of universal existence when striking them
with unmitigated force. Speech is sound in the purest sense of the
phenomenon of sound, but is it music? No, it is not. Then what is
music? Music too is sound, but in what way is it different from speech?
What is it that distinguishes the sound of music from the sound of
speech?

The spoken word as a manifestation of cosmic energies is
immensely powerful inasmuch as it possesses the potential to invoke the
unseen forces of eternity through purposeful emission of the existential
fluids - but where is its emotional appeal? Energies that are multiplied by
way of coalescence do grow into formidable cosmic realities - yet their
impact lacks the ultimate capacity to install the infinite truth in its full
essence. Why? Because this impact yields results that are achieved by
coercion rather than by union, and the emerging spirit is the spirit of awe
rather than that of harmonious intimacy. The sound of speech is the
vehicle *par excellence* to evoke the omnipresence of divine mastery, but
its quest remains an end in itself without extending beyond the limits of
a finite, two-level existence. Based on the concept of supernatural
power, of extramundane potency, the idea of accumulating energies
merely by means of communicative compatibility nourishes the thought
of other-worldliness, of a definite and unchangeable separateness of the

two levels with man and the phenomenal world on the one side, and God and the spiritual world on the other. It is a concept in which

> God is a transcendental Being. He is in the transcendental realm, while we human beings are in the phenomenal realm, and these two realms are separate and unrelated. In this two-level concept, it is difficult for the transcendent God to relate to we humans on the phenomenal plane. Also, how can we relate to a fully transcendent God?[1]

In this two-level perception, speech is the mode of communication sufficient to establish the contact between the two spheres of being - a contact which is yet to develop into a relation. The relation calls for more than just approaching the one level while remaining on the other. A relation requires the dynamism of emotional involvement; it needs the subtleness of emotion which is vital to instigate the interaction between the two spheres. But how is emotional convolution brought about?

> Feelings and emotions can be worked out only in a very informal setting. The more informal the relation, the better. God must be totally informal with his devotees for affective spontaneity to exist.[2]

Informality, however, can arise only where there is mutual responsiveness, and this is not possible in a cosmic configuration dominated by power and uncontrolled proliferation of energies. The potency of speech, of deliberately employed, communicatively potent syllables and sound fragments, aims at the emancipation of power, without cherishing emotional aspirations of any kind. Speech does not appeal to the emotional consciousness of man, because the recited word does not address an emotional object. The sound of the pronounced syllable, powerful and energy-laden though, exposes itself as a bare physical phenomenon devoid of sweetness - devoid of the sweetness of

---

[1] Shrivatsa Goswami, in an interview with Steven J. Gelberg, Vrindaban, 12 March 1982
[2] ibid.

music, devoid of the sweetness which is the quintessence of all emotional pursuits.

It is the naked physicality of spoken sound which binds it to the concept of dualism, to the two-level understanding of universal life. Why? Because physicalness is an expression of the finite which finds its final gratification in the affirmation of the duality. Emotion, however, is nurtured by sweetness which is the essence of infinity. The emotional quest, therefore, directs its ambition not at approval, but at abolishment of the duality. The core motive of emotionality is to transcend the duality which is an embodiment of finitude, and to establish the supremacy of infinity. Consequentially, what does this imply for the conception of the two spheres, the phenomenal and the transcendental realms? The two levels have to be mutually accessible; they have to exist in a dynamism of active exchange, allowing not only for contact, for communication between the two entities, but for reciprocal communication qualified to grow into a relation. What is more, in order to effectuate a communication beyond the ties of the finite, the relation has to be established on an equal level:

> God and the humans have to be on the same
> level, so to speak. There must be a one-level
> relationship. Either you have to rise up to the
> transcendental realm, or God has to descend to
> the phenomenal realm.[3]

How is the equality of relation achieved? How is the emotional quest attempted? Which is the instrument to induce a mutually responsive mode of communication? It is music. It is music which combines in its fluid the energetic power of sound with the transcendental sweetness of joy. Music is superior to speech because, unlike the sound of speech, the sound of music inherits the harmoniousness of the tune, which fills the universe with unbounded delight. If speech possesses the capacity to amass energies by emitting sounds that correspond to the cosmic vibrations, music surpasses the mastery of speech by adding the joy of the melody to the union of matching sound waves. Thus, the impact of music reaches beyond the

---

[3] ibid.

impact of speech because in music, the blankness of bare sound is transformed into the fullness of creative beauty. Speech invokes power whereas music forfeits its claim to power in order to capture the universe with its indwelling melodiousness. The spoken syllable neglects emotion, but for the tune, emotion is the ultimate essence of life. The utterance of words suffices to instigate a communication between two levels, but the musical melody alone can make the two levels meet.

It is music that possesses the ability to transcend the limits of the finite and to transform the duality of the phenomenal and transcendental worlds into an interactive unity, but how does the process of tranformation practically function? Realizing the increased capacity of music over speech, the poet acknowledges that the path towards his spiritual goal is walkable only for the music-maker, and so he decides that "the speech of my heart will be carried on in murmurings of a song". Yet as long as the two levels persist, the ultimate object continues to be inaccessible. Therefore, "either you have to rise up to the transcendental realm, or God has to descend to the phenomenal realm". The two of them have to meet on one and the same plane, because union is not possible if the Supreme Being remains on the one level and man on the other. Consequently union signifies the meeting-point of the two realms; in union, the unity of the two spheres of existence is fully accomplished. But how is this union achieved in the concrete? Is it man who ascends to the transcendental plane, or is it the Supreme Soul who comes down to the human level?

It is neither way - or both ways. The process of cosmic mergence is in reality much more complex than to simply imply the descent of the one or the ascent of the other. Linked to the quest for spiritual accomplishment, it is a process which requires active involvement from both ends. Man alone cannot rise to the level of the divine unless the Infinite Being elevates him, and God on his part has no need to leave his abode of cosmic aloofness without being urged by some compelling commitment. But he does leave, hence a commitment must be there. What is this commitment? It is the bond of love which ties the Supreme Soul to the human soul. It is his love for the human being which makes the limitless one time and again manifest himself in the realm of the limitable, which makes the formless one continually reveal himself in the form, which makes the timeless one constantly revel in the delight of the momentary. It is the love between opposites which instigates the dissolution of the two-level reality into the cosmic truth of oneness. And it is this very love which enables and at the same time requires the communication between the two spheres of existence, because communication is the vital factor to set the flow of love in motion.

What is that to say? Interactive communication arises only when the communicating entities are settled on one and the same level, but in order to establish a one-level relationship, communication is imperative. It is in the process of communication that the two sides approach each other, that the two communicating forces move closer together. Which is the medium of communication? It is music, because the phenomenon of music results from a dialectic process whose object is the dispersal of an existing duality through reciprocal communication. In the process of music-making, therefore, the mergence of the two levels of perception into a single universal entity is accomplished in a most natural way. Music, more than being merely a communicative tool such as speech, qualifies as the adhesive agent that instigates the coalescence of contrary forces, because music functions through its emotional appeal whose impact adds the motivating force to the communicative act.

How is communication through music achieved? Why is it that music extends its influence beyond plain conversational facts? What potency capacitates music to tranform the transmission of blunt power into the transmission of subtle emotional energy? What is it that turns conversation into communication, and communication into communion? The answer lies in the emotional relationship that exists at the basis of each and every musical activity as the vital essence of the creative quest. An instant of music always requires a duality: the one who plays and the one who hears, the music-maker and the listener. The duality necessarily implies a two-level constellation, with music emanating from one plane and reaching out to the other. The sounding creation is conceived on the one level and perceived on the other, and more than that, its only purpose is to transgress the boundaries of its realm of origin. The tune which remains hidden in the singer's mind, the melody which clings to the strings of the unstruck instrument does not liberate itself from the limits of its own level of existence, hence it has no communicative qualities at all. Silence, even if fully charged with musical imagination, is an uncommunicative condition, and only once this silence dissolves into song, only once the sound of music breaks forth is the communication between the realms of the singer and the listener activated.

Music involves the dual presence of a musician and a music-listener, but how does this duality relate to the two-level cosmological order? The primeval constellation in the process of music-making is that in which the music-maker and the listener are settled on different perceptional planes. That is, both the divine level and the realm of humanity are engaged in the creation of the musical reality, and the shifting of the duality on one and the same level, such as in a setting of human musicians and audience, signifies but an extension of the cosmic two-level arrangement. Why, however, are the rôles in the universal game of music distributed between entities pertaining to different spiritual planes? The reason is the function of music within the larger structure of cosmic existence. The two levels of perception are a definite reality, but their dualism is not the ultimate truth which is oneness. The primary quest of being is to dissolve the duality, to melt the two levels into one. How does this object become feasible? The most obvious way is to establish "links between the transcendental and the phenomenal. But although those links are there, God himself remains on the transcendental level"[4] - and that is the problem.

Mere linkage incites the communication between the two levels, but it is not sufficient to bring about their unity. Communication is achieved through links, but communion requires qualified links. Qualified in what sense? The bond that connects the two spheres of existence must be an emotional one. What is more, this bond must have love for its core substance, because it is the positive essence of joy that holds together the strings of cosmic harmony. Love is the fundamental truth at the heart of any spiritual relationship, and it is love that activates the communication between the levels of the human and the divine in the first place. The language of love, however, is the language of emotion, hence it calls for a medium fit to express all strains and nuances of emotionality. Speech is ineligible for lack of an emotional appeal. Music possesses the needed emotive potential, but it is more than its inherent energetic substance that entitles music to endow communication with the

---

4 ibid.

momentum of mutuality and thereby to instigate the communication of love - the communication between lovers.

What is the cause of this increased capacity of music? It is the emotional attitude at the basis of the process of music-making, which is the attitude of creative sacrifice. Every act of music-making is at the same time an act of offering: the musician offers his tune to the listener, the lover his melody to the beloved as a testimony of love. Since the universal course of music-making implies an interaction between the two levels of existence, between the transcendental and the phenomenal realms, musical activity leads necessarily to a continual exchange of emotional gifts between the two planes. The human singer who directs his song to the Divine Listener effectuates more than solely an outbreak of tunes: his first and foremost intent is the spiritual offering, and whether he enwraps it in a mantle of sounds or of different creative material is secondary for that matter. Yet more, the decisive criterion for the spiritual success it is not the offering either, but the contact with the divinity established through the offering. Why? Because an offering of love, an emotional gift exchanged between lovers, prompts communication: mutually responsive communication, that is, communion - and more than that, union.

Is that to say that the human musician, by offering his melody to the Divine Lover, attains union with God? Does this mean that, by dedicating his song to the Supreme Soul, man himself rises from the phenomenal level to the transcendental realm? Yes, it is so, but only on the condition that man commits himself in his entirety, fully and unconditionally. And this is what happens in the cosmic process of music-making: the union of contradicting forces is induced through the act of music-making, which is essentially a manifestation of the quest of love, a sublimated expression of selfless love in its most rarefied essence. Offering through music becomes the means *par excellence* for man to accomplish the ascent to the transcendental level, because it implies self-surrender to the divinity in music. In other words, the musical offering embodies the supreme sacrifice of love, and through this sacrifice, man acquires the capacity to transcend the limitations of his own physical existence and to become one with the Supreme Reality.

But is it always the human being who has to rise up to the transcendental plane in order to instate a one-level relationship with the Supreme Being? No, it is not. Interactive communication takes two ways, and music too takes two directions in the creative cyclism of eternity. The human singer who consecrates his tune wholeheartedly to the transcendental listener may become competent to enter the spheres of the infinite without physically separating himself from the phenomenal world, but what happens to the human listener who conceives the message from his transcendent lover in the guise of the melody sent out by the Divine Music-maker? Does not the arrival of the cosmic song signify the descent of the divine? Is not the message one with the messenger, the tune one with the singer? The music of the transcendental reveals itself as an inspiration in the mind of the human recipient, but is not every strain of divine imagination in reality a manifestation of the selfsame divinity emitting that imagination? And is not the musical message actually a message of love, a message through which the Eternal Lover proclaims his commitment to the human soul? Yes, it is, but how could this commitment be real if not the Supreme Soul would relate to man on one and the same level? How could God's love become consummate if he remains on one plane an his human lover on another?

Yet the communicative mechanism is an intricate, complex framework whose functioning is not restricted to a one-destination process of mergence. For union of the two cosmic spheres to be accomplished, it is not that *either* man has to ascend to the transcendental realm *or* God has to come down to the phenomenal realm, but the dynamism of a creative unity requires man to rise up to the transcendental plane *and* God to descend to the level of humanity. Why is that? Is it not illogical if both man and the divinity move to the respective other realm? Is it not perverse to re-establish the two-level concept with reversed rôles rather than to overcome the duality? Yes, it were so if man's ascent and the Supreme Being's descent would take place simultaneously. But this is not the case. If the human singer and the Divine Music-maker would render their melodies both at the same time, who were there to listen? And if the human listener and the Divine Listener would lend their ears both at once to the cosmic tune, who would generate the tune? The process of music-making is a dialectic process: it requires the duality of the one who sings and the one who listens. The dialectic mechanism calls for exchangeable rôles, but still there will always be the one who creates and the one who perceives.

So what then does it mean that *both* man *and* the divinity have to move to the respective other plane in order to make the mergence of the cosmic realms complete? Union is feasible only on one and the same level, but it is not bound to be accomplished on just one level. To the contrary, the universal current of existence constantly reverses its flow, and so does the current of cosmic music that carries the two realm to confluence. Why? Because creativity, which is the source for all music, hence for all spiritual attainment, can arise only from an active interplay of the two perceptual spheres. The process of universal music-making, therefore, can be nourished by creativity only if it involves *both* the human musician and the Divine Listener, *and* the Divine Musician and the human listener. In the concrete, that means that the musical offering continually commutes between destination and origin, origin and destination: presented by the human singer to the Eternal Listener, it is returned to man as a spiritual offering of musical inspiration. What is it that effectuates this persistent reversal - or rather cyclic flow - of the musical current? It is the principle of mutual responsiveness which is vital to establish and sustain the interactive communication between the realms of the phenomenal and the transcendental. It is the law of reciprocity, of reciprocal exchange that enables the union of dual forces, hence the establishment of a one-level relationship above the two-level actuality.

Communication is necessary wherever there is a relationship, and if this relationship is an active one, communication must take a mutual, two-way direction. A communication that lacks responsiveness fails to establish the desired spiritual bond between the communicating entities: "What is the use of calling someone who does not respond? What evidence do I have that he can hear my heart?"[5]. If the response from the one end does not come, the effort from the other end is wasted, because it is that very response which affirms the existence of a spiritual kinship between the two forces longing to meet. One-way communication without even the expectation of a reply may be sufficient in a passive

---

[5] Gobinda Dās, quoted in Deben Bhattacharya, *The mirror of the sky* (London: Allen & Unwin, 1969), p.60

instant of contact - in an inactive relation free from claims to reciprocity, but it certainly does not work for a relationship whose quest is an emotional one. Why? Because the object of the emotional aspiration is union through communication, rather than communication for its own sake as it is the case with an impersonal approach. That is to say, the emotional intention aims at the entity on the other end of the communicative string, whereas a disinterested attitude can be satisfied with the mere process of communication without yielding an impact on the communicator. With union being the higher goal of the communicative process, communication comes to serve the achievement of that goal by establishing the unity of the two communicative levels. It is this purposefulness which marks the essential difference between communication governed by emotional involvement on the one hand and communication between mutually detached forces on the other hand.

A mode of communication that limits itself to merely exchanging messages between two levels without aspiring a bond of relationship is incompatible with the quest of music whose essence is love, hence reciprocity. But what happens if even the non-appreciative exchange of messages becomes impossible for absolute lack of responsiveness from one level? If communication is continuously activated from the one level, but no sign of reception emitted from the other level? In the cosmic course of action, what is the consequence if the Supreme Being on the transcendental plane constantly withdraws himself from the message sent out by man on the phenomenal level, or if man remains completely irresponsive to the subtle vibrations of the infinite? The ensuent reaction depends on the perceptive attitude towards the relation between the two spheres. In a passive relationship, the response is not needed, because man on the phenomenal plane fulfils his spiritual duty by merely communicating his intents towards the divine forces on the transcendental level; his object is the act of communication rather than its result. The two levels of existence remain separate and detached from each other, and their dualism is accepted in complete disregard of the eternal truth of unity.

In a relationship of love, however, non-responsiveness becomes fatal for the relation on the whole. Determined by the quest for unity, a personally inclined relationship intends to link the two levels of communication, and emotion is the linking substance, the connecting fluid that melts the two spheres into one. The message communicated from the one level to the other in any such relationship, therefore, is an emotional message, which calls for a response from the heart of the one to whom it is directed. Without this response, communication remains a vain effort, for "what evidence do I have that he can hear my heart?"[6]. More so, if one of the two communicators keeps himself aloof, there can be no communication altogether, and without communication, the relationship cannot be tied which is vital to evoke the creative union between separate spiritual entities. Communication through music is the core element of the quest for union, but music becomes eligible as a medium of communication only once mutual responsiveness has been established. The singer cannot render his tune before an indifferent listener, because a disinterested listener is no listener, whereas the process of music-making requires the dual presence of musician and listener in order to activate the stimulative flow of inspiration. And *vice versa*, the listener cannot delight in music without the music-maker to create the melody.

Why is it that music cannot break forth as a process of communication without the mutual interest of both communicative agents involved? The reason is the emotional essence of music, its inborn quest which is the quest of love. Love is primarily an exchange of emotions, and the union of love is the communion of feelings. The love between two souls implies mutual sharing of sentiments, and that means these sentiments have to be communicated to the respective other soul. How are they communicated? - through music, because music as an emotional current is the principal conveyor of cosmic sweetness. If sentiments cannot be exchanged because the way of communication is blocked by non-responsiveness from one end, the resulting effect is pain - an immense sensation of pain arising from the disunion enforced by the unsympathetic attitude of the inconsiderate soul. It is the agony of separation, paired with a deep sense of hopelessness aroused by the fact that the motive of disunion is not a disbandable outside influence but lies within the soul of the beloved.

But can the state of reticence persist for ever? Can the loving soul remain eternally deprived of the message of love? Is it possible for the

---

[6] ibid.

one to permanently withdraw himself from all communication while the call of the other is doomed to fade in an abyss of irresponsiveness? In a relationship of love no, it is not. Because love is truth, hence its quest for union is bound to fulfil. In love, silence as an expression of uncommunicativeness can only be temporary, for the cosmic truth is the truth of union - of music:

> If thou speakest not I will fill my heart with thy
> silence and endure it. I will keep still and wait
> like the night with starry vigil and its head
> bent low with patience.
> The morning will surely come, the darkness will
> vanish, and thy voice pour down in golden
> streams breaking through the sky.
> Then thy words will take wing in songs from
> every one of my birds' nests, and thy
> melodies will break forth in flowers in all my
> forest groves.[7]

The poet knows instinctively that if his love is true, the Divine Lover's response cannot be denied to him forever, and it is this inner sureness that endows him with the strength to transcend the momentary pain of separation and to keep the creative current of his music in motion. What is it that establishes this firm conviction of indifference ultimately yielding to communicativeness, of separateness eventually giving way to union, of agony finally turning into bliss? It is the intrinsic truth, the realness of love and the reality of love's fulfilment. The very fact that the flow of music does not stop in the presence of a seemingly irresponsive listener encourages the musician to play on, because it tells him that the taciturn listener is not uninvolved but, at long last, is certain to respond. The very fact that love persists even against a non-respondent lover affirms the truth of this love and attests the feasibility of its final attainment despite the odds of temporary muteness.

What is the deeper meaning of this existential truth? He who discerns the most subtle reality of cosmic love, who realizes the realness of the ultimate unity of spiritual forces, and who appreciates the

---

[7] Rabindranath Tagore, *Gītāñjalī*, XIX

inevitable instant of their union, acquires the emotional strength to withstand all strains of separation and to enter the realm of universal joy through the door of pain. Singing before a vividly respondent listener is an easy game, but the one who sustains the melody through the desert of non-respondency is acclaimed by eternity. Surrendering one's heart to an affectionate lover is common talk, but the one who keeps his love alive in the face of his lover's indifference becomes truly entitled to the supreme sacrifice of love. It is that same truth about which the Bāul poet reflects when he observes -

> The lunar eclipse / in the night of the full moon /
>   is known to all.
> But no one enquires / about the blackened moon /
>   on the darkest night / of the month...

> *He who is able to make / the full moon rise / in*
>   *the sky / of the darkest night,*
> *has a right to claim / the glory of the three*
>   *worlds...*[8]

Which is the emotive power that enables man to transcend the limits of the impossible? What makes the lover uphold the voice of love against the silence of indifference? Which energy is adequate to accomplish union through separation, to incite communication in the wake of reticence? It is love itself. Therefore, "reaching for reality / is lame talk / to describe the goal / of the lover-worshipper. ... / He will attain / the great unattainable, / stare at the face / of the invisible one, / bearing the nectar of love..."[9].

What is more, it is that same 'lover-worshiper' who qualifies for the highest spiritual union that conjoins the two levels of universal existence. It is not rational links that can unite the worlds of man on the phenomenal plane and of God on the transcendental plane. The only link that can induce their mergence is the cosmic link already existent, the inconceivable yet omnipresent and all-pervading energy of joy that envelopes the spheres of the universe in their full boundlessness. In its infinite subtlety, the unifying flow withdraws itself from the capacity of

---

[8] Gosāiñ Gopāl, quoted in Deben Bhattacharya, op.cit., pp.65-6
[9] Gosāiñ Gopāl, quoted in Deben Bhattacharya, op.cit., p.65

human discernment, hence the Bāul singer admonishes his heart to retain its awareness of this most sublime essence of bliss: "The man that breathes, / lives on the air, / and the other, unseen, / rests above reach. / Between the two, / moves another man / as a secret link. / Worship knowingly"[10]. The elemental truth of universal life lies in the intrinsic oneness of the transcendental and phenomenal realms, of the Supreme Soul and the human soul - so why then the two-level manifestation of cosmic creation? "It is a sport / amongst the three of them. / My searching heart, / whom do you seek?"[11]. It is nothing but a masterful game that the Creator plays in order to stimulate the vital energies of imaginative inspiration. It is the game of universal communicativeness - and the game of cosmic music.

And - it is a dialectic game. "Only from a marriage of two forces does music arise in the world"[12] - hence the eternal truth of oneness must come forth in a two-fold revelation in order to be creative. "Only from a marriage of two forces does music arise" - but how could the marriage be performed if music were not there in the first place? For without music, how would the communication between the two forces be instigated, how their union accomplished? Music is the utmost thing; it is complete in itself, rising "on its own joy from the depths of the heart"[13]. It is music that activates the dialectic game of creation, the eternal play of music-making and listening, of offering and receiving, of separating and uniting in an endless cycle of pain and bliss - only to eventually culminate in the infinite truth of cosmic harmony in which all musical currents merge into one single ocean of silence.

---

[10] Gosāiñ Gopāl, quoted in Deben Bhattacharya, op.cit., p.64
[11] ibid.
[12] Rabindranath Tagore, *Broken Song*
[13] ibid.

Service through music

This is my prayer to thee, my lord - strike, strike
  at the root of penury in my heart.
Give me the strength lightly to bear my joys and
  sorrows.
Give me the strength to make my love fruitful in
  service.
Give me the strength never to disown the poor or
  bend my knees before insolent might.
Give me the strength to raise my mind high
  above daily trifles.
And give me the strength to surrender my
  strength to thy will with love.

Rabindranath Tagore, *Gītāñjalī*, XXXVI

Give me the strength to make my love fruitful in service...And give me the strength to surrender my strength to thy will with love. The poet's modest prayer is more than the personal appeal for divine assistance raised by a solitary heart tried in the world of hardship. A single devoted soul's plea resounds in an unending reverberation from each and every corner of the universe, swelling into a mighty current of devotional energy whose ardent glow fills the transcendent sea with the most sublime fluid of love. The humble entreaty, in an instant of earnest submission, expresses indeed the core quest of cosmic existence: it voices the call for love, for creative accomplishment of love through dedicated worship. Because love is fulfilled in action, in activity: the truthfulness of love consists in its attitude of surrender, hence love takes its prime manifestation in service.

Why is it that love, in order to become consummate, needs to be released in service? Which pressing force compels love to attest its own veracity in the trial of surrender? It is the inherent necessity of inward energies to be discharged in outward action, the need to crystallize the transcendental stream of emotion through definite manifestations of creative activity, which emerges from the existential truth that spiritual entities cannot find freedom within the confines of their own, hence cannot be brought to fulfilment in themselves. The soul accomplishes its emancipation in action, in activity, because being active enables the soul to unfold its full imaginative potential in complete liberation from the strains of inactive freedom. What is that to say? Inactivity implies freedom, action bondage, yet it is in activity alone that true freedom is found, out of which arises the joy that is vital for creation to come forth. Joy is born from freedom - but not from the unqualified freedom of inaction. For joy to take root, the freedom of the soul must be qualified. Qualified in what sense? The freedom that creates joy extends within the rules of cosmic law rather than outside the law, and this freedom is obtained by transcending the bounds rather than neglecting them. It is this very freedom within bonds, the freedom within the bounds of law which leads to the joy that is the cause of all action: "When, verily, one obtains happiness, then one is active. Having obtained unhappiness, one is not active. Only having obtained happiness one is active"[1].

Constructive freedom is not lawless liberty, but is achieved in compliance with the cosmic law of action. Activity, therefore, is the key to the soul's deliverance from the snares of unfulfilled longing:

> ...as joy expresses itself in law, so the soul finds its freedom in action. It is because joy cannot find expression in itself alone that it desires the law which is outside. Likewise it is because the soul cannot find freedom within itself that it wants external action. The soul of man is ever freeing itself from its own folds by its activity[2].

If joy can be revealed only in the freedom of action, love as the quintessence of joy requires the same freedom in order to entirely set free its emotive force. What is the reason? Love is an energetic bond stretched between two spiritual entities, between two souls. This energetic bond is not a static link, but a dynamic vibration that needs to be constantly re-established through constructive action. What is constructive action? It is activity determined by love's intrinsic spirit of surrender: constructive action is service. The soul which is bound by a relationship of love becomes truly free when its love is accomplished in fulfilment, but for this, the soul has to come out of itself in service, in

---

[1] Chāndogya Upaniṣad 7.22.1 *yadā vai sukhaṃ labhate 'tha karoti, nāsukhaṃ labdhvā karoti, sukham eva labdhvā karoti...*
[2] Rabindranath Tagore, *Sādhanā* (London: Macmillan and Co. Ltd., 1914), p.120

constructive action. Why? Because the human soul attains fulfilment, hence finds its freedom only in union with the Supreme Soul, its Eternal Lover. And this union is achieved through service, through activity directed towards the aspired object, through action dedicated to the soul of the beloved.

Of what kind is this constructive action, the service that possesses the inherent spiritual power to establish joy and to evoke the blissful state of consummate love? Which activity is suitable to be performed as service? Basically, it can be anything. Even the most trivial act in human life, if dominated by an indwelling sense of surrender, qualifies as service, as worship. Yet it is music which becomes particularly eligible as a mode of service because of its implicit emotional attitude: music is the sounding embodiment of the idea of surrender, while at the same time music-making represents the core process of outward action needed to incite the emergence of spiritual freedom. That is to say, the tune obtains its freedom only once it is discharged in the sway of relieved musical sounds, not in the hesitant silence of musical thought. Release of the melody, however, calls for readiness on the part of the musician to surrender his song to the listener, for once the tune is set free, the singer inevitably has to part with it. Therefore every act of musical articulation is essentially an act of surrender - of service.

But which is the transcendent substance at the core of the musical fluid? It is love - love that derives its spiritual excellence from the power of submission:

> Only a connoisseur
> of the flavours of love
> can comprehend
> the language of a lover's heart,
> others have no clue.
> ...
> Submission is the secret of knowledge.[3]

Submission is the secret of knowledge - and of love. Music as the fundamental, most spontaneous expression of love lives from its inborn

---

[3] Anon, quoted in Deben Bhattacharya, *The mirror of the sky* (London: Allen & Unwin, 1969), p.41

eagerness to give out its all in complete surrender to its object of emotional aspiration. Consequently, musical activity cannot arise without being governed by the spirit of submission, without the musician's willingness to submit himself through the act of music-making. What is more, the generation of the sounding reality at the hands of the music-maker signifies more than the musician merely parting with his tune: his act of releasing the melody is not forfeiture but surrender, not relinquishment but offering. The musician does not lose his music upon giving up his sole claim to the sounding tune - he rather makes it truly his own by dedicating it to the beloved of his heart. How is that? Dedication is worship, and worship is service - service determined by love, which implies the sacrifice brought for the sake of love. Love's sacrifice, the surrender to the lover can never yield impoverishment, because its core intention is to bring the dual manifestation of a single emotional energy to its creative union. Surrender therefore results in enrichment rather than penury - in enrichment called forth through the unity of creative forces, through the union of the worshiper and the worshiped, the offerer and the recipient, the music-maker and the listener.

Surrender prompts union, but can there be mergence between two souls without mutual submission? Can man attain to the divine without fully dedicating his entire being to the Supreme Soul? And can the divinity become one with the human being without surrendering himself in his entire infinite essence to humanity? No, it is not possible, because without the joy of reciprocal commitment, no soul could exist. Because the soul "only finds the fulfilment of joy in its outward excursions...It cannot live on its own internal feelings and imaginings. It is ever in need of external objects; not only to feed its inner consciousness but to apply itself in action, *not only to receive but also to give*"[4]. And therefore, in order to qualify for the act of giving, the one soul needs to reach out to the other. Yet more, merely reaching out is not enough for an act of offering: the approach must be coupled with the spirit of submission to turn giving into surrender, sacrifice into worship.

Music, which is rendered essentially as a gift of love, emerges as the exemplary symbol of surrender in the course of universal creativity.

---

[4] Rabindranath Tagore, op.cit., p.125

At the same time, the process of music-making represents the archetypal action to affirm the fundamental truth of joy rising up from the freedom established through the bonds of cosmic law. Just as joy is not found outside the rules of eternity, music itself cannot surface as long as these rules are disobeyed:

> it is only when we wholly submit to the bonds of truth that we fully gain the joy of freedom. And how? As does the string that is bound to the harp. When the harp is truly strung, when there is not the slightest laxity in the strength of the bond, then only does music result; and the string transcending itself in its melody finds at every chord its true freedom. It is because it is bound by such hard and fast rules on the one side that it can find this range of freedom in music on the other. While the string was not true, it was indeed merely bound; but a loosening of its bondage would not have been the way to freedom, which it can only fully achieve by being bound tighter and tighter till it has attained the true pitch[5].

Submission to the bonds of truth means to "gain the joy of freedom" - and to gain the joy of music. But what does music as such imply? - submission to the bonds of love. Love is truth, hence submission to the bonds of love is submission to the bonds of truth, and signifies attainment of both the joy of music and the joy of freedom - that is, attainment of the joy of freedom in music. Why? Because music expresses surrender, and surrender implies the freedom of fulfilled love - the joy of pain subdued, the joy of separation vanquished.

The Bāul singer proclaims, "submission is the secret of knowledge", but which intrinsic quality is it that empowers submission to act as the prime force of liberation? Surrender is the key to the door of love, but which energy adds the strength to push the door open? It is selflessness. True love can never be selfish, because the very spirit of

---

[5] Rabindranath Tagore, op.cit., p.128

self-interest contradicts the essence of love which is sacrifice: self-sacrifice. Selfishness disqualifies the soul from the quest for love: "How can you walk / the ways of love, / carrying stolen loot / with impunity? // In the forest of Brinda [Brindāban] / ... / *loving is worshipping*"[6]. Love is worship, love is service, because in service, in worship is it that selflessness finds its fullest accomplishment. What implication does selflessness bear in the concrete? Selfless surrender requires dedicated action and the soul's self-dedication likewise -

> That is to say, the soul is to dedicate itself to Brahma through all its activities. This dedication is the song of the soul, in this is its freedom. Joy reigns when all work becomes the path to the union with Brahma; when the soul ceases to return constantly to its own desires; when in it our self-offering grows more and more intense. Then there is completion, then there is freedom[7].

It is through this dedication that love becomes selfless, and through selflessness that love turns into one single articulation of service immensely deep in its emotional intensity. And it is through that selfsame act of service that love turns into worship, loving into worshiping.

But how is selflessness induced in the first place? - through love. Love is the motivating impetus that prompts the soul to rebel against the strains of selfishness and to commence its crusade against desire. It is love that thus stimulates its own fulfilment, a "fulfilment which is reached by love's emancipating us from the dominance of the self"[8]. Selflessness is the essence of sacrifice, hence service, while at the same time it is the essence of love which finds its most sublime manifestation in the dedicated pureness of the musical melody. Why is it music which symbolizes the flawless substance of self-delivery in the most excellent way? The reason lies in the capacity of music to extract the positive essence from each and every emotional vibration, thereby adding its

---

[6] Hāude Gosāiñ, quoted in Deben Bhattacharya, op.cit., p.69

[7] Rabindranath Tagore, op.cit., pp.128f.

[8] Rabindranath Tagore, *Creative Unity* (New Delhi: Macmillan India Ltd., reprint 1995), p.76

expressive strength to the subtle sweetness of love. Music thus becomes the crucial factor of motion in the struggle against the destructive potencies of selfish desire. In what way is the negative impact of desire practically rendered ineffective? - through reversal of the downward currents of vulgarity implicit in desire: "desires ordinarily flow downward towards animality. The endeavour of the expanding spirit is to turn their current upwards towards the light"[9]. The core effort of the spiritual quest is to upraise the declining currents, but how? "They must be raised by the force of love"[10], for "love is my golden touch - it turns desire into service"[11].

Love is the creative energy capable of reversing the negative currents of selfish intention and to transform them into the positive essence of sacrifice, and therefore the Bāul singer, spiritually enriched by his emotional experience of love, insists that "love is the magic stone, that transmutes by its touch greed into sacrifice"[12]. But love's touch incites yet more than the refinement of crude desire into dedicated sacrifice, more even than the transformation of self-indulgence into selflessness. *Loving is worshiping* - the full meaning of our Bāul's statement extends beyond merely overturning the adverse impact of desire, of selfishness: loving becomes worshiping only when love's play is made meaningful through service, when the fugitive desires of the imperfect are subtilized into permanent values of love -

In the night when noise is tired the murmur of
the sea fills the air.
The vagrant desires of the day come back to their
rest round the lighted lamp.
Love's play is stilled into worship, life's stream
touches the deep, and the world of forms
comes to its nest in the beauty beyond all
forms.[13]

---

[9] Kshitimohan Sen, "The Bāul singers of Bengal", in Rabindranath Tagore, *The Religion of Man* (London: George Allen and Unwin Ltd., 1931), appendix 1, p.218
[10] ibid.
[11] Bāul song, quoted in Kshitimohan Sen, op.cit., p.219
[12] Rabindranath Tagore's translation of the Bāul song quoted above (cf. fn.11), in *The Religion of Man*, p.111
[13] Rabindranath Tagore, *Crossing*, XIV

Love's play is stilled into worship - love's play is distilled into worship, for worship transcends the play of love by making it purposeful, by transforming the idle play of pleasure into the creative play of dedicated service. Worship is the meaningful essence of love; it is active love which fills the lover's heart with a sense of substantiality and makes him conscious of his own life's usefulness. Hence the poet prays -

> Pick up this life of mine from the dust.
> Keep it under your eyes, in the palm of your
>   right hand.
> Hold it up in the light, hide it under the shadow
>   of death; keep it in the casket of the night
>   with your stars, and then in the morning let it
>   find itself among the flowers that blossom in
>   worship.[14]

- and his prayer is the primordial outcry of the devoted soul yearning for liberation from the bonds of aimlessness, for emancipation from the limits of a meaningless existence in which the fulfilment of love becomes but an illusive fancy.

Loving is worshiping - but what is worship, what is service in its true essence? In the Indian tradition, service is regarded as more than merely an end to achieve spiritual attainment. *Sevā hī parama dharma hai* - dedicated worship, *sevā*, is truth (*dharma*), and it is cosmic law (*dharma*). More than that, service is *parama dharma* - the highest truth, the ultimate law of existence.

> That is why I would say that the true striving in
> the quest of truth, of *dharma*, consists not in the
> neglect of action but in the effort to attune it
> closer and closer to the eternal harmony.[15]

Service is worship, worship service, but in its core meaning *sevā* is the active manifestation of the supreme transcendental truth - of the truth of love. And which is the primary tool in the hands of the lover-worshiper? It is music. In the universal game of creation, it is the service of the

---

[14] Rabindranath Tagore, *Crossing*, XVII
[15] Rabindranath Tagore, *Sādhanā*, p.128

singer which is the most called for, because without the motivating potency of the music concealed in his songs, the creative flow of life cannot be instigated. But why then is the singer himself, the creator of the life-giving tune, reluctant to acknowledge the necessity for his presence in the cosmic play? What is it that makes him bluntly state, "I am here to sing thee songs. In this hall of thine I have a corner seat. / In thy world I have no work to do; my useless life can only break out in tunes without a purpose"[16]?

The reason is the transcendent quality of music which makes the melody appear purposeless on the surface: music cannot be wilfully subjected to service in terms of physical action; music cannot be made an ordinary utensil for worship bound to material rituality, such as a flower, a light, or an incense stick. Why? Because music is worship in its very essence; because the act of music-making is in itself an act of service. The fragrance of the flower, the flame of the candle, the smoke of incense alone does not make a statement of love, but music does. Music is the melodious embodiment of self-dedication, hence even the seemingly meaningless tune bears at its core the full significance of love's sacrifice. What is more, the singer has the advantage that his attendance is constantly required to sustain the creative game, hence he partakes of the Supreme Soul's company in every single moment that he fills with his song: "When the hour strikes for thy silent worship at the dark temple of midnight, command me, my master, to stand before thee to sing. / When in the morning air the golden harp is tuned, honour me, commanding my presence"[17]. The singer's music is his worship, and his worship is his music. It is this selfsame music of service, the service through music that makes his "useless life...only break[ing] out in tunes without a purpose" truly meaningful, because the "tunes without a purpose" are there exactly to add purpose - the purpose of worship - to the musical flow.

If it is the attitude of surrender, the object of worship, which makes music intrinsically meaningful, it is the inborn sweetness of the musical melody that attaches the decisive emotional motivation to the act of worship. Music is the tuneful articulation of the sacrifice of love, of

---

[16] Rabindranath Tagore, *Gītāñjali*, XV
[17] ibid.

the sacrifice brought time and again in the process of active service to the lover. The sounding creation thus becomes the immediate fruit of the music-maker's self-surrender to the listener who embodies the spirit of the beloved. But does not self-offering, self-relinquishment imply pain? Yes, in its most immediate sense it does, but the pain of sacrifice is transcended by the fulfilment attained in the purposeful action of worshiping, in the purposefulness of service:

> Pluck this little flower and take it, delay not! I
>   fear lest it droop and drop into the dust.
> It may not find a place in thy garland, *but honour*
>   *it with a touch of pain from thy hand* and
>   pluck it. I fear lest the day end before I am
>   aware, and the time of offering go by.
> Though its colour be not deep and its smell be
>   faint, use this flower in thy service and pluck
>   it while there is time.[18]

How is it possible that the spirit of worship not only transcends the pain of sacrifice, but even transforms that pain into the bliss of attainment? *Honour it with a touch of pain from thy hand* - it is the momentum of love within the sacrifice, the plain truth that the acceptance of pain at the hands of the lover signifies unconditional surrender as the essential quality of love. That is to say, more important than the phenomenon of pain is the fact that by inflicting pain upon his beloved, the lover relates himself to the beloved, hence a contact is established which will ultimately lead to the union of the two. Therefore, the dedicated worshiper does not hesitate to boldly address his Divine Lover:

> Have you come to me as sorrow? All the more I
>   must cling to you.
> Your face is veiled in the dark, all the more I
>   must see you.
> At the blow of death from your hand let my life
>   leap up into a flame.

---

[18] Rabindranath Tagore, *Gītāñjalī*, VI

> Tears flow from my eyes - let them flow round
>> your feet in worship.
> And let the pain in my breast speak to me that
>> you are still mine.[19]

For the one who truly loves, the pain of sacrifice is not felt as pain, because being essentially the pain of love, that pain becomes sanctified by its being an aspect of love. Consecrated to the lover, the pain of sacrifice is made meaningful through the continuity of service against the strains of pain: "[let my tears] flow round your feet in worship" - more so, the pain itself is purified and dedicated to the worshiped soul. *And let the pain...speak to me that you are still mine* - at its culmination, the spirit of surrender defies all pain as meaningless fancy in face of the ultimate reality that through self-surrender alone the lover makes the beloved his spiritual property.

It is the prospect of union, the prospect of being one with the beloved soul that demobilizes the impact of pain, hence the poet's readiness to confront the Supreme Being in the battle of love:

> I hid myself to evade you.
> Now that I am caught at last, strike me, see if I
>> flinch.
> Finish the game for good.
> If you win in the end, strip me of all that I have.
> I have had my laughter and songs in wayside
>> booths and stately halls - now that you have
>> come into my life, make me weep, see if you
>> can break my heart.[20]

The poet says, "if you win in the end" - but can the struggle of love be a struggle of victory and defeat? No, it cannot be, because the concept of love contradicts the idea of combat, and the struggle between souls mutually committed through the bonds of love is playful contest rather than conflict. But what is it that bars combat from entering the realm of love? It is the spirit of self-dedication inherent in the fluid of love, which prevents the loving soul from contesting against the lover beyond the

---

[19] Rabindranath Tagore, *Crossing*, XXIV
[20] Rabindranath Tagore, *Crossing*, XXV

limits of play. It is that very spirit of selfless surrender which makes the dedicated soul forfeit all claims to victory over its beloved, for defeat of the loved one is the loving soul's own defeat. And it is that same spirit of sacrifice which makes the soul accept the pain of love, because it also enables the soul to transcend that pain.

How is suffering turned into joy, pain into bliss? Through dedicated action - through service. More specifically, through musical service, because music arouses the creative spirit in man and thus inspires him to counter the pain of unimaginative passivity. Creativity, coupled with the selfless essence of love, is the vital energy that instigates the spiritual search: "The mystery of life is creative sacrifice. It is the truth central to all religions"[21]. Being an aspect of love, pain acts as the driving momentum to stimulate this search, because the quest for love's fulfilment is the quest to overcome the state of agony:

> Love and suffering go together. No one who really loves can escape suffering. If we are spiritually alive, our capacity for love and service will be ever-growing...Suffering is not punishment or a misfortune. *In the depths of sorrow we receive light.*[22]

Of what kind is this suffering which enlightens the soul rather than defeats it? The musician whose tune misses the correct pitch suffers at the imperfection of his musical creation, but will he resign himself to his incomplete skills? No, he will not. He will try even harder till he masters the perfect melody. Likewise the lover whose call for love remains unheard suffers at the unfulfilled longing of his heart, but does he give in? Does he withdraw his service, his commitment for the beloved? No, he does not - he cannot, if his love is sincere. Because commitment of the soul cannot be retracted, because the statement of true love is irrevocable. Therefore, the pain arising from true love must be accepted, must be faced, must be defeated, and once it is defeated, the soul emerges not only triumphant but also spiritually richer and closer to the attainment of its ultimate goal.

---

[21] T.G.L. Iyer, "Creative Sacrifice, Mystery of Life", in *The Times of India*, 16 September 2000
[22] ibid.

Creative suffering, which carries ahead the quest for fulfilment, is inevitable to sustain the course of cosmic existence, but is it true that "there can be no real enjoyment except in renunciation and sacrifice"[23]? Is it justified to regard suffering as the essence of the spiritual search, to assert that "suffering is the substance of spiritual life, the very flesh of reality"[24]? No, it is not. The substance of spiritual life is the sacrifice, but is sacrifice necessarily suffering? No. Is sacrifice nourished by the thought of renunciation? No - sacrifice bears at its core the spirit of surrender, but surrender is not renunciation, because renunciation implies passive relinquishment, while surrender consists in active service which leads to spiritual gain rather than forsakenness. Spiritual fulfilment, the union of souls is not attained through passive renunciation, but through active worship - through creative sacrifice:

> Who is there that thinks the union of God and man is to be found in some secluded enjoyment of his own imaginings...? Who is there that thinks this secluded communion is the highest form of religion? O thou distraught wanderer, thou *Sannyāsin*, drunk in the wine of self-intoxication, dost thou not already hear the progress of the human soul along the highway traversing the wide fields of humanity...?...Do you in your lethargy desire to say that this car of humanity...has no charioteer leading it on to its fulfilment? ...*He who thinks to reach God by running away from the world, when and where does he expect to meet him?*[25]

Yes, it is true that sacrifice, that creative action nurtured by self-dedication requires the readiness to accept pain in order to transcend it - but this pain, which is defeatable through action, arises out of the separation of souls bound by the commitment of love, and once this pain is abolished, supreme bliss emerges from the union of lovers. The

---

[23] ibid.
[24] ibid.
[25] Rabindranath Tagore, *Sādhanā*, pp.129f.

suffering aroused by passive renunciation, on the other hand, is self-imposed, hence unfruitful.

What is more, the spirit of surrender cannot be captured by materialistic allegories. To explain the essence of sacrifice simply in terms of detachment from material objects, saying that

> when you get detached from it or when that object belongs to someone else, you are free from worry and anxiety to preserve it. When you are riding in your own car on a rough and rugged road you are worried. In another's car you even begin to enjoy riding rough-shod over potholes[26]

is an utterly selfish and materialistic attitude. In reality, quite the opposite is true: surrender signifies consideration for the other more than for oneself, it implies care for that which belongs to the other more than for that which belongs to oneself. For detachment from objects in their material sense does not mean indifference to that which is the property of the intrinsic owner of all things, of the Supreme Soul who carries the universe as the product of his own creative spirit. Cherishing anxiety about one's own rather than another's possessions expresses nothing but the materialistic spirit of inferiority that misses the core attitude of surrender. Surrender is inspired by love, and love in its very essence opposes the idea of possessiveness.

If the sacrifice which is at the heart of creation as the vital cause for all creativity requires detachment in terms of selfish materialism, but at the same time loving attachment in terms of emotional surrender, what object could be more suitable for the creative sacrifice than music, which is in itself an image of detached attachment? The act of music-making is essentially an act of sacrifice in which the musician detaches himself from the musical creation brought forth by him. His detachment is prompted by surrender - it is for the sake of surrendering his melody to the Supreme Soul that the music-maker has to renounce his own claim to it. Yet this is not to say that he ceases to be responsible for his music: offering the song to the Divine Listener, the singer needs to care all the

---

[26] T.G.L. Iyer, op.cit.

more about the perfectness of the tune which he generates not for his own joy alone, but for the joy of the Divine Lover to whom it is dedicated as a gift of love.

Music, in order to emerge from the depths of infinity, requires inspiration, because the sounding manifestation of the musical idea calls for the creative impetus that stimulates the concrete embodiment of emotional vibrations. Of what kind is the stimulus, the imaginative spark that incites the emanation of the musical flow? It is the closeness of the divinity, the spiritual union with the Supreme Being, with the soul of the beloved that inspires the musical mind to break out in tunes:

> I did not know that I had thy touch before it was
>   dawn.
> The news has slowly reached me through my
>   sleep, and I open my eyes with its surprise of
>   tears.
> The sky seems full of whispers for me and my
>   limbs are bathed with songs.
> My heart bends in worship like a dew-laden
>   flower, and I feel the flood of my life rushing
>   to the endless.[27]

My limbs are bathed with songs - the presence of the infinite, even if it is too subtle to be consciously perceived by the human senses, indelibly manifests itself in music. In music - and in service: *my heart bends in worship*, because the outbreak of music is but a vocalization of worship - an expression of dedicated service through the most sublime embodiment of beauty, an articulation of the emotional offering raised through the voice of the highest ideal of aesthetic refinement. The bliss received through the divine vision, through the touch of the divinity, becomes creative through worship, but at the same time, the creative sacrifice needs to be inspired by the divine vision which is represented in its fullest form in the union of love. Without that union, without the joy derived from consummate love, inspiration cannot arise; yet it is this very inspiration aroused by the spiritual union which is released in service to endow the act of worship with its imaginative energy.

---

[27] Rabindranath Tagore, *Crossing*, XXXVIII

What does this imply in the concrete? The spirit of surrender, the core stimulus of any musical activity, can be sustained only if the relationship of mutually committed souls is not hampered by unproductive distance, because distance prevents the dedicated soul from releasing its accumulated energies of love in active service: "What good is distance for a serving soul..."[28]. What is the use of commitment if distance hinders the soul to give out its all in surrender? What benefit yields longing for union if distance persistently bars the soul from meeting the lover? Why listen to the celestial tune if the Divine Music-maker remains aloof beyond unreachable limits?

> My lord is playing his flute / out of the doors, /
>   As I restlessly ache / Listening to him.
> I could not gather / The garland of meeting / And
>   in shame I walk my way.
> I go farther and farther away / And yet still I hear
>   the tune.
>
> *What good is distance for a serving soul...*[29]

Service requires closeness; it calls for intimacy between the souls of the lover and the beloved, the worshiper and the worshiped, the singer and the listener. Surrender can materialize in active worship only once the prospect of love's fulfilment turns real, once the union of love becomes a feasible object - once joy descends into the soul confused by distance, assuring the faltering heart time and again that its call will be heard for "tasted on the tongue of life, / the lord of love is true"[30].

How is fulfilment attained even and especially in the face of distress? How does union withstand separation, commitment defy distance? Through service! Through dedicated worship carried on in spite of the pain of distance, through devoted sacrifice against the strains of aloofness. *The lord of love is true*, and it is love which illumines the path to its union all by itself, holding up the torch of worship fueled by its own essence of surrender to seek out for the remote divinity:

---

[28] Gangārām, quoted in Deben Bhattacharya, op.cit., p.59
[29] ibid.
[30] ibid.

You hide yourself in your own glory, my King.

...

You make room for us while standing aside in
   silence; therefore love lights her own lamp to
   seek you and comes to your worship
   unbidden.[31]

Yet service cannot be instigated until love has acquired the force and
intensity to remove the hurdles of separateness, of separation, of
distance. Just as music does not break into sound until the musical idea
has matured, love is not meant to fulfil before it is fully grown. Active
worship requires the ripeness of love, hence it is not passive lethargy
but apprehensive patience that makes our poet wait for his moment of
worship:

When bells sounded in your temple in the
   morning, men and women hastened down the
   woodland path with their offerings of fresh
   flowers.
But I lay on the grass in the shade and let them
   pass by.
I think it was well that I was idle, for then my
   flowers were in bud.
At the end of the day they have bloomed, and I
   go to my evening worship.[32]

Love is not a static condition of cosmic finality; it is an active, ever-
developing process of increasing and condensing the transcendental
energies of bliss. Maturation of love therefore demands experience -
emotional experience which includes the knowledge of pain. Because
the soul which has not learnt to counter the agony of separation is not
ready for the union of love. It is through the conquest of pain that joy is
attained, not through evasion. The musician who stops his play at the
emergence of a deficient melody will not achieve command over the
tune, but the one who practices yet more eagerly to perfect his skills
certainly does. Once he has acquired sufficient mastery, the musician
becomes eligible to render his music before the listener - to offer his

[31] Rabindranath Tagore, *Crossing*, LVI
[32] Rabindranath Tagore, *Crossing*, LXII

tune in worship to the Listener among all listeners, because then he is truly entitled to emancipate himself in service.

But when is the time ripe for the dedicated soul to make its offering? When has the time come for service, for worshiping? The proper moment is there once the mind of the worshiper has been cleared of all doubts towards the object of worship. Which mind? - the rational mind that appeals to the intellectual faculties in man, from where the constant question about love's truthfulness is raised. Love has attained its full maturity, hence the authority to manifest itself in active worship, when the question about its realness is positively answered once and forever, when the emotional and rational senses within man are no more quarreling over the legitimation of the soul's commitment to the spirit of the infinite. But why do we need to respond at all to the importunate inquiries of the rational mind? Is it not easier to ignore those queries and to follow the call of emotionality, dismissing the voice of rationality alltogether?

It is easier, albeit not possible. Why? Because

> man is a rational animal. He needs to properly understand things in terms of the categories of reason. We do not always operate in a spontaneous intuitive mode. That which we may experience in a mystical state of consciousness has to be in some way translated into the language of ordinary rationality. Even for a predominantly emotional person reason is not dead. It is a question of proportions.[33]

What happens if the proportions are overlooked? If the emotional claim of the heart overturns the rational mind, or the rational argument uproots the stands of emotionality? The impact of such neglect is likewise destructive no matter which way ignorance takes. If the rational side is overemphasized, the mind thus disregarding the quest of emotionality will

---

[33] Shrivatsa Goswami, in an interview with Steven J. Gelberg, Vrindaban, 12 March 1982

fail to realise that while the infinite is always greater than any assignable limit, it is also complete; that on the one hand Brahma is evolving, on the other he is perfection; that in the one aspect he is essence, in the other manifestation - both together at the same time, as is the song and the act of singing. This is like ignoring the consciousness of the singer and saying that only the singing is in progress, that there is no song. Doubtless we are directly aware only of the singing, and never at one time of the song as a whole; but do we not all the time know that the complete song is in the soul of the singer?[34]

Supremacy of reason over man's inborn feeling for the cosmic reality means to deny the completeness of creation; it is like accepting the longing for union but not the fulfilment itself, like acknowledging the melody but not the great truth of music, like recognizing the act of surrender but not the object of surrender. Dominance of reason forsakes the meaningful essence of life for a gigantic question mark, yet the answer is not found in the opposite extreme. Those who rely on emotion alone fail to realize the universal truth of existence, because their "intellect, in its vain attempts to see Brahma inseparable from his creation, works itself stone-dry, and their heart, seeking to confine him within its own outpourings, swoons in a drunken ecstasy of emotion"[35].

So where is the solution? How can the two conflicting spirits, the rational and the emotional minds, be reconciled?

It is a question of proportions. A devotee must have rational and intellectual faculties. He must not only be emotionally satisfied, but must be rationally satisfied as well. A person who is fundamentally a rationalist isn't necessarily

---

[34] Rabindranath Tagore, *Sādhanā*, p.126
[35] ibid. (p.127)

emotionally arid. He has emotions, but those
emotions are subordinate to his intellect.[36]

If proportions are maintained, the path towards spiritual attainment
remains unblocked, because "true spirituality...is calmly balanced in
strength, in the correlation of the within and the without"[37]. If the
rational and emotional faculties interact in a creative harmony, if the
problem of doubt is faced rather than dismissed, then the query of
rationality is bound to be ultimately solved and the truth of love to be
permanently affirmed. Love, in order to become fruitful, requires both
emotional and rational capacities. Why? Because attainment as the
ultimate quest of love arises from the marriage of the rational and
emotional senses, and this union needs to be viable for both.

What is more, the current of love is sustained through the
harmonious interplay of inner essence and outward manifestation, of
state and action - of emotion and its release in the activity of service.
And it is service which helps to establish the proportionality of emotion
and reason in the first place. How is that? The core essence of service is
surrender - selfless surrender to the object of worship. For the soul to
commit itself completely, the question of doubt must not arise, hence the
rational mind has to be gratified before the surrender. And thereafter? In
surrender, there is no space for doubt, because surrender is
unconditional - and this the rational mind has to respect as a fact of
spiritual conclusiveness. It is this very momentum of unconditional
commitment which disarms even the adverse forces of pain, hence the
devoted worshiper, the committed lover has all authority to call out to
his god, "You may hurt me, my lord / go, hurt me / as long as I can bear
the pain"[38], because he knows that his commitment gives him the
strength to bear, nay, to transcend that pain.

His commitment gives him the power: the commitment which is
discharged in service, in worship - in music. Music is the mode of
worship *par excellence* because music possesses all the intrinsic
potencies that are essential for the unfolding of love's imaginativeness.

---

[36] Shrivatsa Goswami, in an interview with Steven J. Gelberg, Vrindaban, 12 March
1982
[37] Rabindranath Tagore, *Sādhanā*, p.127
[38] Podu, quoted in Deben Bhattacharya, op.cit., p.107

Music is in its very nature an act of sacrifice, of service, of surrender, because music is nourished by the essence of love which is mutual submission. Music is the sounding expression of the creative sacrifice through which the Creator establishes time and again the cosmic truth of joy committed to beauty. Music is service, yet all service is ultimately rendered through music, because it is the flow of the musical current, the liquid of immeasurable transcendental sweetness, which motivates the sacrifice at the core of service. And music is worship - the highest, most sublime and most excellent vocalization of the universal call of love.

12

Realization through music

What is it that drives these bees from their home;
these followers of unseen trails? What cry is this
in their eager wings? How can they hear the
music that sleeps in the flower soul? How can
they find their way to the chamber where the
honey lies shy and silent?

Rabindranath Tagore, *Lover's Gift*, X

What is it that drives the human soul from her abode of finite convenience to set out for the ever-continuing pursuit of an unknown freedom? What is it that inspires man to strive for an invisible transcendental reality whose realization carries the prospect of never-ending bliss? What call is this resounding from the human heart's fervid aspirations? How can the soul hear the cosmic melody that rests at the bottom of the ocean of existence? How can she reach out to the immeasurable depths of the infinite where sweetness lies hidden in the modest shred of a tune? How can she know of the essence of essences, of the finest treasure of joy concealed in the inner chambers of eternity?

She knows. Not how, not why - she simply knows. In the realm of unbounded love, in the land of timeless play, there is no question of how and why. In that kingdom of persistent coming and going, of perennial meeting and parting, of constant being and becoming, no soul is answerable for her whence and thence: she *is*, and the mere fact of her being eradicates all queries about her credentials. And the soul knows. She knows her ultimate direction that leads her to the innermost spheres of attainment, just like the bee knows his way to the nectar at the heart of the flower: "honey is hidden / within the lotus bloom - / but the bee knows it"[1]. The bee alone knows it, not anyone else, because the bee alone has tasted the sweetness of honey, because the bee alone has heard "the music that sleeps in the flower soul"- because the bee alone is the connoisseur, and "only a connoisseur / of the flavours of love / can comprehend / the language of a lover's heart, / others have no clue"[2].

---

[1] Anon, quoted in Deben Bhattacharya, *The mirror of the sky* (London: Allen & Unwin, 1969), p.41

[2] ibid.

The bee, the connoisseur of the flavors of honey, can follow the call from the flower soul, not the dung-beetle: "dung-beetles nestle in dung, / discounting honey"[3]. And that bee which is the human soul, the connoisseur of the sweetness of love who has listened to the melody slumbering within the universe and has relished the honey resting in the core of the cosmic soul - that bee thus follows the call from the Supreme Soul and rushes on to their meeting-place where all currents of existence come to confluence in one single, gigantic sea of nectar.

Where is that sacred spot of union from which the stream of life springs forth? Where is the acclaimed land of sweetness where the quintessence of love is kept as the holy of holies? Where is the land of which the Bāul sings, "the forest of Brindā / guards the essence of love - / Rādhā and Krishna, / with cowherds ruling the land"[4]? Where is the land with its *tomāl* trees, its *guñja* flowers and shady *aśoka* groves, for which the poet offers his all as he declares, "I shall gladly suffer the pride of culture to die out in my house, if only in some happy future I am born a herd boy in the Brindā forest"[5]? Where is that realm of realms, the land aspired through the prayer swelling in a millionfold outcry from the heart of humanity, "be I a man in my next life, then be it that same Rasakhāna to dwell in Braja with the cowherds of Gokula village"[6]? Where is it, that land where the bee finds fulfilment in the inexhaustible abundance of honey welling forth from numberless flowers, that land where the human soul, the bee within man, is eternally gratified through the unending presence of the divine? And where is it, that land which is the land of music, where melodies emerge in ever-fresh shapes to unite into an immense flow of transcendental sweetness?

No, the kingdom of kingdoms is not a distant land in some remote corner of the universe beyond the reach of actuality. It is not an unfathomable presence outside the limits of the soul's capacity. It is living reality; it rests within the human soul, within the soul's own essence of devotion, within the soul's own faculties of love. Therefore,

---

[3] ibid.

[4] ibid.

[5] Rabindranath Tagore, *Lover's Gift*, XXII

[6] *Sujāna-rasakhāna* of Rasakhāna, *mānuṣa haũ to vahī rasakhāna basaũ braja gokula ke gvārana...*

we must try to understand the true character of the desire that man has when his soul longs for his God. Does it consist of his wish to make an addition, however valuable, to his belongings? Emphatically no!...when the soul seeks God she seeks her final escape from this incessant gathering and heaping and never coming to an end.[7]

So what then is it that the soul seeks in her quest for realization? "It is the *nityo' nityānām*, the permanent in all that is impermanent, the *rasānām rasatamah*, the highest abiding joy unifying all enjoyments"[8]. But how is this highest quest pursued? How is ultimate joy attained?

Realization of the infinite truth becomes feasible in the same way as does the bee's search for the sweetness hidden at the core of the flower: striving for the essence of essences, the bee submits himself to the flower and tastes the honey in union with the flower soul, but, making the flower his own at the moment of union, he never at one point takes possession of her. The secret of the bee is submission - submission to the flower opening her heart to give out the full sweetness of nectar to her humming lover. And that same secret is the secret of the soul seeking to accomplish union with the Supreme Reality at whose core rests the quintessence of cosmic sweetness: the soul submits herself to the Infinite Being and partakes of the most sublime, transcendental bliss without claiming control over its source. That is to say, "our daily worship of God is not really the process of gradual acquisition of him, but the daily process of surrendering ourselves, removing all obstacles to union and extending our consciousness of him in devotion and service, in goodness and love"[9]. Submission is the secret of attainment, the way to the aspired land of fulfilment:

---

[7] Rabindranath Tagore, *Sādhanā* (London: Macmillan and Co. Ltd., 1914), p.147
[8] Rabindranath Tagore, *Sādhanā*, p.148
[9] Rabindranath Tagore, *Sādhanā*, p.149

... / The forest of Brindā / guards the essence of
love - / Rādhā and Krishna, / with cowherds
ruling the land.

Submission is the secret of knowledge.[10]

Submission is the secret of knowledge - it is the secret that makes the
bee know of the honey inside the flower, it is the secret that tells the
human soul of the sweetness at the heart of the Eternal Lover:
submission is the secret from which the quest for realization is born,
carried ahead, and ultimately accomplished.

Submission is the secret of realization - and the secret of music.
What is music? Music is the sounding fluid of transcendental sweetness.
And more than that, music is the knowledge of that sweetness, and it is
the attainment of that sweetness. Thus the bee not only "hear(s) the
music that sleeps in the flower soul", but also tastes that music only to
realize the music of his own soul in the very act of tasting - just as the
human soul is guided by music to realization, experiences music in
realization, delights in music at the moment of realizing what? - music.
What makes music so universal in its presence? It is the spiritual essence
of music, which is the essence of love. Music qualifies as the primary
way towards realization, because in music, in the tuneful articulation of
cosmic love becomes manifest the core object of the spiritual quest. The
search for realization is inspired by the knowledge of its object;
realization is attained by submission to its object - but what is this object
of realization? It is love. It is the ultimate transcendental truth which is
the truth of love. It is union - the creative unity of imaginative forces
which is fulfilled in the union of mutually committed souls. And it is
music - the melodious embodiment of universal bliss that unites in its
flow all truth, all love, all creativity.

Realization is essentially action; it is an active process of gradual
advancement towards the aspired object, a process that progresses in
different stages of spiritual perfection. Which are these stages? If we
adopt the nomenclature provided by Indian philosophy, we may best
describe the course of realization in terms of *sādhanā, darśana* and *mukti*

---

[10] Anon, quoted in Deben Bhattacharya, op.cit., p.41

or *mokṣa*: realization is accomplishment, realization is vision, realization is deliverance. What is that to say in the concrete? The first and basic stage of realization is *sādhanā*, the way towards attainment, the way of accomplishing, of realizing. The stage of *sādhanā* is not only the fundamental stage of realization, the initial motion towards the ultimate object; it is also a permanent stage, because realization is a continuous process of advancing towards the infinite, of attaining to the infinite, of merging with the infinite - but never of possessing the infinite which is by nature unpossessible, hence the quest for the infinite remains a perennial quest. Is that to say that attainment as such can never be reached? "If the word attainment implies any idea of possession, then it must be admitted that the infinite is unattainable"[11]. But it is not so. Attainment of the supreme reality must be free from possessive strains, because the spiritual quest itself opposes the concept of possession. And it is this very state of being above possessiveness that makes the search for attainment truly accomplishable.

When does realization materialize, attainment turn real? The continual progression of *sādhanā*, of accomplishment finds its culmination in *darśana*, the vision: *darśana* is the moment of attainment, the instant when the spark of realization flashes through the searching soul. *Darśana* is realization *per se*; *darśana* is the spiritual union - more than that, it is the climax of union, the supreme moment of amazement when all currents of music mingle into silence, when the aggregation of compressed energies of bliss has reached its highest density. Yet *darśana* is not the final stage, not the ultimate state of realization, because in *darśana* alone the energies of bliss are not released. When are these energies set free? *Darśana* is silence, not music, so when does the musical flow break forth? The culmination of *darśana* is naturally resolved into *mukti*, into *mokṣa*: into deliverance. What is the meaning of deliverance, of *mokṣa*? Of course, deliverance relates to the liberation of the searching soul through the instant of realization, but first and foremost, deliverance means release of energies - of the accumulated energies of bliss, of the compressed forces of joy, of the repressed sounds of music.

---

[11] Rabindranath Tagore, *Sādhanā*, pp.149f.

What is more, deliverance as a direct result of realization carries at its core the primary impetus for the spiritual search to be instigated anew on a higher qualitative level. *Mukti* emerges from *darśana*, but again it inspires *sādhanā*, that is, the liberation felt at the moment of attainment itself stimulates the constant quest for realization. Why is it so? What is the reason for this continuity in the process of realization, in the progression of *sādhana-darśana-mokṣa*? Is not deliverance the ultimate stage of realization, the ultimate *state* of attainment? Yes, deliverance is the ultimate, but it is not final. Deliverance is the highest state, but it is not static, it is not stationary.

How is that? The reason lies in the nature of the quest for realization. Realization of what? - of the supreme transcendental reality, of the quintessential truth which is joy, which is bliss, which is love. The quest for realization is an innately emotional quest. If deliverance would imply the mergence with an attributeless energy, if liberation would signify the union with naught, then the spiritual quest would surely stop here. But it is not possible: an unqualified deliverance is no deliverance, and the union with a neutral entity is no union, because such deliverance, because such union does not lead to bliss which is the essential object of the quest for attainment. The quest for realization of the supreme transcendental reality, the quest for attainment to the supreme cosmic truth, the quest for union with the Supreme Soul is in its very essence the quest for infinity, for the infinite. And therefore, every attainment can only be partial: it cannot be complete because the infinite reality cannot be comprehended in its entirety in one single instant of realization; attainment cannot be conclusive because the infinite reality is continual, hence the quest for attainment of the infinite reality too must be continual.

Yet attainment, however partial in its momentary appearance, must be true in its spiritual substance. That is to say, the quest for realization must be accomplishable: "our existence is meaningless if we never can expect to realise the highest perfection that there is. If we have an aim and yet can never reach it, then it is no aim at all"[12]. The quest for the highest spiritual truth needs to be attainable, but it must not be satiable, because the moment the soul's aspiration becomes satiated, the

---

[12] Rabindranath Tagore, *Sādhanā*, p.155

joy of attainment is gone. "Thus our soul must soar in the infinite, and she must feel every moment that in the sense of not being able to come to the end of her attainment is her supreme joy, her final freedom"[13]. Attainment is necessary, but attainment must not come to an end - it must not become an end in itself, it must not rest in a static conclusion, just as the union of love, the ultimate goal of spiritual attainment, must not stagnate in a rigid finality that would mar the continuity of universal creativity. How is such a condition of terminal ultimateness, of ultimate termination prevented? - through the motivating essence of love which keeps the current of emotional ambitions ever flowing:

> In all our deeper love getting and non-getting run
> ever parallel. In one of our Vaiṣṇava lyrics the
> lover says to his beloved: 'I feel as if I have
> gazed upon the beauty of thy face from my birth,
> yet my eyes are hungry still: as if I have kept thee
> pressed to my heart for millions of years, yet my
> heart is not satisfied.'[14]

It is the infinite nature of the object of love reaching beyond its material manifestation which makes the quest for love, the quest for the realization of love a persistent, continuous quest. But how is that quest practically accomplished? How is realization brought to perfection in the concrete? Which is the way, which the vehicle to spiritual attainment? It is music. It is the sounding manifestation of cosmic sweetness with its inherent motivating potencies, the subtle resonance of universal love with its inborn imaginative potential that brings the cycles of creation to effectiveness. Music is the dynamic flow of energies, the life-giving liquid of emotion that instigates the process of realization and sustains the continuity of *sādhanā*, *darśana* and *mokṣa*, thereby ensuring the perennial nature of the spiritual quest. What is more, music represents the quest for realization on a two-fold level: on the one hand, music inspires the process of accomplishment on the cosmic level, while on the other hand, music is in itself a continual process of accomplishment. That is, from one point music *is* the spiritual quest, while from the other point music embodies the spiritual quest on the metaphoric level.

---

[13] Rabindranath Tagore, *Sādhanā*, p.152
[14] Rabindranath Tagore, *Sādhanā*, p.150

However, it is from either point that music prompts realization, that music proves conducive to accomplishment, to attainment: music is *sādhanā*, music induces *darśana*, and in music there is *mokṣa*. Being essentially an energy of motion, music qualifies as the prime stimulator for the spiritual quest on the universal level. It is through music that sweetness as the core essence of love becomes perceptible for the human heart, because the sounding melodiousness of music crystallizes the transcendental energies of bliss into a definite manifestation of aesthetic beauty. Therefore, the human soul comprehends her quest for realization in terms of music: it is music that institutes the progress on the way towards accomplishment, in *sādhanā*; it is music that evokes the vision, the climax of *darśana*, and it is the newly released flow of music that leads to deliverance - to *mukti*, to *mokṣa*. But how is music itself brought to perfection? - through *sādhanā*, through the endeavor at accomplishment. How is music attained? - through *darśana*, through the moment of vision in which musical inspiration is conceived, the high-point at which all sound gives way to the charged silence of aggregated imaginative energies. And how is music called forth? - through *mokṣa*, through release of the accumulated musical forces in the liberated current of tunes.

Thus the quest for realization is not only pursued through music, it is itself the quest of music. It is the quest which is attainable but not satiable, because the spiritual essence of music drives the musical reality constantly towards infinity, towards that which is attainable but not capturable, towards that which is relishable but not exhaustible, towards that which is enjoyable but whose joy comes never to an end. So how can the infinite be realized, how music be apprehended? Realization is an active process, but more than that, realization is experience: it is the experience of the infinite realized through the experience of infinity. The soul accomplishes realization through the taste of unbounded freedom arising from attainment that reveals itself in continuous but never conclusive instants. Without experience, realization is unfeasible: "That we cannot absolutely possess the infinite being is not a mere intellectual position. It has to be experienced, and this experience is bliss"[15]. What is that to say? Experience is the clue to attaining the unpossessible,

---

[15] Rabindranath Tagore, *Sādhanā*, p.152

because the very meaning of experience is to make one's own that which cannot be possessed. Therefore, experience is the key to realization - and to music. Music is by its nature infinite, hence music can only be experienced, not possessed. The music-listener only senses the sound of the musical reality and tastes the flavor of its emotional essence, but there is no way of him capturing the tune and making it his own physical property. Why? Because music is uncapturable - as is the sweetness in the flower, which the bee relishes but never owns even if he sucks the last drop of honey from the bloom: he only grasps the nectar, not its sweetness.

Realization is experience, but what is experience? How is experience induced? Experience is knowledge: it is knowledge through feeling. And yet experience is at the same time feeling through knowledge, for "the secret of feeling, / my heart, / is in knowing it"[16]. The secret of feeling is in knowing it, and the secret of knowing is in feeling it: that is to say, the secret of experience is in feeling that which is known, and in knowing that which is felt. And the secret of realization is experience: realization is the ultimate state in which knowledge and feeling unite to accomplish the comprehensive experience of the Supreme Reality in all its rational and emotional qualities. What then is realization through music? Realization through music signifies the prime intention of the spiritual quest: it is music which is experience *par excellence*, because music is knowing, music is feeling, music is the original, the elemental quest for realization inspired by the living touch of the divine.

Music is inspirited by the vision of the infinite, and it is this vision of the invisible, the *darśana* of the unseen reality that instigates the search for attainment in the first place. The poet prays, "stand before my eyes, and let thy glance touch my songs into a flame"[17], because it is through those very songs that he seeks to reach the unreachable; it is through those very songs that he longs to attain the unattainable; it is through those very songs that he aspires to realize the unrealizable. But more important, his quest is not blunt ambition: through music he *does* reach the unreachable, through music he *does* attain the unattainable,

---

[16] Padmalochan (Podo), quoted in Deben Bhattacharya, op.cit., p.102
[17] Rabindranath Tagore, *Crossing*, LIV

through music he *does* realize the unrealizable because the quest of music is the quest of love, and in love, nothing is impossible; in love, even the unfeasible becomes realistic for love alone inherits the power to transcend the intranscendible. Therefore, the quest for the fulfilment of love represents the ultimate quest for realization in cosmic dimensions. Therefore, the quest for the fulfilment of love is not merely the quest for love: it is the quest for love as the quintessence of existence, it is the quest for *nikhil prāṇer prīti*, for universal life-giving love[18] - and it is the quest for the realization, for the attainment of that love.

What is realization in the striving for love's fulfilment? Realization aims at the infinite, and the realization of the infinite signifies union with the infinite, hence realization represents nothing less than the union of love. Infinity is unity, and "the region of the infinite is the region of unity"[19]. Realization of the infinite is experience, is knowledge, and knowledge leads to unity, just as "words do not gather bulk when you know their meaning; they become one with the idea"[20]. Just as sounds do not heap up when you know the melody; they become one with the concept of the song. Realization is union, realization is the way to union, realization is the result of union - realization is in one *darśana*, *sādhanā* and *mokṣa*. And how is that realization accomplished?- through music. Because music is the way of *sādhanā*, music is the object of *darśana*, music emerges from *mokṣa*. What does that mean? Music is the driving energy that instills union, and union is true realization by reason of its intrinsic selflessness, by reason of the complete absence of the spirit of acquisition: "it is not the function of our soul to *gain* God, to utilise him for any special material purpose. All that we can ever aspire is to become more and more one with God"[21].

Realization represents union, realization embodies the union of love, but at the same time, realization implies the constant search for that union which is the highest goal of the spiritual quest. But is union yet to be established? No, it is not - there is no necessity to establish this union which is already perfect: "The union is already accomplished. The *paramātman*, the supreme soul, has himself chosen this soul of ours as

---

18 Rabindranath Tagore, *Ananta prema* ('Unending Love')
19 Rabindranath Tagore, *Sādhanā*, p.154
20 ibid.
21 Rabindranath Tagore, *Sādhanā*, pp.154f.

his bride and the marriage has been completed"[22]. The union has been fulfilled, the marriage of souls performed, but now that love has been brought to perfection, the union of love must be realized. That is, the human soul needs to comprehend the truthfulness of this union in order to become truly blissful.

> ...the marriage of supreme love has been accomplished in timeless time. And now goes on the endless *līlā*, the play of love...When the soul-bride understands this well, her heart is blissful and at rest. She knows that she...has attained the ocean of her fulfilment at the one end of her being, and at the other end she is ever attaining it...Then all her services become services of love, all the troubles and tribulations of life come to her as trials triumphantly borne to prove the strength of her love...But so long as she does not recognise her lover...she sways in doubt, and weeps in sorrow and dejection.[23]

The union of love must be realized: it must be relished, it must be experienced, but experience is only found in the continuity of the play, and that is the crux of realization as a process at large. Realization by itself expresses the "marriage of supreme love [that] has been accomplished in timeless time", while the *līlā*, the ever ongoing play of love, becomes manifest in the soul's continuous quest for realization, and it is this quest, the perennial search for accomplishment, for realization, which enables the experience of the union of love through the play of love.

Why is this experience so essential? Why is it vital for the soul to be aware of the bliss arising from her marriage with the Supreme Soul? Because only "he who knows the ways / of the river of life, / has no sense of fear..."[24]:

---

[22] Rabindranath Tagore, *Sādhanā*, p.160
[23] Rabindranath Tagore, *Sādhanā*, pp.161-2
[24] Phatik Chānd, quoted in Deben Bhattacharya, op.cit., p.106

> He who can seize the vortex
> of the *Tribeni,*
> the confluence of the three streams,
> can swim with the joy of love.
> He is not afraid of the hazard...[25]

Because only he who knows that the union of love is for real can bear the pain of separation. Because only he who knows that the marriage of supreme love has been completed an endure the strains of being apart in the play of love. Because only he who knows that the music of love is true can transcend the silence of aloofness. And that is to say that he who knows the sweetness emitted by universal love is also able to hear its sounding manifestation reverberating from the spheres of eternity in endless currents of joy, of beauty, of music.

Realization through music is more than merely the spiritual quest and its accomplishment. Realization through music signifies the aesthetic emancipation of the soul, the attainment to the Infinite Reality through the joy of beauty. Music carries at its core the spark of creativity which is immanent in all expressions of beauty, and which is the prime impetus of all joy aroused through the manifestation of the formless in the form. The joy of beauty is the joy of creative beauty, of beauty which is ever in the process of becoming, of beauty whose utmost excellence lies in its momentary imperfection, in its yet to be, because in this rests the permanent truth of existence, the "perfectness of being that lends to the imperfection of becoming that quality of beauty which finds its expression in all poetry, drama, and art"[26] - and in all music. More than that, music embodies the constant quest of becoming in the most exemplary way, because music can never be complete in either time or space. Music is a continuous process of interweaving melodious chains of sounds; it is a continual process of creating, but the complete creation, the musical work in its entirety exists only as an underlying concept in the mind of the singer, which, though it manifests itself as musical experience in the heart of the listener, never emerges as a comprehensible monolithic presence.

---

[25] ibid.
[26] Rabindranath Tagore, *Sādhanā*, p.157

Yet the complete creation is there, and it must be there in order to fill the process of creating with meaning. That is to say, if we want to delight in the joy of becoming, the joy of being must be real. Without the perfection of being, without the unifying bond of the underlying idea, the process loses its creative spirit and appears as a senseless sequence of unrelated details:

> We see the gesticulations of the dancer, and we imagine these are directed by a ruthless tyranny of chance, while we are deaf to the eternal music which makes every one of these gestures inevitably spontaneous and beautiful. These motions are ever growing into that music of perfection, becoming one with it, dedicating to that melody at every step multitudinous forms they go on creating.
>
> And this is the truth of our soul, and this is her joy...[27]

The joy of music consists in its higher object of accomplishing the realization of its own joy, but that very realization becomes possible only because music is the way towards joy. Realization through music, therefore, is the realization of music, the realization of the joy of music which enables the accomplishment of realization in the first place.

Why is that? Why is it that all realization takes its root in the realization of joy? The reason is the incompatibility of other faculties for the attainment to the Supreme Reality. The Supreme Soul is perfect, hence

> knowledge which is partial can never be a knowledge of him. But he can be known by joy, by love. For joy is knowledge in its completeness, it is knowing by our whole being. Intellect sets us apart from the things to be known, but love knows its object by fusion.

---

[27] Rabindranath Tagore, *Sādhanā*, p.158

Such knowledge is immediate and admits no
doubt.[28]

Joy is knowledge paired with feeling; it is the knowledge whose secret
is feeling, the feeling whose secret is knowledge. Mere knowledge
bound to the limited capacities of the intellect cannot reach the ultimate
truth: "mind can never know Brahma, words can never describe him; he
can only be known by our soul, by her joy in him, by her love"[29].
Knowledge which arises out of the immediate experience of its object
creates that joy of fulfilment from which is born the spiritual quest.
"Words can never describe" the supreme transcendental reality - but
music can. The rational vehicle may prove incompetent to accomplish
the quest for the infinite truth, but music holds the full ability to enforce
the fusion that capacitates the knowledge which is the knowledge
through love.

In what way does knowledge through love differ from the
knowledge attested by the rational intellect? *Such knowledge is
immediate and admits no doubt*: such knowledge carries the essence of
attainment which is its definiteness. The knowledge nourished by reason
alone, the knowledge that lacks the impetus of feeling can never go
beyond the limits of doubt, because its course is constantly encumbered
by disbelief. Therefore, this incomplete knowledge cannot proceed
towards realization, towards the highest goal which requires the
confidence of its ultimate accomplishment in order to be instigated in the
first place. What is it that makes the preliminary knowledge of the final
spiritual success so essential? The reaon lies in the quest itself, in the
way towards attainment which is by nature burdensome. Why should
the searching soul accept the troubles on her path if that path leads
nowhere? Why should the heart bear with agonies that are never coming
to an end? If the object of realization were fake, it would be utterly
foolish at all to strive for accomplishment. If the musician were to know
for sure that he can never accomplish the melody, his training would be
a sheer waste of time.

---

[28] Rabindranath Tagore, *Sādhanā*, p.159
[29] ibid.

But it is not so, and that it is not so can be comprehended only through the joy of being, through the joy of love, through the "joy [which] is knowledge in its completeness". And it is for the sake of this joy, for the sake of this knowledge which is knowledge in its entirety, that the poet ever continues his wearisome journey:

> The time that my journey takes is long and the
>   way of it long.
> I came out on the chariot of the first gleam of
>   light, and pursued my voyage through the
>   wilderness of worlds leaving my track on
>   many a star and planet.
> It is the most distant course that comes nearest to
>   thyself, and that training is the most intricate
>   which leads to the utter simplicity of a tune.
> The traveller has to knock at every alien door to
>   come to his own, and one has to wander
>   through all the outer worlds to reach the
>   innermost shrine at the end.
> My eyes strayed far and wide before I shut them
>   and said 'Here art thou!'
> The question and the cry 'Oh, where?' melt into
>   tears of a thousand streams and deluge the
>   world with the flood of the assurance 'I
>   am!'[30]

It is in this assurance 'I am' that the true knowledge is found, that the way howsoever tiresome becomes manageable for the truthfulness of its distant aim. It is this very assurance from the Supreme Reality through which the impact of doubt is offset. And it is nothing but this elemental assurance of being that enables the ultimate fulfilment of the spiritual quest, that evokes the actual instant of realization, that prompts the attainment to the infinite, that induces the experience of the most sublime transcendental truth. How is this experience received after all the adversities encountered on the way? With amazement - with an overwhelming sense of astonishment at the stunning easiness of having reached the final destination. *That training is the most intricate which*

---

[30] Rabindranath Tagore, *Gītāñjali*, XII

leads to the utter simplicity of a tune - it is the *sādhanā*, the way of accomplishment which demands most of our spiritual strength, not the *darśana*, not the attainment itself.

What is more, the tune can be rendered only once the training has been completed, only once the musician accomplishes the melody in its full simplicity. That training, "the most intricate [training] which leads to the utter simplicity of a tune", requires the musician's patience. If he attempts to render the tune before it has been fully refined through earnest practice, his play will be spoilt, and the sweetness of the music is hampered by the imperfectness of the musical delivery. Therefore the singer whose ambitions are guided by wisdom waits for the proper moment to come forth with the perfect song:

> The song that I came to sing remains unsung to
>   this day.
> I have spent my days in stringing and in
>   unstringing my instrument.
> The time has not come true, the words have not
>   been rightly set; only there is the agony of
>   wishing in my heart.
> The blossom has not opened; only the wind is
>   sighing by.
> ...
> I live in the hope of meeting with him; but this
>   meeting is not yet.[31]

This meeting is not yet - but it is yet to be. *Only there is the agony of wishing in my heart* - but what happens if this agony of longing becomes too strong for the soul to bear it any longer?

Like the perfect tune, the spiritual quest cannot be accomplished before its time has come; realization can be attained only once the search has been brought to completion; union with the Supreme Soul can be established only once love has grown to full ripeness. If the soul does not afford that moment of patience to hold on till the Supreme Being is

---

[31] Rabindranath Tagore, *Gītāñjali*, XIII

ready to meet her, she is bound to fail in her effort, hence the Bāul's stern admonition -

> O cruelly eager, / Are you going to fry on fire /
>   Your heart's flower bud?
> Are you going to force it to blossom / And let the
>   scent escape / Without biding your time?
>
> Look at my master, God, / Eternally opening the
>   buds to bloom / But never in a hurry. / …
>
> Listen to Madan's appeal / And do not hurt the
>   master at heart:
> The stream spontaneously flows / Lost in itself, /
>   Listening to his words…[32]

The stream spontaneously flows towards the sea, but it reaches the sea only when it has completed its full course through the river-bed. Therefore, forcing the bud to blossom before it has opened will only harm the flower; it will not help extracting the sweetness of the nectar not yet manifest. Realization is not attained before the way has been traversed in full: there can be no *darśana* without *sādhanā*, just as the joy of music cannot arise without the tune, the perfect tune, being played.

But the tune *will* be played - it is bound be played in the same way as the bud is bound to blossom, in the same way as the seeking heart is bound to unite with its eternal lover. Why? "That the bud has not blossomed in beauty in my life spreads sadness in the heart of creation"[33]: because without the continual metamorphosis from becoming to being, the progress of universal creation cannot be sustained. "When the shroud of darkness will be lifted from my soul it will bring music to thy smile"[34]: because the Supreme Being finds his own fulfilment only in the fulfilment of man's longing. There can be no joy without music, and without joy, existence becomes but an immense blunder of reality - devoid of creativity, devoid of love, devoid of life.

---

[32] Madan, quoted in Deben Bhattacharya, op.cit., p.94
[33] Rabindranath Tagore, *Crossing*, IX
[34] ibid.

Music melts into one with the course of existence, inspiriting the creative cycles with the life-giving breath of joy:

It has fallen upon me, the service of thy singer.
In my songs I have voiced thy spring flowers,
    and given rhythm to thy rustling leaves.
I have sung into the hush of thy night and peace
    of thy morning.
The thrill of the first summer rains has passed·
    into my tunes, and the waving of the autumn
    harvest.
Let not my song cease at last, my Master, when
    thou breakest my heart to come into my
    house, but let it burst into thy welcome.[35]

Let not my song cease at last - thus is the singer's prayer, let not silence prevail, conclusive silence that brings the course of the universe to standstill, but let there be music always, music that brings forth unending joy, continual love, eternal life.

And thus is the soul's prayer for the continuity of the creative quest - the quest for realization. Music is the river that flows towards the ocean of the infinite, and music is also the boat that takes the soul ahead: "I know my songs are the boat that has brought me to the harbour across the wild sea"[36]. Music is the vehicle towards realization, but it is at the same time the core object of all realization, because music is joy, music is love, music is one with the Supreme Reality aspired by all spiritual intents. Music is the way of accomplishment *par excellence*, because in music unite all individual approaches; in music multitudinous rivers come to confluence into one ocean of bliss:

Have you tallied, / My heart, / The number of
    ways / Of finding him / In the city of love?
...
He is reached in the way / Each seek to reach
    him: / Through tender passion / Or servitude,

---

[35] Rabindranath Tagore, *Crossing*, LXXIV
[36] Rabindranath Tagore, *Crossing*, LXVII

/ Through loyalty / Or parental care. / Or
through the love / Of tranquility, peace…

Find the feelings / Which are born with you, /
And then worship him / With your own
strength.[37]

Worship him with your own strength - and with your own music.
Worship him with your own strength - but do worship him, for worship
is the essence of realization, the essence of love, the essence of music. It
is through worship that true realization is accomplished: true realization
which is attainment, true realization which is union, true realization
which is the union of love that fuses the human and the divine into the
most sublime liquid of creativity. And that is the attainment to the
supreme land, where the bee rejoices in the unending flow of honey and
the heart of man delights in eternal play with the Divine Lover. That is
the attainment to the kingdom of music, where the air is drenched with
the sweetness of tunes reverberating from the spheres of infinity. That is
the attainment to the transcendental realm of bliss: to Brindāban, the
"forest of Brindā / where…loving is worshipping"[38]; to Brindāban, "the
forest of Brindā / [that] guards the essence of love"[39]. That is the
attainment to the blessed land which is reached along the ways of love:
submission is the secret of knowledge[40], for submission is the secret of
joy - of joy which is love, of joy which is bliss, of joy which is music:

> Let all strains of joy mingle in my last song - the
> joy that makes the earth flow over in the riotous
> excess of the grass, the joy that sets the twin
> brothers, life and death, dancing over the wide
> world, the joy that sweeps in with the tempest,
> shaking and waking all life with laughter, the joy
> that sits still with its tears on the open red lotus
> of pain, and the joy that throws everything it has
> upon the dust, and knows not a word.[41]

---

[37] Punya, quoted in Deben Bhattacharya, op.cit., p.108
[38] Hāude Gosāiñ, quoted in Deben Bhattacharya, op.cit., p.69
[39] Anon, quoted in Deben Bhattacharya, op.cit., p.41
[40] ibid.
[41] Rabindranath Tagore, *Gītāñjalī*, LVIII